Before The Blood Dried

A PSYCHOLOGICAL THRILLER

Written By

J.J. Lucie

Published by Franklin Publishers

Printed in the United States of America

For permissions, inquiries, or additional copies, contact:

Franklin Publishers

www.franklinpublishers.com

Dedication

For Tony, Nicolas, Jaden, Austyn, and Kaison

Who remember what others tried to erase
Who stood by me, even when I didn't know who I was
Who remind me that even the darkest stories need a light to be told

Acknowledgments

For the Ones Who Remember

This book was never just mine.
It was carried by hands before mine—trembling, silenced, stained, steady.

To the survivors of institutional betrayal:
You are not echoes. You are evidence.
This story is stitched in your name.

To those who have lived through memory gaslighting,
who have sat in rooms and been told the pain didn't happen,
or worse—that it didn't matter:
I see you.

To the ones who hum when the silence gets too loud.
To the children whose names were redacted, reassigned, or rewritten.
To the women called hysterical for remembering too clearly.
To the men told to be strong enough to forget..

To the therapists who resist protocol.
To the nurses who smuggle truth into systems designed to erase.
To the archivists, the whistleblowers, the insomniacs,and the ones who stayed to leave a sound behind—
Thank you.

To the readers who carry intergenerational grief like an unfinished sentence:
You are not broken. You are not late. You are the after.

The fact that you feel it means the story was never fully buried. Only paused.

To the team that helped shape this book:
your faith in recursion was its own kind of miracle

To those who held me through the writing of this:
You know who you are. Your names hum beneath every chapter.

And finally—to you.
The one holding this now.
The one who read to the end, even when it hurt.
Even when it felt too familiar.
This book is for the versions of you they tried to overwrite.

You are not a vessel.
You are the voice that returned.
You are the one the Spiral couldn't contain.

With deep, quiet reverence,
-- J. J. Lucie

Table of Contents

CHAPTER: ONE

A Spiral Into Memory

Arlington Hills Psychiatric Hospital – September 1, 1947

The fog parted, and there it was: tall, gray, a cathedral that had forgotten what it once prayed for. Arlington Hills hunched beneath a sky undecided between night and morning. Fog clung to the gables like a memory—or a warning—left behind.

Ellie Hale stepped off the military-chartered bus, ration book folded in her pocket, gloves a half size too small. Her feet struck gravel with the dull certainty of memory. Back in Chicago, they'd called her name—"Nurse Hale." A pause. Too long. As if no one expected her to answer. Not even her.

The wrought iron gate closed behind her with a sound like a verdict. She paused—mud-caked steps, a hand-painted sign swinging in the wind, and beneath it, a bronze placard: Established 1919 for the Care and Convalescence of War-Wounded Minds.

She hadn't expected the silence. It wasn't peace—not the kind you earn. It wrapped around her like an apology no one knew how to speak. There was something in the air—expectant. Like the building had exhaled just long enough to let her step inside.

A soldier brushed past her, young and gaunt, uniform sleeves frayed at the edges. He didn't meet her eyes. None of them did. Not even the ones standing still.

Inside, starch and floor wax filled the air. Paper charts rustled like moth wings. The overhead lights buzzed faintly, but one flickered in a rhythm that didn't match the others. Ellie stared at it too long. Counted the pauses and realized she was holding her breath between flickers—like the room itself was remembering its own darkness, and hesitating before returning to light.

She signed her name on the intake register in careful cursive. Not her real signature—this one more deliberate, more precise. As if she were becoming the version of herself expected to walk these halls.

Ellie.

But even as she wrote it, a whisper unfurled at the base of her skull. That's not how it started.

She used to like that name. Or someone did. But the way it echoed here—too clean, too final—it felt like it had been chosen for her, like a room number or a drawer label.

Her reflection in the intake window held for a beat too long. A double-glass pane. Two Ellies. Neither quite matching—one blinked first. As though the mirror wasn't showing her back to herself but offering her forward, into something she hadn't agreed to yet.

Behind the receptionist, a corkboard displayed scattered artwork— paper suns, rudimentary stick figures, one drawing of a staircase that looped in on itself, spiraling downward like it had no bottom. Beneath the clipboard—a sketch. Just a doodle at first glance. But the figure wore Ellie's coat.

The one she hadn't removed yet.

Her throat dried. She slid the sketch back with trembling fingers. The receptionist didn't look up. She passed through the corridor with the sense of being led somewhere she'd already been. Her fingers brushed the wall. She recognized the coolness of the marble trim. Not from pictures. Not from briefing folders. From dreams.

A memory slid sideways in her mind—the scent of camphor and chalk dust, a child's voice echoing down the stairwell, a metal chair screeching across the linoleum. But when she reached for it, the feeling dissolved.

The fog outside pressed against the windows. She thought of how easy it would be to vanish in it. How many names could be rewritten if you just walked far enough away. And yet, she had come back.

In the hallway beyond admissions, a single piece of paper clung to the wall with yellowing tape. A spiral. Pressed so hard into the paper, it scarred through—like something trying to cut its way out.

Ellie stood there longer than she should have. It was the kind of drawing that didn't belong to one person. It belonged to whoever remembered it last.

The hallway swallowed sound in a way Ellie hadn't experienced before, not like silence. It was stillness—as though the walls had forgotten how to echo. The kind of stillness left after something had been unspoken for too long, where silence starts to carry weight as if holding its breath too.

Her shoes clicked too cleanly on the linoleum, each tap landing with the precision of someone being watched.

She gripped the handle of her suitcase tighter. The worn leather creaked under her palm, a small sound that reminded her she was real. Still here. Still moving.

At the end of the corridor, a clock ticked a second too slowly.

The intake nurse, Travers, was all sharp lines and unblinking eyes, her uniform too white to be real. "Dr. Weatherly will see you now."

Ellie stepped through the open door and into a room that smelled of tobacco, formaldehyde, and wax-sealed folders. The windows were shuttered despite the hour. Dust hung visibly in the thin stripe of sunlight that breached the blinds.

Dr. Weatherly stood without rising—tall even in his seat, collar starched too tight for shoulders bent beneath the weight of unread files. His eyes—clear as glass polished thin. Too thin. Like something had worn the empathy out of them. There was no warmth in his expression—only the precision of someone who'd learned to observe without empathy.

"Miss Hale," he said, without offering a hand. "You've come from Chicago?"

"Yes, sir." Her voice felt borrowed. Too thin in the space between them.

He nodded toward the chair across from his desk. It was cold when she sat, the wooden arms oddly low, like it had been built for someone smaller or younger.

"I've reviewed your intake," he said, thumbing through a file already open. Her name sat typed across the top in bold block font: HALE, ELEANOR J. A red spiral was stamped in the margin, faint but deliberate.

"You've served in rehabilitation wards before?"

"One in Denver," she said, though the memory came fractured. A red basin. A man coughing up teeth. A name she never wrote down.

Weatherly's eyes didn't flicker. "You'll be stationed in Ward C."

Something in the air shifted—like the temperature dropped just enough to make her breath tighten.

"Most of the men there are veterans," he continued, "though what they've returned from varies... depending on who's asking."

Ellie hesitated. "I was told I'd be working trauma-recovery."

"You will be," Weatherly said. He closed the file with a soft thud. "But here, trauma doesn't recover in straight lines."

He slid a folder across the desk. She opened it slowly. A sketch was paperclipped to the front—charcoal, dark and slanted. Her breath caught in her throat.

It was a figure. A woman in a nurse's coat. Her coat.

Before she could speak, Weatherly added, "That was drawn by a patient three days ago. Before your train arrived."

Ellie looked up sharply. "Who drew it?"

"Silas. Subject 7C. Former infantryman. Arrived in February under temporary sedation. Highly intelligent. Increasingly unstable."

"And he drew me?"

"He drew someone," Weatherly said, voice mild. "But it seems we've filled the outline." She didn't know what chilled her more—that a stranger had drawn her… or that Weatherly didn't sound surprised.

Ellie set the paper down with care as if it might burn. The lines were simple, almost childlike. But there was something uncanny in the angle of the shoulders. Like it had been drawn from memory. Or something deeper.

"Patients in Ward C tend toward recursion," Weatherly said like it had once happened to him, or worse—through him. "They report events before they happen, often in fragments—drawings, words, mirrored gestures. You may see things you believe to be a coincidence. They are not." He said it like it wasn't a warning but a blueprint. As if he'd seen it before—and let it run anyway.

She nodded, not because she agreed, but because she couldn't speak.

"You'll write everything down," he said. "No carbon copies. Ink only. The administration reviews your notes. But more importantly—he'll review you."

Ellie looked at the sketch again. The nurse's eyes were scribbled out with spirals where pupils should have been.

"Report to Ward C at 0600. There's a chair waiting for you. You'll know it when you see it."

He didn't stand when she rose. But just before she reached the door, he said, without looking up, "If he mentions the orchard—don't ask questions. Just listen."

Ellie turned back, her voice barely audible. "What orchard?"

Weatherly finally looked up. "You'll dream of it, eventually. They all do."

"Not me," Ellie wanted to say. But the words didn't come.

Because some part of her already knew—she'd dreamed of worse.

"Meet me in the screening room in 10 minutes," he demanded flatly. Ellie turned with a simple, "Yes, sir."

The corridor beyond the intake desk extended down like a vertebrae of the institution—rigid, cold, and inescapable. Ellie's footsteps echoed too perfectly, each tap a sound too crisp to be natural. The building seemed to absorb her presence like it had been waiting.

To her left, a bank of old clocks lined the hallway. Each ticked with its own rhythm, slightly out of sync with the others, like soldiers returning from different wars. One had stopped at 11:12. Another, smeared with soot, jumped ahead every seventh second. The largest had no hands at all. Just the spiral symbol scratched into the face.

Ellie slowed, the clipboard in her hands pressing into her ribs like a shield. The silence pressed back harder. It wasn't the kind of silence that followed stillness—but the kind that followed hiding.

A crooked mirror above the fountain. Silvered to distortion, as if it had swallowed too many faces. Ellie caught her reflection, but it lagged. Her mirror self paused too long. A breath out of sync. A blink that didn't belong to her. A flicker of vertigo snapped through her, sharp and personal — not the building's fault. Hers. As if the bones beneath her skin had known this place before she did. She reached for the fountain—but stopped. Her reflection was already drinking. And smiling. Her fingers curled back from the cold metal spout like it burned. A sour-sweet tang clung to the air, like old blood left too long in sunlight.

Farther down, she passed Room 9. Its placard had been removed and replaced with a patch of beige paint that didn't match the wall. Still, beneath the cover-up, letters bled faintly through—scrubbed but not erased. LILI—maybe. Or CLAR—She stepped past—but paused.

A sound. Not loud. Not even clear. Just the faint scrape of something wooden—like a chair leg shifting across linoleum. Then silence. Then breath. But not hers. She strained to place it—a chair dragging, or a body turning too slow.

Ellie turned back to the door. Nothing moved. The paint still flaked around the corners. The knob didn't turn. But a pressure lingered in the air, subtle as static. She reached out, one gloved hand brushing the frame. It felt warm. Too warm for a sealed room. Her pulse flinched.

A child's voice whispered from somewhere she couldn't see. Not a word—just a breath, shaped like memory. Then it stopped.

She blinked hard, took one step back, and the hallway reasserted itself. Lights overhead hummed faintly. Her breath returned.

Room 9 was silent. But the silence didn't feel empty. It felt sealed.

The hallway bent abruptly near the records annex. Here, the lights dimmed as if the voltage struggled. Ellie's shadow split into two. One curved with her shoulder. The other didn't.

She stopped before a door marked OBSERVATION–CANDIDATE SCREENING. The brass knob chilled her glove.

Inside, Dr. Weatherly sat at a desk angled toward the window, one hand resting near a closed file. A cigarette burned itself out in a tray beside him, untouched. The smoke coiled in a spiral, lazy and precise.

"Miss Hale," he said without looking up. "Do you always walk like someone else is watching?"

Ellie didn't answer. Not because she didn't have a response. But because she wasn't sure who he meant.

Dr. Weatherly opened the file. "We've run your transfer file twice. Once from the Chicago index, once from Edenbrook."

She shifted. "Edenbrook?"

"That's where your file originated. But we don't have evidence you ever served there. No intake date. No peer reviews. No termination slip."

Ellie's throat went dry. "That must be a clerical error."

"Clerical errors don't sign their own transfer papers."

He slid the file toward her. It contained her name in two columns: HALE, ELEANOR, and beneath it, in smaller handwriting: Subject 1C – Provisional Clearance.

Her hand moved toward it, unsteady.

"We don't expect perfection here," Weatherly said. "We expect containment."

"Of what?"

"Memory," he said. "Yours. Theirs. Ours." But it didn't sound like a theory. It sounded like a decision that had already been made.

The spiral stamped into the lower right corner of the file looked embossed. When Ellie touched it, it felt warm.

"I'm ready," she said.

"No," Weatherly replied. "But the chair is."

Behind her, the hallway lights buzzed again—faster now, like something approaching.

And just for a moment, the file's photograph of Ellie blinked.

Before she had.

The intake room was warmer than the corridor, but only just. It felt like the kind of warmth that didn't come from the radiator in the corner—it came from papers stacked too close to the lightbulb, from bodies having sat here too long with thoughts they didn't want to voice. Ellie sat at the far edge of the table, a clipboard resting on her knee, the edge of it digging into the fabric of her skirt.

Dr. Weatherly stood across from her, arms folded as he read a file that should've belonged to a stranger. Her file. But there was no picture clipped to it—only a series of typewritten notes, one line underlined in red:

"Observation recommended. Subject has been here before."

Ellie's hands remained still, but her pulse tapped a rhythm against her glove seams. The sentence echoed in her head, dislodging something she couldn't name. Her throat felt tight.

"I see you've read the orientation material," Weatherly said without looking up.

"Yes, sir."

"And you've signed the consent memorandum?"

"I... believe so." She hesitated. The momentary lapse tightened his gaze.

"We ask because memory distortion is common in this department. Names, dates, intentions. It is important to establish control variables early."

Ellie gave a small nod. Her posture was perfect, but her spine felt like glass.

Weatherly stepped closer, laying the file down with deliberate precision. "Tell me, Nurse Hale. Why did you apply to Arlington

Hills?"

The answer had been rehearsed. She opened her mouth to say it—but the words fractured before they arrived. A long pause filled the space.

"I don't think I did," she said.

Weatherly's expression didn't shift. If anything, the stillness in his eyes became more pronounced. "Interesting. The file lists you as a transfer from St. Agnes, Chicago."

"I've never worked there."

"No?"

She blinked. "I… don't remember."

"Memory is a fragile construct," he said, moving behind her. "Particularly in places like this. We find it's not what was taken that haunts most subjects. It's what returns without invitation."

She felt a chill gather at the nape of her neck. Weatherly circled back around and laid a photograph on the table. Black and white. Blurry. A woman in a nurse's uniform walking down a hallway.

"Do you recognize her?" He didn't ask how it was possible. He already knew.

Ellie stared. The figure was in profile, but there was no mistaking the tilt of her head. The coat. The posture.

"It's me," she whispered.

Weatherly nodded. "The problem is, this photograph was taken three years ago." Her breath caught.

"We reviewed your previous file. Notes were inconclusive. Terminated mid-study. No record of reassignment. Yet here you are."

The room spun slightly. Ellie closed her eyes. When she opened them again, Weatherly was closer. His voice had the calm of someone who'd watched this happen before—and documented it. The hum from the overhead light deepened until it sounded almost like breathing.

Weatherly tapped the edge of the photograph. "While you are assigned to Ward C, you are to maintain distance, precision, and control. The men there don't respond to empathy. They respond to consistency."

"Yes, sir." Her voice didn't sound like her own.

"And Nurse Hale—" She looked up.

"Do not ask about Room 9. Do not enter the west stairwell. And if you see your reflection blink first, leave immediately."

Ellie nodded. A mechanical gesture. She folded the photograph into her coat pocket, though she didn't remember choosing to. The spiral on the file's cover glinted faintly in the dim light.

"Dismissed," he said. She rose, turning toward the corridor. As she reached the door, Weatherly added one final note:

"You may not remember your first assignment, Miss Hale. But the ward does. It always does."

And for one flicker—no longer than a blink—she thought she'd seen this exact hallway in a dream. Same shadow. Same ticking clock. Same spiral stamped in the dust.

Her hand trembled on the doorknob. And behind her, the hallway's final light blinked. Not broken. Not weak. Just... watching. Something was waiting on the other side of the door. Not just the ward.

Something that remembered her — even if she no longer remembered herself.

CHAPTER: TWO

Echoes in the Archive

The hall curved like a spine no one dared to straighten, its bones locked in a quiet spiral the building had long since forgotten how to undo. Overhead, the fluorescent lights buzzed with a warbled hum, low and steady. Ellie moved slower now, her heels striking the institutional tile in a rhythm too even, too rehearsed. Five steps between doorways. Six, if she allowed her breath to pause mid-stride.

A nurses' station sat abandoned at the bend, its desk scattered with forms and amber vials. One bottle lay on its side, its handwritten label curling away from glass. Chloral hydrate. Beside it, a typewriter sat with its metal arms fanned like fractured wings. A single sheet waited half-typed in the carriage, ink faded with the final sentence unfinished.

Her eyes stared back—flat, too bright. Still. But not blank. Waiting. As though her reflection knew the next step before she did.

She turned sharply, heart tapping faster than her footsteps. The hallway was empty, but a door halfway down remained ajar. The plaque read: PHASE ONE FILE ARCHIVE.

Dr. Weatherly appeared as if conjured, leaning against the doorframe, clipboard in hand, his cap tilted off-center. "You'll want to watch Ward C," he said without preamble.

Ellie straightened. "What for?"

"Not what. Who."

His coat flared slightly as he stepped back, motioning her to follow. "The boys in C aren't just broken. They're... rewritten. They forget the war remember things that didn't happen. And the ones who do remember?" He paused, voice tightening. "They paint it."

"Paint what?" Ellie asked.

Weatherly's eyes met hers. "You."

Her breath caught. "What do you mean?"

"I mean, Silas has already sketched half this ward. Faces we hadn't seen yet. Names we hadn't spoken. And last week, he drew your eyes before he even knew your name."

They stepped into the archive room. It smelled of vinegar and iron filings. Floor-to-ceiling shelves held files yellowed with decades, some tied shut with red string. Ellie's gloved hand brushed a box labeled Classified: Drift Protocol – Inception Series. A stamped line across the top: MEMORY IS A FUNCTION OF CONTROL.

The lid was unsealed. Inside, a stack of patient reports. Some had been blacked out with thick strokes of charcoal. One file bore the mark of a different era—typed on yellowed paper, stamped not with Weatherly's initials but "M. Weaver." The handwriting in the margins was tight, precise, and unrepentant. A faded note in red ink ran along the margin:

"A mind that loops can be rewritten. A name that repeats can be replaced."—M.W.

She pulled the one for Subject 7C. Male. Identifiers: withdrawn, pre-verbal during reactivation, responds only to mirror stimuli. Recurrent themes: orchard, name transfer, identity displacement.

Ellie's eyes paused on the word orchard. Not because it was strange—but because it wasn't. A tree. A ribbon. Soil packed into her palms—someone else's memory or her own?

"What is the Drift Protocol?" she asked.

Weatherly didn't look at her. "That's above our clearance."

"But we're reading it."

"That's how it works here." He gestured to another file. "They give us just enough truth to drown in. Besides, truth doesn't prevent recurrence," Weatherly said. "It documents it."

Ellie reached for the next report but stopped. Her name was printed across the top.

HALE, E. – Phase One Observer. Clearance Level: Conditional. Memory bleed observed.

"I didn't consent to any observation."

Weatherly looked at her, his voice quieter now. "Doesn't mean you weren't chosen."

A voice cleared gently behind her. Ellie turned. A woman—elegant in the way steel sometimes is—stood at the edge of the hallway. Her coat was charcoal gray. A clipboard tucked under one arm.

"Nurse Hale," she said. "You'll want to write down everything Silas says. Even when it doesn't make sense."

Ellie blinked. "You've worked with him?"

The woman's expression didn't soften. "I've worked with all of them."

"Dr. Gretchen Weaver," the woman offered. "Clinical Research Coordinator and Head of the Cognitive Rehabilitation & Experimental Therapy department."

Ellie nodded slowly. "You were with Edenbrook?"

Gretchen's eyes flickered. "In a way. I've followed some of the longer threads. Especially the ones that keep reappearing."

She handed Ellie a folded page.

"The building won't follow this," she said, gesturing to what appeared to be a floor map. "But it helps some people sleep."

Ellie unfolded it. Standard wards. Therapy rooms. But one area wasn't labeled. Just a shape. A spiral.

"What's this?"

Gretchen's voice dropped. "That part isn't drawn to scale. Because it isn't built to be. Some architecture is metaphorical."

Ellie's brow creased.

Gretchen turned to leave but stopped. "Careful with Room 2-C," she said. "She isn't one of yours."

Ellie blinked. "What do you mean?"

Gretchen didn't smile this time. "She remembers more than she's supposed to. And less than she needs."

The words sat heavy between them, unanswered. Gretchen turned away first, her gaze fixed somewhere past the hallway like she was watching a memory retreat.

She didn't say more. Just walked past. But as she moved, Ellie noticed—her reflection in the frosted glass didn't move with her. It stayed behind. Watching.

She doesn't observe them, Ellie realized. She collects them.

Like proof. Or warning.

Ellie set the file down with trembling fingers. The paper smelled faintly of ozone—like a storm that had already passed but left its charge behind.

From the corner of her eye, a folder slid off the desk. No one had touched it. She bent to retrieve it. A sketch had fallen out. The spiral orchard. And standing in its center—two figures. One was clearly Silas. The other was a nurse. Wearing Ellie's coat.

Her stomach dropped—not because it was strange, but because it wasn't. The shape felt remembered. The angles too precise to be imagined. It pressed behind her ribs like déjà vu turned inside out—

too familiar to deny, too wrong to accept.

Her hand hovered above the page like it might bite.

"I've never been there," she whispered.

Weatherly's voice barely reached her. "Not yet."

The corridor to Ward C bent left like a secret withheld, the kind that grew heavier the longer it stayed unsaid. Ellie walked the length of it slowly, boots brushing the linoleum in a rhythm that didn't quite match the tempo of her thoughts.

She passed a wheeled gurney with a buckle strap still hanging off the side, then a wire cart with three cracked porcelain trays stacked too neatly, their silence louder than motion.

Room 3-C sat at the end of the corridor—its name etched by hand on a tarnished plaque, not standardized like the others. Something about that deviation made her hesitate.

She turned the handle, and inside, the lights flickered once, then steadied. The room was small, the walls the color of old gauze, shadow pooling in the corners as if it had nowhere else to settle. A steel-framed bed sat against the far wall, but it was the figure at the desk who drew Ellie's attention, Silas.

He was seated, slightly hunched, one leg crooked beneath the chair and the other tapping a jittering rhythm against the floor. His shirt was clean but misbuttoned. Charcoal-stained fingers hovered above a sketchpad, motionless. His eyes lifted the moment she entered—not startled. Expectant.

"You're late," he said.

Ellie checked her watch. "I'm early."

"Not for this."

She blinked. "Have we met before?"

He didn't answer. Instead, he gestured to the page in front of him. A sketch—unfinished. A spiral. Faint at the edges, darker toward the center.

She sat across from him, clipboard poised. "You've been here since July, is that right?"

His eyes didn't move from the paper. "I've been here longer than anyone thinks."

"What makes you say that?"

He picked up the charcoal. "Because I remember people before they arrive."

Ellie looked down at the sketch again.

"Have you drawn me before?"

"Every night since the power came back on."

He didn't blush. Didn't flirt. He said it like it was a responsibility. And she didn't recoil. She stared. And for a second, she didn't feel studied. She felt... remembered.

He tilted the sketchpad. There she was, drawn in fine lines—her coat, her gloves, even the small fold in her collar that she'd adjusted that morning without knowing why.

"I drew you," he said.

"Before you arrived. Before they gave you that name again."

He handed her a page. Her face, caught in profile—hair damp, collar crooked. The exact way she'd stood last Tuesday.

"You always arrive the same way. Not new. Just rearranged."

Her breath stilled. "When?"

"Before you forgot the orchard."

A pulse behind her eyes. A branch. A ribbon. Soil under her nails. Not a memory. A fragment. Buried.

"What orchard?" she asked, voice thinner now.

Silas didn't answer. Instead, he began to hum—a slow, circling tune that vibrated through the air like static searching for a forgotten frequency—a signal too old to trace but impossible to turn off. Ellie didn't recognize the melody, but her breath caught, her spine tightening with some embedded memory that didn't belong to her.

"You're not the first," he said suddenly. "They tried it before."

"Tried what?"

"Taking out the name and putting a new one in."

Her voice sharpened. "Who did?"

Silas looked at her then, eyes sharper than they had any right to be. "The same ones who taught you not to ask."

A beat passed. Then he smiled faintly, tapped the sketchpad once, and said, "But you're here now. That means it's happening again."

"I don't want to be part of this," she said—too fast. Too honest.

But even as the words left her mouth, they sounded wrong. Like someone else's refusal.

She stood to leave, breath unsteady. Behind her, the fluorescent lights buzzed louder. She turned back. Looking more closely at the drawing, she noticed in the corners the numbers 14-9-1-3 were scribbled.

"Is that a date?" she asked.

Silas didn't answer. His eyes twitched toward the numbers, then away again, like they stung.

"No," he finally said, barely audible. "That's what they called it. Before the Spiral."

Ellie's breath caught. "Before?"

His hand hovered midair as if drawing from memory he didn't trust. "NIAC... Neural Integration... and Control." Ellie mouthed the letters. N-I-A-C. Her stomach turned. Not just initials. A key. A cipher. A protocol they buried and called something else.

She froze. That acronym wasn't in any of the patient files, not in the intake records, not on any ward.

"You remember that?"

Silas's gaze snapped to hers. For a moment, his expression changed—not frightened, but furious. "I don't remember. I was made to forget."

He looked back down at the sketch, his voice hollow.

"The Spiral doesn't begin anything. It finishes it. By the time you see it... it's already too late."

On the paper, the spiral had widened. It reached the edges now. And in its center, where her figure had been drawn—was no longer her. Only a blank outline. And beneath it, written in rough, all-capital letters:

SHE WAS NEVER NEW.

The phrase pulsed behind her eyes, not as information but as recognition. Ellie walked the corridor on autopilot, her footsteps too even, clipboard too tight in her grip. She kept thinking of the sketch— of the outline where her figure used to be. The absence drawn like a scar.

She didn't sleep that night. Not really. The hours unraveled in a series of half-dreams and lightbulb flickers, the kind of sleep that felt more like surveillance than rest. At some point, she remembered hearing the hallway clock chime three, then four. Each toll echoed like a pulse against her ribs. By morning, the light outside had turned the color of bleached paper, and her reflection in the medicine cabinet looked a shade too pale to be alive.

She dabbed at her eyes with a cold cloth, reapplied her lipstick from muscle memory, and buttoned her uniform like armor. Whatever had shifted in her wasn't gone—it had only settled deeper, like dust in the lungs.

She kept hearing the phrase in Silas's voice.

You're the new variable.

In the corner of her vision, her reflection in the glass seemed slower again. Not reversed. Not flickering. Just… lagging. Like it was waiting for a cue she hadn't given.

The hallway beyond Ward C stretched too long, as if someone had quietly unspooled it overnight. The lighting buzzed faintly—soft, steady, but uncomfortable. Ellie kept her pace measured, though the soles of her shoes stuck faintly with every step, the institutional wax catching just enough to resist. Something about the rhythm felt off.

She passed a glass window outside the nurse's station. Her reflection caught the corner of her vision—and froze her mid-step. Not because she looked different but because she hadn't moved. The reflection had. It had stepped forward a fraction before she had, then stood still as if waiting for her to catch up.

She blinked. The image snapped into sync. But her skin crawled with the wrongness of it.

Farther down the hall, she paused near a rust-edged cart. One of the drawers was slightly ajar, an orderly's oversight. She nudged it closed. Her fingers, tremoring now, brushed the metal frame—and suddenly, she felt it again: soil. Cold. Wet. Packed into her palms like she'd been digging. Somewhere far away—or deep inside—the sensation of childhood clawed its way to the surface. Not her own.

A whisper bloomed behind her ear. They planted the names here. She turned. The corridor was empty. Ellie inhaled through her nose, trying to steady the breath that was already unraveling. From somewhere behind the walls, a hum began. At first, it sounded mechanical. A pipe groaning. But then it shifted—human.

A voice. No, not a voice. A humming. Low and circular. The Spiral Tune. She pressed her hand to the wall, cold against her skin. The hum dissipated—but her eyes caught another detail.

Scratched into the baseboard near the stairwell, so small she nearly missed it, was a shape. A spiral. Etched faintly but deliberate. She crouched to touch it. Her fingertip traced the line. It felt warm. The warmth traveled up her arm—not like heat, but like recognition. Her fingers knew the shape before her mind did.

A sudden whisper passed through her like wind. Not outside. Inside.

"Ellie..."

She stood too fast. The hallway tilted, then righted. The silence returned. But it didn't feel like absence. It felt like something holding its breath. She quickened her steps toward the , her pulse knocking hard behind her ears. She needed answers. And she was starting to fear she wasn't the only one asking the questions.

At the hallway's end, a door clicked open. Dr. Gretchen Weaver stepped out, her clipboard hugged tightly to her chest. Her expression was unreadable—but her eyes flicked once to Ellie's hand. The one still tingling from the spiral.

"Nurse Hale," she said calmly. "Let's walk."

They moved in silence past the old records room, past a corridor where the wallpaper curled like peeling skin until Gretchen slowed near the door to an unlit office. She opened it with a key from her coat pocket, ushering Ellie inside without a word.

The room was sparse—just two chairs, a desk, a lamp that flickered once before catching. Gretchen shut the door gently. No click. Just the hush of weight finding wood.

"You've had your first interaction with Silas," she said, stating it rather than asking.

Ellie nodded. "Yes."

"And?"

"He… knew things. About me. About a place I don't remember."

Gretchen's mouth tightened, but she smiled. Politely. The kind that never touched the eyes.

"That's normal. Well—normal for here."

Ellie sat rigid in the chair, fingers folded too neatly. "He mentioned an orchard."

Gretchen looked away, adjusting a folder on the desk that didn't need adjusting. "Patients in Ward C experience projected memory episodes. Environmental hallucinations. It's not uncommon."

"He also said I'd been here before."

That made Gretchen pause just half a breath too long. She picked up her clipboard.

"And how did that make you feel?"

Ellie bristled. "I'm not a patient."

Gretchen gave a soft chuckle. "Forgive me. Habit. I only mean—this place can evoke powerful associations. There's a reason it's often called the Reflection Ward."

Ellie frowned. "By who?"

"By those who've stayed too long." The room settled into a strange stillness.

Gretchen finally met her gaze. "I understand the temptation to… interpret things. To find meaning in stray comments or scribbles. But I'd caution against chasing shadows. You're new. That makes you vulnerable."

Ellie opened her mouth, but Gretchen's voice dipped just above a whisper.

"There was another nurse before you. Thought she saw too much. Heard things. Went looking. We're still writing the report."

Ellie's breath slowed.

"You're not her," Gretchen said, leaning forward, voice gentle now. "You're stronger. You'll adjust. Just... stay present. Observe. And don't dwell on dreams. They aren't yours to keep."

Ellie's throat tightened. Her thoughts felt crowded.

"I'll… keep that in mind," she said.

Gretchen rose, brushing invisible dust from her coat. "Good. Now, get some air before your next rotation. And Nurse Hale?" Ellie paused at the door.

"If you see something again—something that doesn't belong—don't write it down. Some truths only take root when given ink."

Ellie didn't answer. The hallway outside was colder than she remembered. And behind her, the mirror on the wall flickered. This time, it wasn't her reflection that looked back. It was someone else. Smiling. The smile in the mirror was hers—but only from the mouth down. The eyes were already remembering something she hadn't written yet—holding it, shaping it, as if memory itself were preparing to speak through her hand.

2-C: The Echo in the Mirror

Arlington Hills Psychiatric Hospital – September 4, 1947

Room 2-C – Post-Intake Observation

The door was labeled 2-C, but the corridor skipped Room 3. Ellie blinked. The floorplans she'd memorized bore no trace of a Room 2-C—like a line erased, but never fully forgotten. They told her the girl in Room 2-C had come from Edenbrook. No file. No prior intake record. Just a sealed envelope with a transfer stamp and a date that didn't make sense.

August 31st, 1947.

Three days before the facility reopened. Three days before Ellie arrived.

"Standard observational protocol," Dr. Weatherly had said, offering her the sealed case file with the redacted intake summary. "Just assess. No therapeutic engagement yet. You'll know if she's ready."

Ellie hadn't asked what that meant. No one ever clarified at Arlington Hills.

They just watched.

The girl sat at the far end of the room, perched at the edge of a chair too large for her frame. Her shoes barely touched the tile. Her shoulders curled inward—not from cold, but from the weight of a memory her body hadn't yet been permitted to forget.

One hand clutched a graphite pencil in a grip too tight for comfort. The other hovered inches above the blank intake page before her. It hadn't moved since Ellie entered.

The clipboard in Ellie's hands grew heavier by the minute. She made standard notations:

- Motor delay – present

- Eye contact – evasive

- Pupillary response – heightened, untriggered

But the air between them was thicker than the symptoms on the page. This wasn't just an observation. It felt like trespassing.

The tray gleamed, catching light the way a mirror catches breath—offering back only the faintest suggestion of her shape, as if afraid to reveal too much at once.

Each time her eyes drifted too close, her head jerked away—as if the reflection were trying to speak before she was ready to hear it.

Ellie softened her posture, crouching slightly. "You're safe here. You can look wherever you want."

The girl didn't answer. Her eyes flicked once—just once—to the polished tray beside her. Then flinched. Ellie followed her gaze. In the warped shine of the metal, there was only the child's reflection. Pale. Silent.

But the girl whispered, not to Ellie—"It looked back like it remembered her."

"Can you tell me your name?" Ellie asked gently.

The girl blinked. "That's the name they gave me."

A chill moved under Ellie's coat. The pencil twitched. The girl finally touched it to paper—first with a tremor, then with certainty. One curved line. Then another. A spiral. Shaky at first. Then deliberate. Three loops. Four. The tip of the pencil snapped. She didn't flinch. She reached for another.

"What are you drawing?" Ellie whispered. The girl's voice came softly:

"It's not what I see. It's what I remember seeing."

She drew faster now—shapes forming without reference. A chair, child-sized, curved slats like a spine. A tree with no branches, its roots splaying outward like veins sketched from above—as though it had grown down, not up. An orchard. The loops were too clean—measured. Not natural. The spiral's center bled outward as if the paper itself resisted being named.

Ellie's stomach dropped—not because it was strange, but because it wasn't. The shape felt remembered. The angles are too precise to be imagined. She leaned closer.

Then, without lifting her gaze, the girl wrote something in the corner.

E. HALE

Ellie recoiled like the name had burned through the page. Her pulse flared. Her grip on the clipboard faltered. That wasn't just handwriting. It was memory.

"Where did you see that name?" she asked.

The girl tilted her head. Her eyes met Ellie's for the first time.

"Isn't that you?"

Ellie's breath caught.

"Yes," she said slowly. "But no one told you that."

The girl looked back at her drawing. And kept drawing. Behind them, the mirror flickered. Not visibly. But subtly. Ellie's reflection blinked out of sync—just half a second late.

The girl in Room 2-C whispered:

"She looked at the mirror. And it looked back like it remembered her."

Ellie walked the rest of the way in silence, the floor beneath her feet too clean, too bright. The drawing still gripped in her hand.

The hallway air was sour at the edges—like spoiled paper, like breath that had nowhere to go. Cold sweat prickled at her collarbone. Even the shadows held their breath.

She entered the records archive with caution—not because of silence, but because of the strange way sound warped here. The rustle of paper echoed too loudly. Footsteps came from the wrong direction. The walls themselves had absorbed too many secrets.

She closed the door behind her. A soft latch. No lock.

The ledger lay on the center table—a massive, leather-bound book, cracked at the spine and ribboned with yellowed tabs. She'd passed it before, dozens of times, but never opened it. It was too ceremonial, too permanent.

Now, she did. Her fingers trembled as she turned the pages. Intake years stretching back to the twenties. Children listed by initials, not names—as if identity were a variable best kept small, containable. A page marked "Phase One: Observational Drift." Then "Phase Two: Pre-merge Simulation."

She paused at "Phase Three: Proxy Implantation." Her stomach clenched. She turned one more page.

There—folded between entries—a form had slipped loose.

A misfiled intake report.

HALE, ELEANOR J.

Date of Intake: August 17th, 1945

Status: Unresolved – Memory Schema Retained

Stamped diagonally across the top: Subject 1C – Provisional

Ellie's breath caught. Her name. Two years too early. The margins were filled with red ink: "DO NOT DISCLOSE TO SUBJECT."

"Monitor for reintegration bleed."

"Use alternative surname if reactivated."

She turned to the ledger and there it was.

1C | The Retained

No discharge. No reassignment. No formal treatment notes. Just one line in the margin:

The subject who could not forget.

Ellie's throat tightened. Her hand hovered over the entry, wanting to erase it, to strike it through, to make it disappear.

But she couldn't move. Her fingers wouldn't close.

She stared down at the ink. It wasn't fresh, but it felt alive—bleeding through the paper like memory through skin.

Behind her, the overhead bulb flickered once. Just once. But in its momentary stutter, her reflection appeared in the glass cabinet across the room.

The glass wavered—subtle at first. Then, her reflection came into view. Same coat. Same stance. But the face wasn't hers. Not younger. Not older. Just… wrong.

A mouth she didn't recognize. A left eye slightly out of alignment. A smile—slow, knowing—unfolding just a second too late, like it had waited for her to look first.

Ellie stepped backward. The cabinet remained closed. But her own image didn't. It kept watching even after she turned away.

The room was empty. A shiver trickled down her spine. She closed the ledger with care but not reverence. The kind of care one uses when returning a weapon to its place.

Outside, the hallway had quieted. But something remained. The knowledge she couldn't unknow. She had been recorded before she arrived. She was already in the book. And the name she answered to wasn't the one that started this. And maybe it wouldn't be the one that ended it, either.

She turned from the archive door, but the hallway blurred around its edges—just slightly as if it had been redrawn without warning. The lights above flickered, but not in rhythm. In pulse.

Ellie stepped forward, but the floor softened beneath her like old earth or memory not quite settled. Her hand reached instinctively for the wall but found glass instead—cold, mirrored, humming.

A flicker shimmered in the air ahead—soft, shifting light, like oil on water. But as Ellie moved closer, she realized it wasn't light. It was pattern. A spiral, luminous and slow, turned just above the floor. Not drawn. Not projected. Present.

With each rotation, the hallway thinned—became less real, more remembered. Silas had sketched this shape before. She hadn't believed it then. Now, she wasn't sure she'd ever doubted it at all.

It didn't spiral like a symbol. It twisted like scar tissue—old, knotted, impossible to heal.

Like something old rising through memory's sediment. Walls warped. Angles dissolved. She saw a tree. A chair. A child's hands in the dirt. A voice pulsed through the spiral—not sound, but structure. Memory woven into breath.

"You're remembering out of order." Her vision snapped back. Normal hallway. Standard light.

Except on the tile—an ash-like spiral imprint, smudged but

unmistakable.

And on her fingertips: graphite. She didn't remember picking up the pencil. Her hand trembled. The graphite dust clung like ash. Maybe she hadn't picked it up at all. Maybe it had remembered her first.

CHAPTER: FOUR

The Orchard's Recall

The hallway bent toward the east wing, folding in on itself—long, hushed, and rank with bleach and something older, the stench of a memory left to rot. Ellie hadn't meant to come this way. The room wasn't on the floor plan Gretchen had shown her. It shouldn't have existed at all. Yet here she was.

The corridor was colder here. The walls seemed narrower, the overhead light dimmer, as if the current flickered just beneath perception. Her shoes clicked with a stutter she couldn't account for. She counted the steps anyway. She always did. As if naming the rhythm could stop it from changing. But this wasn't rhythm. It was recursion.

That thought didn't feel like hers. But it fit her too well to ignore. The doors were numbered. Except this one. This one had no number. Just a brass placard above it that read:

WHISPER ROOM

The letters had been carved deep, but time had worn their edges thin—as if the room had whispered back long enough to sand them down.

She paused with her hand on the knob. The air held that tight stillness—the kind that thickened before a thunderclap. The brass was warm like someone had just let go.

Inside, the room was small. Square. And wrong. Mirrors lined the walls—floor to ceiling, edge to edge. No seams. No frames. The ceiling bore a pane as well, reflecting her back on all sides like she'd entered a prism made of herself. The floor was wood, scuffed, and old, except for the center was a single chair. Child-sized. It looked wooden from afar, but as she stepped closer, she saw the grain shimmered faintly, as though it wasn't made of wood at all.

Ellie sneezed. Not delicately. Loud. Full-bodied. The kind of sneeze that belonged in a different building entirely. A puff of dust billowed from the folder. She wiped her nose with the sleeve of her uniform and muttered, "Guess mildew doesn't loop." Silence followed. Then, absurdly, she chuckled. Just once. The chair across from her creaked in agreement.

A tag hung from the back of the chair: E.H. Ellie's breath faltered. The letters weren't printed. They were carved. Small, clean, deliberate cuts. Her initials—but not from any tag she'd ever worn. She stepped further in, breath slow, uncertain. Her reflection multiplied with each pace, surrounding her in imperfect repetition. One blinked too soon. One smiled a half second after she did. Another seemed to breathe before she had inhaled.

She turned in a slow circle. No matter where she stood, the chair remained at the center. She reached out. Her fingers met glass. There was no chair. Just its reflection. She turned quickly—only to find her reflection standing behind the chair. Not in the glass. In the room.

Ellie backed away. The walls closed in—not physically, but perceptually as if the mirrors were collapsing in on her sense of distance. She turned toward the door, but something stopped her—a breath on the back of her neck, cold and scentless.

She spun. In the reflection of the Whisper Room's ceiling, the stitched-eyed girl reached upward—but this time, she wasn't mimicking Ellie. She was mirroring herself. Not a ghost. Not a warning. A version practicing return. Her eyes were sewn shut, but her lips parted—as if caught mid-scream. Or mid-memory.

Ellie froze. Her mouth moved, but no sound came. The girl raised a hand. Her stitched eyes wept dark threads. She reached forward—no, outward. Then the mirror fogged.

Words began to appear across the central pane as if traced by a fingertip she couldn't see:

DO NOT REMEMBER

Her breath hitched. The phrase melted away—replaced by another. I'm still in here.

Then another, as the mirrors around her pulsed one by one:

The mirror pulsed faintly, as though holding its breath between sentences.

Stop digging. Stop asking. Stop being me.

Ellie's hand flew to the glass—but her fingertips left no mark. Then, one final phrase appeared in fog above her head, reflected in the ceiling pane:

"It's okay if you forget again."

Her lips had moved before the sentence appeared.

Ellie backed into the door, heart slamming against her ribs. Her hand fumbled for the knob.

The mirror pulsed.

She turned, wrenched the door open, and fled into the corridor. The hallway yawned back to normal—blank walls, blank air—but the echo of her breath was still tangled with something else's.

When she turned back, the door was gone. No placard. No frame. No sign the room had ever existed. Just the smooth stretch of plaster and the echo of a memory she hadn't yet made. Ellie leaned against the wall, eyes wide, breath shallow. The whisper came again, not from outside but within her own skull:

"It started here. But it never ends."

A scraping sound echoed faintly through the hallway beyond the mirrors—slow, deliberate. A chair leg? A breath?

Room 9 again. Still locked. But never silent. It came from past the administrative hall, too distant to trace. Yet too familiar to ignore. Far down the hall, she thought she saw movement—a figure retreating too quickly to identify. A clipboard. A dark coat. But no footsteps echoed.

If someone had seen her enter the Whisper Room, they hadn't stopped her. The corridor outside didn't echo. It absorbed. Her footsteps vanished beneath the silence, swallowed by walls that had forgotten how to reflect sound. Ellie moved quickly but without urgency, as if her body were being guided by instinct rather than intention. Her fingers still tingled from the mirror's static, the spiral still pulsing behind her eyes like an afterimage burned into thought.

She didn't know where she was going—only that something inside her had already chosen.

She didn't remember deciding to go outside. The building blurred behind her like breath on glass. All she knew was that she needed space—to breathe, to forget, to remember. The orchard felt like the only place left that wasn't curated. But even that wasn't true.

The orchard behind Arlington Hills was quiet in a way that felt rehearsed—too symmetrical, too still, like a dream that had practiced being real. Ellie followed the gravel path that curved off from the eastern ward, past the rusted wheelbarrow that always seemed to be in a different place each day. Her shoes sank slightly in the soft earth, each step whispering something just beneath the threshold of hearing.

She'd found the map tucked inside a book left outside Silas's door. Not a map in the traditional sense, but a charcoal sketch—a spiral orchard drawn from above, with a child-sized figure at its center. She hadn't told anyone about it. Not Gretchen. Not even Dr. Weatherly.

The real orchard looked like the drawing had been plucked from it. Each tree curved just slightly inward as if growing under pressure. Their bare limbs twisted toward a central clearing where the snow never seemed to stick.

Her thoughts spun, loud against the unnatural stillness. How could she have known where to go? She had walked the path without hesitation. Her hand had known which branch to brush aside. Her breath came shallow and sharp.

You're just unraveling, she told herself. This is what stress looks like. Memory confusion. Pattern fixation. Emotional displacement.

But her body disagreed. Her knees ached in recognition. Her coat tugged like it had knelt here before.

Ellie paused just past the first tree. Her boots crunched frost into the loam, but the sound was swallowed quickly as if the earth had grown used to holding its breath. She knelt where the ground rose slightly, a bulge beneath the mossy carpet, and brushed away the top layer of leaves.

Beneath them: a flat stone. Worn smooth. The kind used in old military gardens or forgotten graveyards. No name was etched into it.

But someone had carved a symbol—lightly, not recently. A spiral, half-erased by time. She touched it with her gloved fingers, and the chill that bit her palm felt older than winter. The spiral didn't mark an ending. It fed downward—like roots. Not growing. Devouring. Feeding on whatever name had been buried here last.

A sharp cry broke the silence. Not an animal. Not human. Something in between. A fragment of sound that didn't belong to this moment. It pulled her upright, breath caught, and for a second, she thought she saw someone else kneeling across the orchard—mirroring her position. Same coat. Same boots. Same motion. But no one was there. Just trees. Just shadows.

Ellie stopped. The wind shifted. Her breath caught in her throat.

"I was here before," she whispered to no one.

"No," said a voice behind her. "You never left."

She spun—nothing. Just wind in the branches. But the air tasted like copper. Like blood on a coin. Then—flashes. Not memories. Something else.

Ellie on her knees, digging. Her fingernails caked with soil. A ribbon clenched in her fist.

The girl's voice, again, layered through time: "They planted the names here."

The memory fractured. Another layer. A child's hand gripping hers in the dark, tugging toward the center. "Come on, Ellie. They said I could show you."

The name caught in her throat. She crouched. Brushed away a thin layer of snow. Below it, scratched faintly into the soil, was a mark: a spiral, curling inward, pulsing like a heartbeat frozen in dirt.

Ellie's hand hovered above it. "I remember…" But she didn't. Not clearly. And maybe that was the point.

What if memory wasn't being restored… but replaced?

What if she wasn't digging something up—but down?

But what came next wasn't hers. The words pushed through her like echoes in someone else's voice.

"They drew me first. Before I had a name."

She staggered upright. The trees now bent closer, their shadows warping against the earth. The wind circled back. This time, it carried the scent of antiseptic and burning paper.

She reached into her coat pocket and pulled out the sketch. A second figure had been added. A nurse's silhouette. Standing beside the child. No charcoal dust on her gloves. No memory of drawing it. Only the echo.

Ellie turned as if called by name—but not by voice. By memory.

The tree at the center of the orchard shifted. Its roots curled like fingers. She stepped toward it. She should have been afraid. Instead, she felt... homesick. Not for a place. For a self, she didn't remember losing.

"Who did you make me into?" she whispered—to the tree, to the Spiral, to no one.

Behind her, a whisper tickled the frost:

"She didn't forget. She was made to remember."

The orchard bent. The snow fell sideways. And the spiral glowed faintly beneath her feet. Not drawn. Etched. Alive.

She turned away from the grave-stone spiral and walked back toward the service stairwell, clutching the clipboard tighter against her chest. She didn't know what she'd been before. Only that this version had been waiting here a long, long time.

CHAPTER: FIVE

The First Subject

The records room smelled of iron and ink—like a machine trying, and failing, to remember itself. Ellie stepped inside and closed the door gently behind her. The overhead light flickered once, then steadied, casting a jaundiced glow across the shelving.

The place was colder than usual. She didn't shiver.

She moved toward the wall labeled "Experimental Intakes" and crouched beside the second-to-lowest drawer.

Phase One: Observational Drift

Phase Two: Mirrorline Initiation

Phase Three: Proxy Implantation

She ran her fingers along the tabs until one caught beneath her nail. The folder was thinner than it should have been. She pulled it free and opened it across her lap.

No intake name. No birth year. No release form.

Just a subject ID: 1C – The Retained

Her breath stilled. She had seen this before. Or thought she had. A corner, a glimpse—a memory trying to convince her it was new. A redacted corner of a larger file. A forgotten number.

But this time—her name wasn't listed. Not anywhere. And still, it felt like she was the one being described. A line at the top read:

"Subject exhibits recursive resistance. Memories rebound instead of dissolve."

Below that, someone had scribbled in faint pencil:

"Mirror rejection confirmed. Retains memory fragments during overwrite."

The note wasn't written like a warning. It read like a symptom chart. Memory, here, wasn't just recorded. It was implanted. Like skin that won't take the graft. Ellie blinked. Her reflection shimmered—slightly delayed, slightly wrong, like the glass was waiting for her to believe it. The lighting overhead buzzed again, and for a moment, her image smiled when she didn't.

She turned back to the folder.

Tucked into the back pocket was a photograph. A grainy black-and-white, edges warped from age. A child sat in a chair too large for her, shoulders hunched, eyes wide. She held a drawing pad.

And watching her—from behind the mirror—was a boy.

Silas. But younger. Barely fourteen. And the girl… she couldn't place her. Couldn't name her. But her posture was identical to the one Ellie had seen mirrored in the orchard. She had drawn something—though the paper was turned away from the camera.

Ellie turned the photo over. Written in red pencil:

S. Reeve – Observation 3A

Emotional convergence confirmed. Child #1C shows high absorption rate.

Another line scrawled sideways in rushed handwriting:

"The girl they used before the others."

Ellie's hands trembled. She hadn't met this girl. Yet her skin prickled—as though her own memories had been folded through this stranger's body and pressed back into her bones.

She set the folder aside and rose to her feet. The cabinet's reflection no longer held her image. Instead, the child from the photo sat in the mirrored seat, head bowed, spiral drawn across her lap in thick crayon lines. The reflection didn't just differ. It disobeyed. It was like the mirror had stopped pretending. Like it had remembered something, Ellie hadn't.

Ellie reached toward it. The reflection blinked—and vanished. She stepped back. The room absorbed the air around her.

The file still trembled in Ellie's hands as she climbed the stairs to the west wing. Gretchen's office beckoned her without her awareness. Her heart didn't race. That was the strange part. It just... sank. Like something inside her already knew the answer. Knew who she was asking about.

Her body had simply moved like it already knew the route—like the thought had been there before she had the words for it.

Outside the glass-paneled door, the hall was quiet. Too quiet. She knocked once. Inside, Gretchen sat at her desk, a cup of untouched tea steaming faintly beside a folder she wasn't reading. She didn't look up.

"You're early," Gretchen said.

"I wasn't scheduled," Ellie replied, setting the file on the edge of the desk.

Gretchen's eyes finally met hers. Then dropped to the file. The color in her face didn't change. But her stillness sharpened.

"That drawer hasn't been accessed in years," she said.

Ellie's voice was steady. "You know what's in it."

"I know what's been buried." A beat passed between them.

"There was no name," Ellie said. "Only a number."

Gretchen nodded slowly. "That's how they kept the subjects clean. Numbers don't dream."

"But they remember. And worse—they make us remember them." Ellie's voice sharpened. "And you let them?"

Gretchen looked down. "We cataloged them."

Ellie opened the folder again, laying the photograph on the blotter pad between them. She tapped the corner of the image with one finger—the place where the boy watched the girl from behind the mirror.

"Silas was there," Ellie said. "He saw her."

"I know."

"You knew?"

"He was never supposed to. But trauma doesn't respect protocols. It bleeds."

"Who was she?"

Gretchen's silence lasted too long. "She was…" Gretchen began, then stopped herself. "Someone who believed she was saving the others. Someone who volunteered."

Ellie's chest tightened. "She was a child."

"She was a prototype." Ellie recoiled.

Gretchen flinched. "That's not how I wanted to say it."

Her voice cracked. Just once. "I tried to stop the merge."

Then quieter, like she'd buried the memory beneath protocol: "But they'd already named her." The tea on the desk had gone cold. Neither of them moved to touch it.

Ellie turned the photo over. "You wrote this. The line about her being used first."

Gretchen's fingers curled. "I didn't want to forget her. So I wrote it where someone would one day find it."

"Someone like me." Gretchen looked away.

Ellie leaned in. "Is that what this is? You think I'm her?"

"I think that memory chooses its own record-keeper," Gretchen said quietly. "That doesn't mean you're the same girl."

Ellie walked toward Room 2-C like someone is trailing behind her. Her gloves stayed on—she didn't want to see if the spiral had reappeared beneath her skin.

Room 2-C's door stood ajar.

The girl was still there, posture unchanged, pencil in hand. But the drawing had changed.

She had drawn the orchard again. This time, the spiral wasn't just implied—it was explicit. Burned into the clearing at the center, like a map etched in ash.

And beneath it: a name. Not hers. Not Ellie's. Not even the girl's. Just a single letter: C.

"Who asked you to draw that?" Ellie asked.

"No one asks. It just starts. The shapes remember themselves."

"Why the orchard?"

The girl blinked. "Because that's where she began."

"She?"

"The first one. She stayed there when they took her name."

"And the spiral?"

"It's the part that refuses burial. The part that digs its way back up."

The pencil moved again. A figure. Seated. A chair with slats like roots. Another girl behind her—unfinished. Ellie's breath caught. Not Clara. But close enough to remember her wrong.

"Who is that?" Ellie asked.

The girl flipped the page. Drew a hallway. Curving. A mirror at the center.

Name beneath it: E. Hale.

"Where did you see that?" Ellie whispered.

The girl didn't blink. "It saw me first."

Ellie fled the room.

Silas hadn't moved since the morning session.

"You saw it, didn't you?" he said before she spoke.

"Saw what?"

"The one with her name in your handwriting."

"No one said anything about names."

Silas tilted his head. "Not what you read. What you remembered."

He handed her a drawing. Two figures. One beneath a tree. The other—mirror for a head. The tree bark etched with the letter: C.

In the corner: her initials. E.H. But the graphite was old.

"I didn't draw this."

"You didn't need to. You remembered it enough."

"What's it offering?"

"The part of you that stayed."

He smiled faintly. "Clara, you—"

Ellie froze. The name caught in her chest like a fishhook. Not "Ellie." Something older. Something she shouldn't have recognized—but did. Her mouth opened, a reply caught on her tongue. Not "Ellie." Something older. Something that didn't belong here.

She swallowed it. Hard. Like a name she hadn't earned.

"What did you call me?"

Silas blinked. "I didn't."

She stood.

"Just remember," he murmured, "the mirror shows what you owe. Not what you want."

In the restricted archive, Ellie found the file: PR-1 / OBS-PROT-1C

PROJECT SPIRAL: EARLY SUBJECTIVE COGNITION TESTING

Test Name: OBSERVATIONAL DURATION

Merge Type: Phase Zero (Non-consensual)

Subject Classification: 1C

Handwritten:

"RECURSION BEHAVIOR PRESENT PRIOR TO TRIAL." "EARLY RESPONSE TO MIRROR CONTAINMENT SHOWS SELF-FRAGMENTATION AHEAD OF MERGE." —MW (Marcus Weaver, Ph.D.)

In the margin:

Subject unknown to self. Identifiable only through pattern.

"Let the orchard tell her."

A spiral had been drawn on the opposite cabinet. Light. It was faint—but not fading. It looked like it was thinking. Like it had waited long enough—and was now remembering her deliberately. Behind it—A breath.

Ellie turned. And ran. She ran because the Spiral wasn't done. It was still telling her who to be. And part of her—God help her—was starting to listen.

CHAPTER: SIX

The Unveiling Protocol

The older nurses didn't talk much about Hazel Greer—but they all deferred to her. She wasn't listed as a supervisor, didn't sign disciplinary reports, and rarely appeared in meetings. But she knew where the archived ledgers were kept—and more importantly, which names had been scratched out and written back in. She knew which keys opened which stairwells. And more than once, Ellie had seen junior nurses pause when Hazel entered a room like something in the air recoiled around her.

Ellie hadn't spoken with her often—not directly. But the few times they'd crossed paths, Hazel had looked at her the way one looks at a mirror too long left uncovered. Not afraid. Not curious. Just watching. Like Ellie was a reflection Hazel wasn't ready to face—but knew she'd have to.

Today, Ellie needed to ask. Not for permission. For clarity. Or whatever passed for it here. The classified memo sat folded in her pocket like a second pulse. She knew every word. But one line circled back again and again: "Allow identity bleed to complete, then reassign under fabricated intake alias."

She passed the corridor to records, walking through dim light that pulsed in a spiral cadence. A reflection blinked ahead of her in the glass above the stairwell—but it wasn't hers. Not exactly. It flickered, delayed, like a thought half-forgotten trying to find its shape again.

The art therapy wing was quiet. The hum of the building softened into something more organic. She stopped at Hazel's office. The door was ajar, a thin line of lamplight bleeding out across the floor. Inside, Hazel sat at her desk, flipping through patient logs like she was trying not to be caught revising the past.

Ellie stepped into the doorway and offered the folded memo.

"I need to ask you something."

Hazel didn't look up right away. "You're not supposed to have that file."

"I think we passed 'supposed to' a long time ago."

Hazel met her eyes then—tired, rimmed in red. Recognition flickered, followed by something deeper. Regret.

"Where did you find it?"

"Vault B. Behind a false panel labeled DRIFT FAILURES."

Hazel's shoulders fell. "That drawer was meant to stay shut."

"Why?" Ellie stepped forward. "What is going on here? Who is Marcus Weaver?"

Hazel hesitated. "Dr. Weaver was a decorated trauma researcher. He pioneered mirror-phase rehabilitation for shell-shocked soldiers. Led the NIAC program before it was... restructured."

Ellie pulled a sketch from her pocket—charcoal, frantic. A chair. A tree. A spiral of roots. The initials E.H. written in a hand just slightly off from her own.

Hazel took one look and paled. "That's from the 1C ledger. Pre-coded. No subject name."

"But it's in my hand," Ellie said.

Hazel's reply was soft. "Memory doesn't live in the mind. It lives in the motion." Ellie's fingers flexed—reflexively. As if her hand knew something her head still denied. Hazel's lips moved — not to speak, but as if shaping an apology she would never say aloud. Her hands, briefly, folded as if in prayer. Then unfolded. Flat. Empty. Hazel turned back to the logbook. Her hands trembled just once—before she stilled them.

"What does that mean?"

Hazel didn't answer. Not directly.

Ellie stared at the sketch. The hum behind her eyes was rising again.

"Who was she? 1C."

Hazel swallowed. "Clara."

Ellie turned to the window. The orchard loomed in the fog behind the hospital. The spiral tree. The chair. Roots too deep to dig up. She blinked—but the image stayed. Not in her vision. Somewhere else. A deeper register.

"Thank you for your time," she said and left before Hazel could reply.

The east wing breathed differently than the rest of Arlington Hills. Not the clinical hush of sterilized wards. This corridor sighed in drafts and groans—too old to lie. Ellie walked it with her breath held between caution and certainty.

Signs flickered past: Music Therapy, Reassignment Evaluation, Intake Overflow. Most scratched out. She brushed one peeling placard, revealing blue paint beneath—the same shade as the orchard chair.

A sound behind her—slow, dragging. She turned. Empty. She kept going. Room 9 had no plaque. Just a faint spiral etched into the baseboard. It hadn't been there the day before.

She opened the door. Dust clung to the air. A child-sized chair faced the mirror wall. A file lay open beneath it. She crouched. The orchard again. Spiral trees. At the center: a dark smudge, pressed into the paper like a wound trying to scar over but failing.

Only one word. SUBJECT.

Her reflection met her gaze from the mirror—but didn't blink when she did.

Then it spoke.

"Ellie…"

She staggered into the hallway.

The map Gretchen had given her was incomplete. It had never shown this. But her feet found the Orchard Archive anyway. The room was warmer than expected. A manila folder sat at the table's center.

SUBJECT 1C – PHASE ONE. She opened it. Spiral drawings. Names overwritten. In margins: "They planted the names here."

Another line: "Still naming them. Even the ones that don't last."

One sketch showed a girl at the spiral's center; the face was erased. Beneath it: "This was where they started to forget me."

Flashes broke across Ellie's mind. Shovel. Ribbon. Frost. A whisper:

"You buried it. But it bloomed anyway."

The door shut on its own. She knew this turn. This breath. This page waiting open.

This wasn't discovery. It was re-enactment.

Memory wasn't showing her the way. It was dragging her down it.

When she reopened it—the hallway had changed. A voice, distant, hummed the Spiral Tune. Her own. She moved deeper. Past rusted stairwells. Down to the Orchard Transfer log.

The hallway curved like a memory bending under pressure. Each file whispered. A single sheet lay waiting. A spiral orchard. Two figures now. A child. A nurse. The badge: Hale. Beneath the roots, a third name—erased. But the curve of the first letter was unmistakable. A C. Not Clara. Not exactly. She reached for it. A whisper at her ear:

"I'll wear it next."

Then, almost as an responsive echo, "Stability is not healing. It is silence." The paper warmed in her hands.

Ellie whispered, "I was here." But the name she whispered wasn't a seed she'd planted.

It was a graft — pressed into her mouth, stitched into her breath.

A breath responded.

"You never left."

Ellie stood at the threshold of the west stairwell, breath caught between steps. The lights overhead dimmed, not from failure but from choice. On the landing below, where no chalk had ever marked the floor, a new spiral had been drawn—deliberate, damp, and fresh. It wasn't drawn in chalk. It was ink. Still drying. As if someone had expected her to find it. Its lines weren't childlike. They were clinical. Surgical. A message meant for her. She crouched without realizing, fingers trembling as they hovered above the symbol. And for the first time since she'd arrived, she didn't ask what it meant. She asked what had drawn it.

It wasn't a symbol anymore. It was the memory of a memory.

Layered. Breeding. Waiting for a host. Like a graft ready to root where the body split open.

She should have recoiled. Instead, her hand hovered — not to erase it, but to finish it. Behind her, a door creaked open. But no footsteps followed. Only the sound of charcoal snapping under pressure.

CHAPTER: SEVEN

The Unassigned Memory

Arlington Hills Psychiatric Hospital – September 6, 1947

The stairwell door groaned shut behind her, but Ellie didn't flinch. Her gaze stayed fixed on the spiral—its chalk lines still moist, as if time itself kept circling back, refusing to let it set. The symbol curled inward, tighter than the others she'd seen, as though it had been drawn not to warn… but to contain.

She reached out and touched the edge with her gloved fingertip. The chalk was warm—not from sun or skin, but from memory. The kind that loops. The kind that roots. Her hand jerked back instinctively. But not before she saw it.

In the spiral's center, where chalk usually thinned, a single word had been scratched in reverse:

Clara.

Her breath caught. When she looked up, the hallway ahead had shifted. Same walls. Same lights. But the air had thickened like she'd stepped through a seam that shouldn't have opened. She backed away from the spiral, heart pounding, and turned—expecting silence.

Instead, a voice whispered from behind the stairwell grate.

"Clara didn't vanish. She was buried."

Ellie froze. The whisper didn't echo. It folded inward like it had only ever been meant for her.

"Who's there?" she said aloud, but her voice cracked—too loud in the quiet. The grate behind the wall exhaled softly, as if releasing something that had waited years to speak. Nothing moved. But she felt watched, not by eyes, but by the building itself. By the memory, it kept breathing back into her.

The chalk spiral had begun to smudge—slowly unraveling as if the message had been delivered and no longer needed to remain. Ellie turned and walked fast now, back through the hall that had changed behind her. Each step echoed differently than the one before.

She needed to find the original orchard blueprints. Not the ones Weatherly gave her. The ones no one wanted her to see. Because Clara hadn't disappeared. And Ellie wasn't sure anymore which one of them had come back.

Ellie didn't knock this time. She pushed open the door to Room 3-C with more force than she meant to, her breath sharp, her gloves dusted faintly with chalk. The room was dim—just the way Silas kept it. The blinds were drawn, slats angled to slice the afternoon light into thin ribbons across the floor. He sat in his usual place: near the radiator, sketchbook resting on his knees, fingers stained black at the edges like he'd been drawing since dawn.

"I found the spiral," she said, skipping any preamble. "In the stairwell below the orchard archive. Chalk. Fresh."

Silas didn't look up.

She crossed the room in three long strides, heart pounding. "And in the center, a name."

His charcoal stopped mid-curve.

"Clara," she whispered. "It was Clara."

Now, he looked at her.

His eyes weren't startled. They were tired, like someone who'd waited a long time for someone else to catch up.

"She was the first," Silas said quietly. "She knew how to carry it."

Ellie stepped closer. "The spiral?"

He nodded. "The name. The recursion. The weight. All of it."

"Then why is it mine now?" Her voice rose, unsteady. "Why do I keep finding her drawings in my handwriting? Her memories stitched into mine?"

Silas stared down at the paper on his lap. "Because she left pieces behind."

A beat passed. The overhead light buzzed faintly.

"I think I was her," Ellie said, voice low. "I think I was overwritten."

Silas finally looked up again. His expression was unreadable. "You're not Clara."

She flinched.

"You're what came after."

He turned the sketchpad around. Ellie leaned in.

A girl beneath a tree. Spiral roots beneath her feet. And beside her—another girl, mirrored in pose. But fading at the edges. Unfinished. Unstable.

"They buried her," Silas murmured, "but they didn't let her rest. And when they pulled something new out of the orchard... it remembered the shape of the first."

Ellie's throat tightened. "Then what am I?"

Silas tilted his head. "You're the reason I didn't forget."

She staggered back a step. Her fingers grazed the edge of the chair as she steadied herself. "You called me Clara once, before. In the drawing. You said her name."

He didn't blink. "Did I?"

"You did," she snapped.

He shrugged faintly. "Then maybe I forgot again."

His gaze drifted to the window.

"Or maybe," he added, "you remembered too much."

Ellie's hand went to her coat pocket—the folded sketch was still there, pulsing like a second heartbeat. She looked back at Silas, unsure what she wanted from him. Answers? Reassurance? A name that wasn't hers? Ellie recoiled.

"No," she said—too fast, too loud. "I'm not her."

Silas didn't flinch.

"I remember Chicago," Ellie continued, her voice rising to fill the sterile silence between them. "My transfer. My apartment. The snow. The train. I remember me."

Silas turned the sketchpad back toward himself. "Do you?"

"I'm not some… overwritten copy," she whispered, more to herself now than him. "I have memories."

"Memories are just what the mind agrees to replay," he murmured, not looking at her.

Ellie's chest tightened. She took a step back, then another, until the doorknob hit her spine. Her hand curled around it.

"You said Clara was the first," she whispered, voice trembling. "If that's true… why me?"

Silas finally looked up again. His gaze was hollow, worn down to something raw.

"Because you came back."

[INT. MONITORING STATION – SUBLEVEL D]

The room was silent, but for the soft tick of a wall clock, two minutes slow.

Gretchen sat alone, her lab coat draped neatly over the back of a steel chair. In front of her, a grainy black-and-white monitor flickered with static, then steadied. The feed was labeled: WARD: C – 3C – UNLISTED OBS.

She watched Ellie retreat from Silas, hand still clutched around the doorknob like it was the only thing holding her together. Her breathing was too loud through the old audio feed. Distorted. Frantic.

Behind Gretchen, the observation logs for that room sat open. No longer assigned. No longer reviewed. Except for her.

Her fingers hovered over the volume dial. She didn't turn it up. She already knew the cadence of what was coming.

Onscreen, Ellie said, "I remember who I am."

And yet—Her reflection in the room's window lagged a full second behind.

Gretchen's jaw tensed. She reached for a sealed manila envelope marked "MERGE RECORD – SUBJECT 1C" and slid it back into the drawer she kept locked with a brass key tucked into her pocket.

She whispered, not to the screen, but to herself:

"She was never supposed to survive reentry."

The monitor flickered. The spiral glyph in the upper corner of the feed pulsed once—slow and deliberate—before fading.

Gretchen didn't flinch.

But her voice caught on the edge of the truth as she whispered:

"She doesn't know how close she is."

ARCHIVE FILE: SPIRAL—INTERVIEW 047

DATE: November 3, 1941

SUBJECT: Patient C.M. (Unnumbered at time of recording)

INTERVIEWER: Dr. Weatherly, Lead Clinical Examiner, Spiral Phase I

[Recording begins. Slight hum of tape reel. Child breathing softly.]

DR. WEATHERLY:

Tell me what you see, Clara.

CLARA (age 8, voice soft):

I see the orchard.

DR. WEATHERLY:

DATE: November 3, 1941

SUBJECT: Patient C.M. (Unnumbered at time of recording)

INTERVIEWER: Dr. Weatherly, Lead Clinical Examiner, Spiral Phase I

[Recording begins. Slight hum of tape reel. Child breathing softly.]

DR. WEATHERLY:

Tell me what you see, Clara.

CLARA (age 8, voice soft):

I see the orchard.

DR. WEATHERLY:

And where are you standing?

CLARA:

In the middle. With the tree that bends funny. The one with the face.

DR. WEATHERLY:

There's no face, Clara. You've been told that. What does the spiral mean?

CLARA (hesitant):

You said it's where the remembering goes. But it… hurts when I follow it.

DR. WEATHERLY:

It only hurts if you turn against it. Let the memory loop. Let it settle.

[Paper shuffling. A soft scratch—possibly chalk.]

CLARA:

I didn't want to forget her.

DR. WEATHERLY:

Who?

CLARA:

The girl before me. The one in the mirror. I think she cried. I didn't… I didn't mean to take her place.

[Pause. Static rise.]

DR. WEATHERLY (voice cooler):

Clara, there was no girl before you. That's recursion. A fragment.

You must trust the mirror. It shows who's still here.

CLARA (after long silence):

Sometimes, I see myself blink… before I do.

DR. WEATHERLY:

That means the process is working.

[Long pause. Tape clicks softly.]

CLARA (barely audible):

If I forget…will I disappear?

DR. WEATHERLY:

Not disappear.

Just become who you were always meant to be.

[Tape clicks. Silence. Then a faint voice, hard to place—perhaps from the playback tape, perhaps not:]

"You can't overwrite what never erased."

[End of recording.]

Ellie blinked. The words lingered like dust in her throat. She didn't remember hearing the tape. And yet… it felt like a memory replaying from behind her eyes. The spiral sketch in her hand pulsed faintly—like heat through paper.

Outside the archive, the corridor was silent again. But something had shifted. And down the hall, behind one locked door, a girl was drawing the orchard from above… with Ellie's name already written beneath the tree.

The intake bell rang twice. Once sharply. Once as if it had been struck from inside the wall. Ellie stood at the far end of the vestibule, clipboard in hand, posture stiffer than usual. She hadn't been assigned this shift, but something had pulled her here. A hum beneath the tile. The kind of instinct that didn't come from training—but from memory.

The new arrival came in without escort. A boy—sixteen, maybe seventeen. Gaunt, with a long scar curving beneath his left eye like an unfinished sentence. He wore an oversized army coat that hadn't been issued to him. And though the protocol required silence during intake, he spoke before his name was ever asked.

His eyes met hers, wide and too clear.

"You're not supposed to be here," he said. "They said you were gone."

Ellie's grip tightened on the clipboard. "I'm sorry?"

The boy stepped forward, ignoring the nurse reaching for his sleeve. "They called you Clara. Clara M., I saw you in the orchard. You were drawing with your eyes closed."

Ellie froze. The air in the vestibule thickened.

"Who told you that name?" she asked carefully.

He tilted his head. "You did."

He smiled faintly, almost apologetic. "But not like this. You were younger. And you said not to let them name you again."

Behind her, the intake door slid closed with a mechanical hiss. A gust of cold swept through the vestibule, curling around her ankles like breath.

Ellie stepped back. The clipboard slipped from her hand. And for a flicker—no longer than a blink—her reflection in the vestibule glass was no longer alone. The girl from the orchard stood behind her. Smiling.

The lights in the monitoring room buzzed with a low, insectile hum. One of the overhead bulbs pulsed with a faint spiral of filament burn—barely visible, but enough to make Gretchen's jaw clench.

Dr. Weatherly stood beside the projection reel, arms crossed, eyes fixed on the grainy black-and-white playback footage. On-screen, the boy from intake stared directly into the vestibule camera—though he shouldn't have known it was there.

"He said her name," Gretchen murmured. "Clara. Without prompting."

Weatherly didn't speak right away. His gaze remained locked on the boy's face, tracking every micro-expression with mechanical calm. Behind him, a red-inked file sat unopened on the desk: Subject 3B – Provisional Drift Exposure.

"That wasn't in his prep file," Gretchen added. "He was cleared for delayed activation. Memory prompts shouldn't have surfaced until Phase II."

Weatherly's voice was quiet. "Unless something seeded early."

"You think she triggered it?"

"I think he remembered something he was never told."

The reel clicked forward. Ellie's figure appeared onscreen now—backlit, frozen in place. The boy's voice barely carried over the audio strip: "You were drawing with your eyes closed."

Gretchen's knuckles whitened around the file. "He shouldn't know that. Not even she remembers the orchard."

Weatherly turned away from the footage, his expression unreadable. "They're starting to synchronize."

"We need to reset him before the bleed worsens."

He shook his head slowly. "No. Let it run."

Gretchen stiffened. "You want the recursion to escalate?"

"I want to see what memory does when it's no longer assigned. They weren't supposed to recognize each other this early." His voice lowered. "But they did."

Silence returned to the room—tense, coiled.

On the screen, Ellie stepped back. The clipboard fell. The reflection behind her flickered and smiled. Weatherly reached forward and froze the frame.

"Monitor them both. Daily. And increase the dose on Silas."

Gretchen's voice barely rose above a whisper. "And if she asks questions?"

Weatherly finally turned toward her.

"Lie."

ELLIE'S QUARTERS – NIGHT

The room held still, too still—as if the walls themselves were bracing for a truth they'd already heard.

Ellie sat on the edge of her cot, her gloves still on, though her fingers ached beneath them. The drawing from earlier rested on her lap. The girl beneath the tree. The spiral pressed into the orchard floor. The second figure now scribbled faintly in—unfinished, like memory struggling to finish the sentence it had started years before.

She hadn't spoken to anyone since Silas said her name. Not Ellie. Clara. She didn't remember responding.

Did she speak? Or had the Spiral spoken through her?

The mirror above the sink had fogged from the radiator's hiss, even though she hadn't run the water. She stared at it now—blank silver smeared by breath she hadn't exhaled. She stood. Crossed to the mirror. Wiped the fog away.

For a second, her reflection stared back—normal, tired, real. Then, the spiral appeared behind her. Not drawn. Reflected. Etched into the floorboards just behind her heels. The Spiral wasn't an image anymore. It pulsed—a heartbeat stitched out of memory she couldn't unhear. She turned. Nothing.

When she looked back at the mirror—the reflection had shifted. It smiled first—too early, too certain—before she even knew what feeling she was supposed to have. Now, it showed her from behind, kneeling in the orchard. Her hands were dirt-stained, a ribbon wrapped around one wrist. Not the one she wore now. An older one. Faded red.

She blinked. The image rippled—and this time, the girl in the mirror was not her. She was younger. Wide-eyed. Lips moving but no sound escaping. She clutched a drawing—of the Spiral—and scrawled over it in smeared charcoal:

"You're wearing what they gave me." Ellie whispered, "It's not mine." Then blinked—confused. Because she hadn't meant to speak. Not that. Not then. The voice had come from her throat, but it didn't feel like hers.

This makes Clara's infiltration explicit without killing the slow dread. Ellie stepped back, breath caught in her throat.

"No," she whispered. "That's not me."

But the mirror girl's mouth moved again. This time, the voice echoed in Ellie's head, layered over her own thoughts:

"You didn't forget. You were repainted." Ellie didn't move. Didn't blink. The words didn't echo. They settled. Like truth finally given shape.

The mirror cracked—not with force, but with memory. A web of fractures spiraled outward from the girl's reflection like it had been waiting for her to finally look.

Ellie staggered away. The drawing on the bed had changed. Now, the girl beneath the tree was facing forward. She had Ellie's coat. But the name scribbled beneath her read: Clara. Ellie sank to the floor, the spiral behind her eyes glowing white-hot. The room buzzed faintly— then stilled. She didn't cry. She didn't breathe.

She just whispered:

"Then who the hell am I?"

INT. WARD C – OBSERVATION ROOM – NIGHT

The halls of Arlington Hills hummed behind her like something breathing through cracked tile and sealed doors. Ellie moved like someone underwater—purposeful but slowed by pressure she couldn't name.

The drawing was still in her hand.

Clara.

The name wouldn't let go.

She passed Room 3-C. Her hand lingered at the frame, inside: stillness. Silas sat at the edge of his cot, head bowed, one leg bouncing slightly like a metronome, keeping time with something unspeakable. His fingertips were smudged again with charcoal, his sleeves rolled above his wrists like a soldier bracing for field dressing.

Ellie stepped inside. The air changed.

"Why did you call me Clara?" she asked.

Silas didn't lift his head.

"Because that's what you were when I remembered you."

Ellie's throat constricted. "But I'm not. You said it like you knew."

"I did." He finally looked up. His eyes were clouded but lucid. "And then I didn't."

Ellie moved closer, every step louder than it should have been. "Tell me the truth."

He shook his head. "Truth doesn't survive here. Only memory. And memory lies."

"You drew me before I got here."

"I remembered you before you arrived," he said, voice sharper now. "And when they wiped you—when they gave you her name—I saw it. I saw it all again."

She handed him the drawing. The one with the girl beneath the tree.

"Who is this?"

Silas's hand hovered over the image, then dropped.

"That's her."

"Clara?"

He didn't answer.

"She looks like me," Ellie said. "She draws like me. But she's not me."

Silas tilted his head. "Then why do your drawings change when hers does?"

Ellie blinked. "What are you talking about?"

"You haven't noticed? Every time you forget, the spiral moves."

He reached beneath the cot and pulled another sketch from the mattress seam.

Two girls now. One kneeling. One standing behind with a nurse's badge.

Both wearing Ellie's coat.

He pointed to the second figure.

"That's what they made. A proxy."

Ellie's knees buckled slightly. She caught the edge of the desk. "They made me?"

"You were part of her return." He looked at her—steady, not cruel. "I tried to forget the words they made us memorize. But they loop back eventually." He leaned closer.

"Do not restore the name. Do not disrupt anchor."

A pause engulfed the room and the space between them.

"But you're doing both, aren't you?"

He stood, stepping closer. "You're not a nurse. You're a mirror."

Two memories snapped into focus at once—one where she boarded a train in Chicago, another where she dug her fingers into frozen orchard dirt.

 Both tasted real. Both tasted wrong.

She reeled. "Stop."

"I called you Clara because I wanted you to be Clara. But you're not."

"I said stop."

"You're what they left behind. A copy of a copy. A memory with edges."

He reached out. Ellie stepped back, shaking.

"No," she whispered. "I'm real."

Silas smiled—not cruelly. With pity. "That's what she said, too. I tried to anchor you once.

But they unmade it faster than I could hold you."

A light overhead popped. The flicker shadowed the room for half a second. In that moment, Ellie saw her own reflection in the glass behind Silas—just briefly. Her mouth moved. But the voice wasn't hers. Maybe real was never the point.

Maybe remembering was the only thing that survived.

CHAPTER: EIGHT

Recursive Truth

Arlington Hills – Ward C, Dusk

The hallway outside Ward C was quieter than usual. Not silent. Just… waiting. Ellie moved slowly, clipboard pressed too tightly to her chest, the edge biting into the crook of her arm. Every step felt heavier, like she was stepping into a memory, still deciding whether to keep her shape.

Room 3-C sat at the end, its nameplate dulled by time, the paint around the doorframe peeled like something inside had scraped and scraped—then stopped. She paused with her hand on the knob. A beat. A breath. Then stepped inside.

Silas was awake. Not just conscious. Awake in a way that suggested calculation. Intent. He sat at the edge of the bed, hands folded with the precision of someone waiting for the next command. The sketchpad lay open across his knees, the charcoal stick gripped in fingers stained black to the second knuckle. His posture was still, almost reverent like something outside of him had done the posing. He didn't look up.

"You came back," he said quietly.

"I said I would," Ellie replied, softer than she meant to. Her voice felt borrowed, like something she'd already said in a version of this room that hadn't happened yet.

"Most don't," Silas said. "Not after the second drawing."

Ellie stepped further in, letting the door click closed behind her. The shadows in the corners seemed deeper today—receding just enough to imply they were listening.

Silas drew one final stroke, then set the charcoal down. "You're not ready to see this."

"Then why did you draw it?"

He looked up, and for the first time, their eyes locked.

"Because you're not supposed to remember yet. But the orchard does." Her spine prickled. He flipped another page. Ellie saw her own posture—head tilted, one cuff unbuttoned. A detail no one had seen but her. The image was weeks old. Or older.

"You drew me?"

"I drew what the Spiral remembered. You're just what it held."

"Silas… who am I to you?"

His smile didn't reach his eyes. "I could answer that. But you'd call it delusion."

She crossed the room in measured steps and sat across from him. Not close. But not as far as she should have. He flipped the sketchpad around and slid it across the table. Ellie leaned in.

The orchard again—drawn from above. But this time, the trees didn't spiral inward. They branched outward like antennae, each tree tipped with a spindled mark that looked more like wire than root. And at the center: a circle. Not a tree. Not a chair. A node. Mechanical. Embedded. Pulsing.

A silence settled between them. One that felt older than the hospital. He turned the page. The next sketch was almost identical. But this time, the spiral wasn't drawn. It was pressed into the paper. Smudged in with something darker—thicker than charcoal, too matte for ink. Whatever it was, it stained.

And in the center: a nurse. Her figure half-erased but unmistakable.

The coat. The clipboard. The stance. Ellie. Her throat tightened. "I didn't draw that."

"No," Silas said. "But it's still yours."

She tried to control her breath, but it stuttered.

"You think I'm part of that program," she said.

He tilted his head. "I think you never left it."

Ellie stood, fighting the rising tide behind her sternum. "Silas, I need you to focus. This drawing—what do you remember when you make these?"

He gave a small, sad smile. "You keep asking the wrong question."

"Then tell me the right one."

He leaned forward, voice a whisper now. "Why do the mirrors keep remembering what you forget to unlearn?"

Her stomach flipped. Something about that sentence—too close. Too real. She saw her reflection again, the one that didn't blink when she did.

She rose abruptly, the chair legs screeching against the tile.

"I need to—"

"Run?" he asked, voice steady. "Or hide?"

"I need to review your file," she said, retreating toward the door.

"Just remember the numbers, Nurse Hale."

Silas stood just slightly. "They're not just coordinates. They're instructions."

Ellie stepped out into the hallway, pulse thudding. Behind her, the door didn't close. It watched. Ellie didn't realize she was holding her breath until she reached the end of the hallway. Her shoes clicked against the linoleum in the wrong rhythm—half a beat behind, like her own steps, didn't trust her anymore.

She ducked into the empty medication closet, closed the door gently behind her, and leaned back hard against the shelves. The light buzzed above, one bulb flickering out every third second. She counted. Not because it helped but because it kept her from thinking too loudly.

NIAC. Neural Integration and Control.

She whispered the words under her breath, but they sounded older than she meant them to. Like someone else had already said them here. Her hands still trembled.

She reached into her coat pocket for the patient chart she'd stashed before heading to Ward C. Just routine cross-reference, she'd told herself. Something clinical to make her feel like a nurse again. But what she pulled out wasn't a chart. It was the drawing.

The same orchard sketch Silas had shown her minutes ago—only this one wasn't in his charcoal. It was in blue pencil.

The kind clipped to her clipboard.

And in the corner, below the spiral tree and the nurse figure standing in its shadow, a name had been signed in the bottom margin.

E. Hale

Her breath caught. She hadn't signed it. She was sure. But the letters were hers. Not just the shape—the pressure. The slant. The looping curl on the H that only happened when she was writing too fast. Her own fingers had made this. Or something wearing them.

She dropped to a crouch, laying the paper flat against the floor tiles, trying to explain it away. Had Silas somehow slipped it to her? Had she copied it unconsciously?

But she'd seen him draw it. In real time. This was different. This one had notes in the margins. Dates. Arrows. Names she didn't recognize scribbled out and rewritten. And then—at the center, beneath the spiral tree—something she hadn't seen before.

Numbers. The same four.

14 – 9 – 1 – 3

But this time, the letters had been decoded below them:

NIAC Command Pathway 1C: Do not disrupt anchor: Do not restore name. She traced the words with her thumb. The paper felt warm. No, not the paper. Her hands. They burned faintly. Like a current had passed through them.

She glanced up at the mirror above the sink—small, round, meant for checking bandage wraps and blood smears. Her reflection looked... misaligned. Pale, yes, but more than that—like a duplicate laid slightly out of register.

Behind her—just behind her shoulder—the girl from Room 2-C stood in the reflection. Still. Watching. Drawing. Ellie spun. The closet was empty. She turned back to the mirror. Her reflection was there again—but off. The girl stood behind her now, just barely out of frame. Not the girl from Room 2-C. Older. Familiar. Clara. In the glass, Ellie's reflection blinked—and then its mouth moved. Faster than hers. Whispering a sentence Ellie didn't say:

"They kept me for you."

The mirror fogged instantly. A breath that wasn't Ellie's clung to the surface in a spiral pattern. Ellie backed away. The breath faded. But the message lingered.

Now, there were two figures beneath the spiral tree. Both female. One child. One adult. Both labeled.

Clara. E.H.

Her breath hitched. She folded the paper slowly, methodically. She pressed it between the pages of her logbook like it was just another observation. Just a note. But her hands wouldn't stop shaking. Ellie pressed her palm against the cabinet, steadying herself. Her throat was dry, her pulse sharp. Then— "I remember burying her," she said aloud.

The words came too fast. Too clear. Her lips tingled. Her voice still echoed in the tight room, but her mind had not formed the thought. Not yet. She blinked hard, breath dissolving into vapor. I didn't mean to say that, she thought. I don't even know who I meant.

But her body had known. Her mouth had moved. Like muscle memory answering before the mind could interrupt.

Outside the door, the hallway had gone quiet again. The kind of quiet that waits. Ellie didn't knock. She pushed open the office door with more force than intended, the doorknob biting into the palm of her glove. Gretchen looked up from a stack of intake ledgers, her brow lifting only slightly.

"You're early," she said, not unkindly—but not surprised, either.

"I need to talk to you," Ellie said, shutting the door behind her. "Now."

Gretchen gestured calmly to the chair across from her desk. "Then sit. You're shaking."

Ellie didn't sit. She stepped forward and placed the folded sketch on the desk—unfolding it carefully, like a trap she was setting. The paper made a sound too loud for its weight.

Gretchen didn't touch it. She looked at it. Once. Then again. Then slower. Her silence was answer enough.

"You recognize it," Ellie said.

"It's a spiral orchard," Gretchen replied, voice cool. "They appear often in patient renderings. Especially in Ward C."

"This one wasn't drawn by a patient," Ellie said. "It's mine."

Gretchen met her gaze.

"I didn't draw it. But it's in my handwriting. The pencil pressure, the initials, the notation style—it's mine."

Gretchen's fingers tightened slightly over the armrest. "And yet you're not sure when you made it."

"No," Ellie said. "I'm not."

She leaned in, voice low, nearly shaking. "So you're going to tell me why I signed something I don't remember drawing. You're going to tell me what NIAC is. What 1C means. Why Silas knew my name before I arrived. Why he said, I never left the program. Why this sketch shows the same orchard I dreamed about before I set foot on this property."

Gretchen said nothing. Ellie took a breath. Then another. Her pulse roared in her ears, but she kept her voice steady. "No more riddles. No more metaphors about memory or mirrors or rooms that aren't really rooms. I want the truth."

A long silence stretched between them. The kind that felt like it had already happened once.

Gretchen's tone didn't falter. But the line of her jaw tightened.

"I used to believe in tests. In baselines. Now, I study the ones who fail them. Because they remember too well."

A beat.

"Sometimes I think the Spiral was never about forgetting.

Just—classifying those who couldn't."

Then Gretchen spoke—softly. Measured. "Do you believe memory can be transplanted?"

Ellie didn't respond.

"I'm not asking philosophically," Gretchen continued. "I'm asking clinically. With enough stimulus. Enough repetition. Enough...

recursion.”

“I don’t know what I believe anymore,” Ellie said.

“That’s how it begins,” Gretchen whispered. “The space between what you believe and what you remember. That’s the gap the Spiral was designed to control.”

“You’re admitting it, then. There was a program.”

“There was a theory,” Gretchen said. “Then an experiment. Then, a failure. Then another.”

She looked at the drawing again, and her voice broke—just slightly.

“That’s not a map. It’s a retention test. You didn’t draw it today. You drew it a long time ago. Someone buried it. Someone else unearthed it. And now it’s… recursive.”

Ellie’s stomach churned. “That doesn’t answer my question.”

Gretchen looked up, something sharp flashing behind her calm.

“I don’t know how much of you is the original record, Ellie. That’s the truth. I don’t know what the orchard gave back when it let you out.”

Ellie’s throat closed. She stepped back from the desk like the paper might burn her if she stayed close too long. “So that’s what I am to you. A result. A retention test.”

“No,” Gretchen said, rising now too. “You’re the one who came back.” They stared at each other—mirror-still.

Then, quietly, Gretchen added, “But the Spiral never gives back the same version it took in.” Gretchen looked away, just once. Her mouth moved like she was about to apologize—then stopped.

As if she’d already apologized once. And it hadn’t worked.

She didn't go back to her room.

She didn't go anywhere that had walls she might recognize too easily.

Instead, Ellie found herself descending into the archive wing again—past the cracked radiator, the flickering bulb near the intake stairwell, the half-covered mural someone had once tried to scrub out of memory. The Orchard Ledger had been moved weeks ago, according to staff. Relocated. Rebound. But it hadn't. It waited. Just like everything else in this place that refused to forget.

Ellie entered the lower records chamber, the lights humming with the slow insistence of a memory just about to surface. She didn't turn on the overheads. Her fingers knew which drawer to open.

The Orchard Transfer Log was buried beneath old census forms and requisition slips, but it pulsed beneath her palm like it had a heartbeat. The leather was cracked. The stitching uneven.

She slid the book onto the nearest table and opened it. Not to the first page. Not to the last. Her hands turned straight to the middle—like her bones remembered the page number her brain had never learned.

Page 141.

It was blank. Or so it seemed. She tilted the book toward the yellow light of a desk lamp. At that angle, faint graphite lines surfaced—erased once, but not completely. Time hadn't let the memory go.

Lines. Notations. Scrawl. A child's handwriting. Uneven. But… familiar. Ellie's breath caught in her throat. Because it was hers. Her own hand. From another version of herself. Or another life.

The first line read: "Today they buried another name beneath the spiral."

The second: "Gretchen says we don't plant the names—we grow them."

The third: "Dr. W said I passed the test. I don't remember what the test was. But they keep calling me by her name."

Below that, a drawing in pencil, half-erased. A tree with too many roots and no trunk. Spirals tucked inside the soil, like they were feeding something.

Her name—E. Hale—was signed at the bottom. Except... the 'E' was backward. Like a child had written it. Or like someone was remembering how.

She flipped the page. In the margin, in another hand—precise, slanted, clinical: "Subject 1C retained partial recall. Identity bleed confirmed. Maintain orchard exposure. Do not inform."

—M.W.

She reached for the pencil on the desk. Slowly, shakily, she tried to correct it—just a small mark, a clean line. A forward-facing E. But her hand wouldn't move. Her knuckles stiffened. The pencil hovered. Her fingers trembled. It should be easy, she thought. But something deep in her bones recoiled. As if the muscles remembered a different alphabet.

The light above her buzzed louder. She looked up. And in the dark reflection of the glass cabinet door, the mirror had fogged. Words appeared slowly—traced as if by breath and fingertip from the other side.

"You came back."

She pressed a hand to her chest—half expecting to find a spiral pulsing there instead of a heartbeat.

Am I writing it without knowing? Am I leaving myself breadcrumbs in the dark?

Then another line.

"But you're not the only one who remembers."

The fog receded. The words disappeared. But the handwriting was hers. Exactly. Ellie closed the ledger with trembling hands. Not because she couldn't face the truth—but because the truth was already inside her.

She turned toward the hallway. The light above the mirror flickered once. The mirror fogged—softly, slowly, from breath, she hadn't exhaled. Then, traced as if by fingertip:

You were me before you knew. She caught her reflection's eye—and for one sickening second, she thought:

The mirror remembers better than I do.

The words blurred. Then vanished. But Ellie's chest ached. As if the message had come from inside her lungs. And from somewhere inside the archive, the spiral hummed softly— just enough to rattle her teeth. The spiral wasn't waiting anymore. It was breathing her. The spiral was breathing her.

In. Out. In. Out. Until the line between thought and muscle dissolved. The hum rose.

Not just a sound now.

A pulse. A heartbeat not her own. Counting down what little she had left.

CHAPTER: NINE

Subject 1C: The Record

Ellie didn't knock. She entered Dr. Weatherly's office with her pulse thudding loud in her ears, the ledger from the Orchard Archive gripped too tightly beneath her arm. The door closed behind her with a weighted hush that didn't match its actual sound.

Weatherly stood behind his desk, one hand resting atop a sealed folder. A red spiral stamped in its corner caught the lamplight—curled tight like it was bracing to move.

"You've been in places you weren't cleared for," he said without looking up.

"I found something," Ellie said. "Pages in the ledger. Handwriting that matches mine."

Weatherly's eyes lifted. Calm. Unblinking. "You've been experiencing memory recursion."

"This wasn't just memory. It was documentation." She stepped forward and placed the ledger on the desk. "You stamped my intake as Subject 1C. Why?"

He didn't answer right away. The silence felt deliberate, like a held breath. Then, "Some records aren't meant to be read out of order."

"I'm done with fragments. I want the truth."

"The truth doesn't always stabilize well," he replied. "You, of all people, should understand that."

Ellie's fingers clenched at her sides. "Then stabilize me."

Weatherly circled to the front of the desk. "Do you remember Edenbrook?"

She hesitated. "Only in fragments."

"Then you remember enough."

"What was I doing there?"

Weatherly's voice lowered. "You were chosen. Not for what you were—but for what you could hold."

Her mouth went dry. She stepped back. "Is Gretchen part of this?"

"She's been monitoring outcomes. Nothing more."

Ellie turned toward the hallway. She didn't look back. She didn't want to give him the satisfaction of watching her unravel. But as she passed the windowed wall outside his office, her reflection didn't follow. It paused, then pivoted to face him—as if she'd been left behind and something else had moved on. And in the glass, just for a flicker—the orchard trees replaced her eyes.

She paused at the threshold of the records room, her hand hovering just above the handle.

Not fear. Not quite. More like the hush before recognition.

The air smelled of graphite and ink, but beneath that—formaldehyde. And something older. Like memory turned to mildew. She stepped inside.

Her breath fogged faintly, though the air wasn't cold. No draft, no vent. Just a weight behind the skin. A silence that remembered too much.

Files lined the walls—thin, bloated, warped with time. They didn't hum. But they held something. As if the room had been waiting for her fingerprint to finish the sentence.

Dust swam in the overhead light but didn't fall. It circled. Slowly. Like something hovering before choosing its host.

She told herself she was here for a dosage audit. Just a routine cross-reference. A misfiled chart from Ward C. Maybe an intake discrepancy. Something small. Something clinical. She told herself that again. And again. But the folder already waiting on the center table said otherwise.

HALE, ELEANOR J.

Beneath it, stamped in clean, mechanical type: SUBJECT 1C

Her pulse didn't race. It paused. Like her heart was waiting to see what she'd do next.

Not handwritten. Not initialed. Not meant for her.

She sat. Slowly. The chair beneath her creaked—not in protest, but in memory. The fluorescent light buzzed. Once. Then again—three short pulses. She looked up. It stopped. But her chair—It creaked. Not under her. Around her. As if someone else had just stood up.

She opened the file. The folder creaked as she opened it—slow, uneven. Inside: an old intake photo slipped loose from its clip. Her own face, barely older than a child's, eyes not yet taught to flinch.

A corner of the photo was stained—brown, brittle. Not ink. Not quite blood. Beneath it, a graphite smudge ran along the margin. As if someone had tried to erase the handwriting, but the pressure remained. She touched it. Her finger came away dark. No welcome page. No summary. No context. Just entries. — Integrity drift noted. — Mirror-phase recall elevated. — Identity retention: stable under controlled recursion.

Ellie blinked. "I don't remember this." A pause. "Or maybe I do." Her voice sounded tired. Not scared. Not defiant. Just… worn thin. Like a song played too often. Like remembering had cost her something she didn't agree to give.

The words came in her voice—but didn't sound like her thoughts. They sounded like something she'd once whispered into a mirror and then flinched away from hearing.

She turned the page. Scrawled in pencil across the bottom margin: Observation successful. Spiral retention without recursion. Maintain field identity. Do not inform subject of intake origin.

Her fingers went cold. Her stomach turned—but it didn't twist with shock. It twisted with muscle memory. As if her body already knew how to survive the knowledge. As if it had done this before. She hadn't transferred to Arlington Hills. She hadn't arrived. She had been retrieved.

Her fingers moved without conscious direction, rifling backward through the drawer: 9C. 8B. 7C… Patient codes. Not names. Each a number with a file. Each a story overwritten. Each identity paused. Like hers.

And then—another file. Not hers. But open. Already waiting.

CLARA M.

A photograph clipped inside. She looked down. Her own face stared back. "You're reading your own erasure. And still—You turn the page. Because some part of you already knew. Didn't you?" A small voice — too small to be hers — whispered:

"Maybe it's just a clerical mistake. Just bad filing. Just a name written wrong."

She almost believed it. That was the worst part.

Beneath the photo, typed in red: Subject memory erosion initiated October 1942. Integration stabilized under proxy conditions. Signed: Dr. M. Weaver

Ellie's hands tightened around the desk edge. Too hard. The skin on her knuckles blanched. Weaver. This is the name she needed to know now more than any other. She had seen it on most of the documents and files she had been reading, and on the edge of a chart, Gretchen had folded shut a moment too quickly. She hadn't thought to ask then. Now, she couldn't stop asking.

She turned toward the hallway, knees weak, breath stammering in the cold. But the room wouldn't let her go. The air thickened. A pane of glass caught her eye—mounted high above the filing cabinets. Just a mirror. Slightly warped at the edges. She looked. And froze.

Three reflections stared back. The first—her present self: pale, rigid, breath fogging faintly. The second—eyes weeping spiral ink. Lips sewn. Head tilted. Doll-like. Stitched. Broken. The third—smiling. Not kindly. Not cruelly. Just… knowingly. If she stared too long, she didn't know which of them would blink first. Ellie moved. Only the first reflection followed. The others waited.

A low static buzzed in her skull. Like a voice had been turned down just low enough to pretend it wasn't speaking. "You kept the name," said a voice she didn't recognize—but felt inside her own throat. "I kept the memory."

Her legs buckled. The smiling reflection stepped forward. Then vanished.

She staggered back from the table. Her coat felt too tight at the shoulders. Wrong in the sleeves. Like it had been tailored for someone else. Maybe it had.

From the corner of the room, a mirror didn't move. But she felt it shift. Like gravity had tilted sideways and forgot to realign.

She turned, trying to leave. The mirror nearest the cabinet fogged. Slowly. Deliberately. There was no warmth. No condensation. But letters still formed across the glass:

YOU WERE NEVER GONE

She turned away—but the mirror cracked. Not from impact, but from pressure. A hairline fracture split across the surface in a spiral pattern. In the fog that remained, one final phrase appeared—etched as if breathed onto the glass from the other side:

"They left me here for you."

The words faded—melted—like steam pulled back into a machine. Ellie pressed a hand against the glass. Her own reflection didn't meet her.

Behind her, the drawer labeled PERSONNEL RELOCATIONS clicked open.

Her badge felt heavier than it should. She pulled the drawer open. Inside—folders sorted by year. She scanned for 1947.

HALE, ELEANOR J.

The first page: TRANSFER RECORD FROM: Chicago Ward 5B TO: Arlington Hills Psychiatric Hospital No date. No signature. No departmental stamp. Only her name.

She flipped the next page. Standard intake questionnaire. But the handwriting wasn't hers.

Under Known Aliases: Subject 1C – Retained Construct

Her throat closed. Retained. Not reassigned. Not relocated. Preserved.

The next sheet wasn't a form. It was a memo. Frayed. Written in haste. DO NOT DELETE. Embedded pathways stable. Subject unaware of recursion. Maintains functional persona. Resume observation until drift manifests. A faint blue spiral stamped beneath it. Barely legible signature: M. Weaver

Ellie flipped the rest. No medical history. No evaluation. No intake photo. Just one note, repeated in varying hands across multiple sheets: SUBJECT 1C – SEE PHASE I LEDGER

She turned toward the far wall. There—One cabinet stood apart. No label. Only a spiral. Embossed, nearly invisible. Her feet moved. She wasn't sure they waited for permission. Inside—weathered folders, older paper, tighter script. She pulled one.

1C

Inside: a child's drawing. A nurse. A child beside her. Spiral eyes. The date: 1935. Twelve years ago. Below it, a note in black ink: Merged subject shows reflexive identity defense. Memory loop stable. Maintain drift field.

Ellie took a step back. The air thinned, not from temperature—but pressure. Like the memory itself was using up all the oxygen.

She turned. Ready to leave. But a dull rectangle in the wall caught her eye. A small hatch. Half-open. A maintenance slot. Inside—misfiled records. Photos. Sketches. Among the sketches, brittle with age, one page felt thicker—crayon on construction paper. Ellie unfolded it gently. A crude outline of a hallway. A crooked door labeled in a child's hand: "Room 9." A girl stood beside it. No face. Just the word written beneath in blocky letters: "Me." The Spiral wasn't trapping memories. It was feeding. Feeding on every abandoned self left too long in the dark.

Her breath stilled. The paper trembled in her grasp. Not because it was eerie. But because her fingers knew the grip. Her palm curled into the shape of the child who'd drawn it.

Ellie folded the sketch. Slipped it into her coat. But her fingers didn't feel like hers anymore. The ledger drawer behind her was still open. She turned to close it. Her hand froze. She couldn't lift it. Something inside her resisted. Not panic. Not pain. Recognition.

And in that moment, a final annotation surfaced. Not typed. Not spoken. Remembered.

No transfer. No assignment. Just a loop. She never left.

CHAPTER: TEN

Memory Saturation:

The rain hadn't let up all morning. It veiled the windows like condensation on memory—thin, but impossible to see through. Holding. Steeping. It tapped on the slanted glass of the administrative annex with a persistence Ellie couldn't tune out. She stood just inside the records vault, the door creaking softly as it latched behind her. The narrow space was suffused with the damp paper scent of a room long sealed—wood polish, dust, and the faint acidity of ink that had aged into the pages like a bruise. Ellie whispered without meaning to: "I am Ellie Hale. I am—" The words didn't finish. They curled back on themselves, unfinished, like a breath that forgot how to exhale.

She hesitated in the threshold, eyes adjusting to the dim yellow of the single desk lamp illuminating the archive shelves. Rain streaked the tall windows. Lightning flashed, briefly catching on the brass drawer handles lining the wall like teeth.

Clutched in her gloved hand was the card Gretchen had slipped into her pocket the night before—no explanation, no words. Just a drawer number: 273-B. Written in careful black ink.

She moved slowly down the aisle, passing ledgers stacked spine out, stamped with decades of names and numbers. Some were too brittle to touch. Others practically buzzed beneath her fingertips. She found the drawer. Exhaled. Pulled—like tugging loose a thread she couldn't rethread once unraveled.

Inside, a manila folder lay atop a collection of wax-sealed envelopes. Her fingers trembled as she lifted the folder—typed labels in military standard font, patient numbers, long case designations. No names. Only designations like 7C, 9B, 3F… And one with no identifier at all.

The page inside was faintly yellowed, creased at the corners. The ink had bled slightly from water damage, but the spiral emblem at the top was unmistakable: the same symbol from her intake file. Triangle enclosing a spiral. Beneath it, the words:

RECORD OF SUBJECT 1C – RETAINED

She ran a thumb along the margin. No intake date. No discharge. Just one note typed faintly near the bottom:

Subject cannot be erased. Recommend procedural reinitiation only upon memory saturation.

She sank into the lone wooden chair by the desk, the folder heavy in her lap. Silas had said the name was planted. Clara had said it didn't belong to her. But here—here was the ledger that proved the name wasn't a birthright. It was a designation. She traced her name—Eleanor J. Hale—on a separate sheet tucked near the back. Then saw it crossed out. Beneath it, another name.

Clara M.

And below that:

RETENTION: ACTIVE

Lightning split the window again. Ellie flinched. Her reflection blinked late—then held her gaze a beat too long like it was deciding who moved first. Her pulse surged as she flipped to the last page. Taped there—so old it had browned at the edges—was a drawing. Charcoal. A figure seated in a spiral-marked chair. The face had been smudged out.

But the name beneath was typed in all caps:

HALE, ELEANOR — SEE PROTOCOL PHASE III

She remembered something sharp: Her mother parting her hair with a comb made from bone. "Don't move, baby," she'd say, even though Ellie never had. Memory could be gentle. But not here.

Ellie stood abruptly, the chair scraping loudly against the tile. Her fingers were shaking too hard to return the pages properly. The folder slipped from her hand. Pages scattered across the floor like shed skin.

Her hands went to her temples. A pressure now. Not pain—recognition. Not memory—return. Behind her, a soft hum began.

The drawer that had been empty… clicked. Another envelope now sat inside. Crisp. Stamped today's date. To be opened upon reactivation.

Her name was typed on the label. Ellie Hale. But beneath it, handwritten in faint red ink, was 'Clara.' She stared at the handwriting on the envelope. Her name. Neat. Curved. Familiar. But she didn't remember learning to write it. Or maybe she remembered learning it wrong. A name stitched to someone else's breath. Before she could think, her hand had already reached for it. Before she could reach, her mind had already accepted it.

The rain stopped all at once. The quiet pressed in. And for the first time, Ellie didn't know which name she would answer to.

She clutched the envelope in shaking hands and backed out of the vault-like it might close behind her, and seal her in with everything she didn't want to know. Her thoughts fractured as she walked. Images resurfaced and dissolved. The orchard, the sketch Silas had made, the whisper in the mirror, the girl in Room 2-C drawing Ellie's name before she knew it. Before Ellie knew herself.

The hallway to the east archive stretched like a ribcage, holding her in place. The walls breathed differently here, exhaling memory instead of air. Every step became a contradiction—forward motion with the weight of regression. Her mind struggled to keep pace with the moment.

Am I remembering this? Or am I being written by it? A door that hadn't existed before marked STORAGE B.

Inside, a circular room. Spiral sketches on every wall. The spiral chair. Real. Waiting. As if the room had been drawn into being around her. She stepped closer, and something inside her flinched. Not her nerves. Something older. Something quieter. This is the place I was written.

A vision came—not superimposed, not imagined—but remembered. Herself in the chair. Younger. Still. Blank. Watching the spiral carved into the floor, like it might unlock something if stared at long enough. Her reflection vibrated in the mirror across the room. She blinked. Her reflection didn't. It waited. Then, blinked first.

Ellie stepped back, breath caught. For a moment, she didn't know which one of them had seen it coming. She turned to leave, breath catching. The door had disappeared. Ellie's knees nearly buckled.

She pressed a hand to the mirror's surface. It fogged with breath—but she hadn't exhaled.

YOU NEVER LEFT

A second drawer clicked open across the room. She hadn't touched it. Her breath caught. Inside: a folder. Labeled in red.

RETURN SCHEMA — SUBJECT 1C

She reached for the folder. But before she could lift it, the mirror across the chamber fogged again—slow and deliberate. Her reflection stepped forward. Ellie hadn't moved. In the glass, her reflection's mouth parted first. It whispered a name Ellie didn't give voice to.

"Clara…"

Not spoken aloud. Just breathed. Like memory exhaled through silver. Ellie staggered back. Her own lungs burned like she'd been holding the air for someone else. She turned, but the room hadn't changed. The reflection stood waiting, lips still moving—slow, rehearsed, like a child mouthing the lines of a play they were never meant to star in. And then her voice—no longer Ellie's, not quite—whispered one line that didn't sound remembered but returned:

"They kept me for you."

A fracture curling inward, not breaking outward. Like the glass wasn't splitting—just remembering itself from beneath. A spiral fracture blooming from behind the glass like frost chasing heat. The crack bloomed like a wound that couldn't scab over—slow, glistening, alive. Ellie backed away, heart hammering. The folder pulsed faintly where it waited on the desk. It didn't pulse like paper. It pulsed like something remembering its own heartbeat. She reached for it. And everything began to loop.

Recovered from Arlington Hills Archive

FILE 1C–THETA | SPIRAL COGNITION MODEL — INTERNAL DIRECTIVE

AUTHOR: Dr. Marcus A. Weaver | DATE: January 1943

CLEARANCE LEVEL: ALPHA RESTRICTED

———————————————————

CONFIDENTIAL — DO NOT COPY

Memorandum: Project Spiral Cognitive Recursion Model

"Stability is not healing. It is silence."

The mirror may receive if recursion is sustained. Patient exposure to mirrored stimuli accelerates dissociation and reacceptance of transferred identity.

We must prioritize candidates with:

Pre-symbolic trauma imprinting

Emotional mutability

Familial or biological resonance with prior subjects

Overwrite viability increases when identity anchors are fully destabilized. The subject should no longer respond to prior naming.

Case Reference: Subject 1C

Age: 7

Status: Reactive, nonverbal

Origin: In-house

Selected for containment under continuity model

Subject 1C does not speak.

But she retains.

Stitch the mouth.

Leave the ears.

She must remember without speaking.

She is the ideal mirror.

Not because she forgets—

But because she loops.

Handwritten Note — Margin, red ink

"She reflects what she is told to forget. That is the shape of recursion." – M.A.W.

CHAPTER: ELEVEN

The Rewritten

The rain hadn't let up all morning. It clung to the windows like condensation on memory—holding, steeping, whispering like it knew something she didn't. The steady tap against the slanted glass of the administrative annex seemed synced to her pulse, each drop, another beat in the rhythm of something waking inside her.

Ellie stood at the threshold of the records vault, her gloved hand still curled around the brass doorknob. The door had clicked softly behind her, sealing her in with the quiet throb of history. She hadn't even realized she'd walked here until she was already halfway down the hall.

The room smelled like aged paper and unfinished sentences—wood polish, stale ink, and the acidic bite of moisture eating away at old truths. The single desk lamp cast a yellow haze across the rows of archive drawers, brass handles gleaming like bared teeth in the storm light.

In her hand: the card Gretchen had slipped into her pocket. No explanation. No instructions. Just a drawer number—273-B—written in neat, meticulous ink.

Her feet carried her forward before her mind caught up. The aisle stretched longer than it should have. Drawer 273-B waited near the far wall, nestled between older ledgers that hummed with a weight she didn't dare acknowledge.

Ellie pulled the drawer. It opened smoother than expected. Inside—A manila folder. Wax-sealed envelopes stacked beneath it like forgotten confessions. A small stamp near the folder's clasp: U.S. Public Health Service – Experimental Neuropsychiatric Authorization, Circular 17-B. The same stamp she'd glimpsed in a faded margin of the Orchard ledger. She reached for the folder first, fingers trembling with a reverence she didn't fully understand.

Typed labels. Military font. No names. Just designations:

7C. 9B. 3F.

And one file with no identifier at all.

The page inside was brittle with age, ink blurred where water had once tried to erase it. But the emblem remained intact: a triangle enclosing a spiral.

RECORD OF SUBJECT 1C – RETAINED

She ran a gloved thumb down the margin. No intake date. No discharge. Just a single line typed at the bottom:

Subject non-erasure confirmed. Recommend reinitiation only at terminal saturation threshold.

Ellie sank into the wooden chair beside the desk. The folder felt like it weighed more than its paper. Like it held something living.

Silas's words came back to her: The name was planted. Clara's whisper: It didn't belong to me.

She flipped through the pages with increasing urgency. Her own name—Eleanor J. Hale—appeared on a back sheet. Then was crossed out. Beneath it:

Clara M. RETENTION: ACTIVE

Lightning forked across the sky. She startled. Her reflection in the window blinked—late. Off-tempo.

She turned the final page.

Taped there—aged and brittle—was a drawing. Charcoal. A single figure seated in a spiral-marked chair. The face smudged out.

Beneath it, typed in all caps:

HALE, ELEANOR — SEE PROTOCOL PHASE III

Ellie stood sharply. The chair scraped loud against the tile. Pages slipped from her lap, scattering across the floor like molted skin. Her hands went to her temples. The pressure wasn't pain. It was return. Behind her a soft hum.

The drawer she hadn't touched clicked. She turned slowly. A new envelope sat inside. Crisp. Stamped with today's date. To be opened upon reactivation. Her name was typed across the front: Ellie Hale. But beneath it, handwritten in faint red ink: Clara.

She stared at the handwriting. Curved. Neat. Familiar. She didn't remember learning to write that way. Or maybe she remembered it too well. Maybe it wasn't hers at all. The rain outside stopped mid-drop. The silence that followed was total.

She turned toward the mirror near the filing cabinet. Her reflection remained. But then—its mouth moved. Not hers. The girl's. It whispered, "Clara." Ellie didn't move. But the glass fogged—just enough for the name to linger between them.

Not absence—but anticipation. She didn't know which name to answer to. And for the first time, she wasn't sure who would respond if called.

The air inside thickened, squeezing her ribs until she could hardly breathe. The walls swam around her. Ellie stumbled sideways, palms scraping against cold, crumbling stone.

Who was she?

The thought struck harder than the fall. It unspooled inside her — a raw, scraping unraveling. Was she the girl Clara had left behind? The girl who survived? Or just a hollow vessel stitched together from borrowed grief and secondhand memories?

Her reflection fractured in the shards of glass around her—dozens of broken Ellies staring back, not scattered like glass, but spinning, spiraling, like petals sheared from a single dying flower.

She pressed her forehead to the wall, the stone damp and pulsing under her skin, as if the building itself remembered what she couldn't.

Maybe she had never been whole to begin with.

Maybe memory wasn't a path home. Maybe it was a spiral too — a descent. A drowning.

A shudder clawed up her spine. She gritted her teeth against it, but the mirrors were inside her now, rooting deeper, whispering not who she had been — but who she had never truly become.

Her hands trembled — she pressed her palms against her eyes, but the mirrors still burned behind her lids, shimmering, whispering, refusing to be unseen. Maybe she wasn't real at all. Maybe she was nothing but a hollow reflection, seeded by grief, shaped by absence, doomed to wander through a world stitched from someone else's memories. She wanted to scream—or shatter. But what terrified her more was the growing suspicion that the mirrors didn't want to break her. They wanted to keep her whole—just... not as Ellie.

But from the darkness inside her mind, something stirred. Not a memory, but a weight, a pull, a thread coiling toward her from the mirrors. A name. A laugh. A sliver of sun flashing against broken glass.

The mirrors weren't breaking her.

They were planting something inside her.

Ellie lifted her head slowly, her vision blurry, her throat raw. She didn't recognize the face in the nearest shard — not completely — but somewhere deep beneath the surface, something familiar moved. Something growing.

She backed out of the vault-like it might shut its mouth behind her. The hall outside stretched impossibly long. The light bulbs flickered in delayed patterns. Her feet carried her forward as her thoughts circled backward.

Am I remembering this? Or becoming it? She dragged herself upright, blinking hard, and forced herself to keep moving down the corridor.

The Spiral hadn't finished with her yet.

She didn't find the next room. It found her. STORAGE B, the door read. She hadn't seen it before. Hadn't walked this far.

Inside: circular space. Spiral sketches wallpapered the walls. The chair at the center matched Silas's drawing. Worn. Wooden. Waiting. And then she saw it. On the far shelf, face down: a fresh sketch. She turned it over slowly.

Silas's lines were unmistakable. Two figures beneath the orchard tree. Both girls. Both with spiral-marked eyes. One was drawn with a nurse's coat, hair pinned like Ellie's.

The other had Ellie's face, too—but younger. Scrawled between the figures:

They made you hers. A chill spiked down her spine. Behind her, someone entered. Gretchen.

She crossed the threshold slowly, eyes landing on the sketch in Ellie's hand. Her breath caught. Just for a second. But Ellie saw it. Panic.

"Where did you get that?"

"He drew it. This morning. Before I said anything."

Gretchen tried to collect herself. "It's just a drawing, Ellie. Silas sketches what he's told. He's impressionable."

"But he knew," Ellie whispered. "He knew before I did."

She didn't raise the sketch. Didn't need to. They both saw it.

Gretchen stepped forward slowly, her voice soft but strained. "Let's sit. You're tired."

"He said I belonged to her," Ellie murmured. "Clara."

The name hung in the air. Neither denied it.

"I think you need to rest," Gretchen said, softer now, almost like an apology stitched into a command. But it was too late. The silence between them had already said too much.

Ellie looked down at the paper again. At the mirrored faces. The orchard tree behind them.

And in the corner of the page, in her own handwriting, a note she didn't remember writing:

REASSIGNMENT SCHEDULED UPON FAILURE TO MERGE. Gretchen moved too fast to hide the panic this time. Her voice dropped—barely a whisper, splintered with an old guilt Ellie couldn't yet translate. "We were supposed to keep her contained," Gretchen said. "But you... you're waking her up."

Ellie stepped backward. "What did you do to me?"

Gretchen didn't answer. She couldn't. And in that quiet, Ellie finally heard what had always been waiting beneath the Spiral:

She hadn't just forgotten who she was. She had been rewritten. And somewhere, Clara still existed. Even if only in her place.

The rain had stopped, but the sound hadn't. Ellie sat with her back against the far wall of the stairwell between wings, legs pulled close, forehead resting on her knees. The echo of her breath barely reached the tiled floor. Somewhere, a pipe clanged. Somewhere, a nurse called for someone who wasn't her. But all she could hear was that soft, interior rustle—like pages turning inside her own head.

Clara.

The name didn't hurt. That was the problem. It didn't sting, didn't resist, didn't push back. It just... settled. Like a coat left too long in someone else's closet.

She remembered the ribbon. Damp from rain, clutched in her palm, the cold seeping into her bones—not from the weather, but from the knowledge that the hand offering it was smaller than it should have been. She remembered the orchard not as a place but as a rhythm. The sound of leaves crunching when they shouldn't have been dry. The way breath fogged in patterns too symmetrical to be natural. Spirals in frost. But even as the memories unspooled, she held tight to one simple truth: That was Clara's story. Not mine. Not yet.

She remembered the feeling of being seated before she realized she had chosen to sit. The feel of old wood, warm under her legs. The way mirrors hummed like they knew too much and wouldn't say it outright.

And the way Silas had looked at her. Not like a stranger. Like a witness. Like someone who saw something beneath her skin that even she had been too afraid to name.

Ellie. Clara. 1C.

Not versions. Not names. Just layers. She wasn't losing herself. She was accumulating. That terrified her. Because if she was made to forget, and now she remembered—What was she supposed to become?

A footstep echoed above her. She didn't flinch. Didn't move. Her voice came out hollow, like something practicing its lines in her throat: "If I'm not the beginning... I'm the echo."

"You are," a whisper said—not hers. Not Silas's. A voice inside the Spiral. Inside her.

The stairwell light buzzed once and held. Then she stood. Time to see what he drew next.

CHAPTER: TWELVE

The Confession

The next morning, Gretchen was already waiting in the records room.

When Ellie stepped through the doorway, she noticed it immediately: the temperature hadn't changed, but the atmosphere had. Not colder—emptier. The kind of emptiness that followed someone trying to tidy away something they couldn't explain. The lights buzzed in the same uneven rhythm, but the shadows felt longer, stretched too thin across the floor. Dust curled in the air above the filing cabinets like breath that had been exhaled—but not received.

Gretchen sat at a small metal table, spine straight. One empty chair waited across from her. Ellie didn't sit right away.

A file lay between them—its tab read: WARD C: ROSTER – PHASE ONE. Stamped across the bottom: U.S. Public Health Service – Circular 17-B (1946) Neuropsychiatric Research Authorization.

Gretchen motioned toward the chair. "Sit, please."

Ellie did, slowly, careful not to meet her eyes.

"You're not the first nurse to come here thinking you're part of something larger," Gretchen began. Her voice was calm. Almost tender. "This place does that to people. The Spiral was never a protocol. It was a metaphor. A coping mechanism. That's all."

Ellie frowned. "Then why do I keep seeing evidence that I've been here before? That I'm connected to something I can't explain?"

Gretchen folded her hands. "You've been through trauma, Ellie. I've seen it in your intake—not your employment—chart. You fixate on patterns. That's not your fault. It's the brain trying to make meaning out of pain."

"I'm here as an employee," Ellie snapped. "Not a patient."

"You are," Gretchen said softly. "But you weren't always."

Ellie's vision clouded for a moment. Her gloved hand tightened around the folded paper in her coat pocket—the drawing Silas had given her. She didn't pull it out. Not yet.

Silas's door stood crooked on its hinges, the numberplate half-torn—like someone had tried to erase him and given up halfway.

Ellie hesitated, clipboard pressed to her chest, fingers twitching beneath her gloves. She knocked once.

No response.

She stepped inside.

The room was dim. The blinds had been drawn with surgical precision—angled just enough to allow a blade of fractured light through, slicing the dust into drifting geometry.

Silas sat rigid on the edge of his cot, back to her. His shoulders were too straight, like a soldier awaiting orders from a war that never ended.

"You're the nurse," he said. Not a question. A diagnosis.

Ellie paused. "Silas…?"

She stepped in, closing the door gently behind her. "It's me. Nurse Hale. I'm here to—"

"—record my deterioration," he finished.

His voice was flat. Measured. Like he'd practiced the phrase.

She stopped mid-step. "No," she said softly. "I'm here to listen. That's all."

"Then you better start early," he said. "I don't speak when the mirrors are uncovered."

She looked around. The wall-mounted mirror above the sink had been crudely taped over with strips of torn linen. "You covered that?"

"I covered all of them," he murmured. "The ones I could find."

"Why?"

He stood, slow and stiff, like something beneath his skin had started to calcify. He turned to her, eyes dark-ringed, glassy. Not vacant. Contained.

"The mirrors hum when the Spiral's awake. They remember too much."

Ellie blinked. "Silas…"

He stepped closer, voice low. Almost reverent.

"I am 1C," he said. Not defiant. Not proud. Almost… regretful.

Ellie's breath caught. "What do you mean?"

He gave a broken half-smile. "They told me that once. When Clara wouldn't stabilize. When she started naming the orchard before they let her see it. They said I could hold her memory until the signal took root."

"The signal?" Ellie asked.

"The recursion imprint," he said. "It's not stored in thought—it's stored in pattern. Images. Sound. Shape. Chalk on tile. Bark on trees. It doesn't spread like memory. It spreads like rhythm."

She stepped closer. "Silas, why would they tell you that you were

1C if—"

"Because I was supposed to be her mirror," he cut in. "That's how the early protocol worked. One host. One echo. They put the Spiral between us to see which mind bent first."

He turned his face toward the covered mirror.

"She bent. I fractured."

Ellie's pulse thundered.

"I don't understand," she said.

"You're not supposed to," he replied. "That's how recursion works. The mind protects itself by overwriting clarity with containment. You feel it, don't you? The bleed?"

She flinched. "Silas…"

He reached beneath the mattress and pulled out a folded page—creased, aged, smudged with graphite.

He handed it to her.

A child's drawing.

An orchard in spiral geometry, drawn from above.

In the center: two figures. One small. One taller. The smaller one, labeled: Clara. The taller: E.H.

Her throat closed.

"They made you hers," Silas said, voice soft.

She looked up.

"They made me watch the merge," Silas said. "I wasn't the first. But I was supposed to be the last—until you arrived."

Ellie looked up.

"Me?"

He nodded slowly. "You carry the pattern. It recognizes you. That's why the system replays you—why the mirrors shift when you pass."

Her voice cracked. "What do you mean 'replays'?"

Silas stepped in close, his voice down to a whisper.

"Because you're not just remembering. You're being remembered." "They told me that once. When Clara wouldn't stabilize…"

Ellie's pulse hammered. "You were 1C?"

Silas's gaze flicked toward the mirror, haunted. "No. I was the placeholder. You—" his voice cracked—"you were always the source."

The overhead light buzzed. In that second, his face wavered—not physically, but in her vision. Like a reflection struggling to catch up.

Ellie staggered back. "I—I'll come back tomorrow."

"There won't be a tomorrow," he said. "Not for Clara. Not for me. Only for the version that survives. The name that holds."

He lifted his hand. Pressed two fingers to his temple.

"They called me 1C. But she's the one the Spiral kept."

There was a lull in the air, stifled, halted.

"You're not the nurse, Ellie. You're the next recursion."

Ellie backed out of the room slowly, Silas's words still echoing behind her ribs.

You're not just remembering. You're being remembered.

The door closed with a soft hiss.

She turned down the hall, heart pounding, the folded drawing in her pocket suddenly heavy, like it carried a pulse. The hallway outside

Silas's room seemed quieter than usual. Too quiet. As if the building itself were holding its breath. Ellie didn't turn back toward the nurse's station. Instead, her feet moved on their own—carrying her past the linen closet, past the east stairwell, until she stood in front of Room 9.

The door was still locked. But the handle gave when she twisted it. Inside, the room was dim and airless. The bed untouched. The mirror across from it partially covered with gauze, as if someone had started to tape it off but never finished. A small desk stood in the corner. And on it—something Ellie hadn't noticed before. A sketchbook. Worn leather warped by moisture. Its spine cracked in two places. Pages curled from age—or from being opened and reopened too many times.

She hesitated, then stepped forward and opened it. The first page was smeared—black swirls, finger-blurred spirals that looped without pattern. But on the second page, words appeared. Scrawled across the top, in uneven pencil: "ME." A child's hand. Not practiced. Letters are too large for the lines.

Below is a drawing of a girl. No face. Just a shadowed outline. The figure sat in a chair too large for her, eyes blank, with a mirror behind her that shimmered like water. Ellie turned the page. And there—more versions. More hers.

The same figure repeated over and over, each time altered— different hairstyles, different ribbons, different shoes. But the same pose. The same spiral was drawn on the floor beneath her chair.

Some were labeled "Clara." Others "C." And one—Ellie's breath caught. One was labeled "E.H."

The letters had been scribbled over. Erased. Then, redrawn in darker pencil below the scratch out: "ME AGAIN."

Her throat tightened. She turned the page. This time, just a single word written across the top in all capital letters: "WHICH ONE?"

Below, a mirror. But instead of reflecting the girl, it reflected the sketchbook itself. As if the page had drawn her into it.

A final note in the bottom corner: "The name doesn't stay. But the drawing does." She closed the book. Her gloves were shaking. And she could still feel the groove where the pencil had pressed too hard—deep into the paper. Or into memory.

The wind outside had a different bite now. It didn't sting. It searched. She walked blind through the gray pathways, her hands shoved deep in her pockets, carrying the weight of a hundred forgotten faces — and the fragile seed of something she almost remembered.

She passed through the outer gate to the eastern yard, following bootprints she hadn't noticed before. Faint. Chalky. Too small to be hers. Too steady to belong to a patient.

The orchard emerged from the fog like a diagram drawn in breath. The trees were bare—but not dead. They leaned toward her. Their branches creaked in unison, not with the wind, but with memory. She carried no clipboard. No watch. No badge. Just the weight of the drawing in her coat and the name Clara pulsing behind her eyes. Ellie gripped her coat tighter—as if pressure alone could keep Clara out. But deep down, she felt it: this wasn't intrusion anymore. It was overlap. This is where they planted the names.

She moved between the spiral rows with the reverence of someone entering sacred ground. Each tree seemed carved, not grown. Their bark furrowed in patterns that matched Silas's drawings—repeating curves, nested loops, and spiral fractals, like trauma etched into the wood.

At the center of the orchard, the air thickened. The soil darkened.

She knelt. Her gloves brushed something beneath the top layer of earth—resistant but not solid. She pulled gently.

A ribbon. Red. Faded. It smelled faintly of iron and rain-soaked cloth—like grief that forgot how to dry. She lifted it. Blood-browned at the center. Too deep to be rust. Too dry to be fresh. As she touched it, a whisper shivered across her spine.

"Please remember me."

It wasn't heard. It was remembered. And then—she saw it. A child, gripping the ribbon. Not in play. In panic.

The girl's face flickered—hers and Clara's, shifting between versions like a projector losing its alignment. Beneath her knees, the earth cracked slightly. She dug again, slower this time, and uncovered the edge of something buried just beneath the surface.

A slatted box. Wooden. Warped. She opened it. Inside:

hundreds of intake forms. Cloth-bound. Fragile. All stamped with the Spiral. Each dated before the project was officially sanctioned. And all labeled with names that didn't exist in the public records. Her fingers found the final file. Folded carefully.

Patient Name: CLARA M. Alias: Subject 1C Handwritten beneath: "Mirror instability unresolved. Recursive reactivation prohibited. Witness exposure must remain suppressed."

Ellie's pulse roared in her ears. She stood slowly. And then she saw it. A spiral chalked faintly into the bark of the nearest tree—and below it, a name carved deep.

E.H. Her name. But not a signature. A stamp. A proof of something she hadn't yet agreed to become—but had already been made. Her own. The wind shifted. A laugh rippled across the orchard. Not mocking. Not joyous. Recognition.

Ellie clutched the ribbon and the sketch tighter.

She turned to leave—but her heel caught on a root that hadn't been there before.

The trees groaned—not from the wind, but from the strain of remembering. One branch swayed low. Not randomly. With intention. And the clearing whispered in a voice not spoken aloud:

"They only forget if you do."

Ellie stepped back inside. The rain clung to her coat, but the air inside the hospital tasted scorched—like paper set alight but never allowed to burn through. The red ribbon was still clenched in one damp glove.

She didn't remember crossing the threshold—but the sound of the hospital was back in her ears. The hum of the overhead lights. The whisper of a file drawer closing two corridors down. The faint clatter of a typewriter no one had touched in years. And footsteps. Soft. Approaching from the wrong direction. Hazel Greer rounded the corner.

She wasn't carrying a clipboard. She wasn't pretending to file something. She just stood there, coat buttoned too high, eyes tight at the corners like she hadn't slept in days.

"I was hoping I'd catch you before you made it to Gretchen."

Ellie didn't respond. Hazel's eyes dropped to Ellie's hand. To the ribbon. Her mouth tightened.

"They told me not to speak about it," Hazel said. "But you deserve to know. At least one thing."

Ellie's throat felt full. "What thing."

Hazel swallowed. "I cleaned the Merge Room."

The words landed like a dropped scalpel. Ellie didn't move. "When?"

"The day after. After the lights went out. After the file marked '1C' was removed."

Hazel took a shaky breath. "The chair was still warm."

She looked down as if remembering something she'd tried too long to forget.

"There was blood beneath the bolts. Not from injury. From nosebleed. Cranial pressure. It happens sometimes during recursion instability."

Ellie said nothing. Hazel pressed on. "They didn't say who the subject was. But the chart they left behind said, 'Retained, not stabilized.' And then they told me to bleach it all. Seal the mirror. Scrub out the spiral. And then forget it."

She met Ellie's eyes.

"But I couldn't. Because I saw your initials on the clipboard left behind."

Ellie's stomach turned.

Hazel's voice cracked. She pressed the heels of her hands against her eyes as if she could squeeze the memory out. 'I was told it was under the Committee on Neuropsychiatric Rehabilitation,' she whispered. 'Same line they used at Topeka. At St. Elizabeths. We thought it was federal oversight. Thought it was science.'

"I thought I was helping," she whispered. "God help me, I believed that. I believed if I stayed quiet, if I followed orders, if I just...pretended hard enough, it would all settle down eventually. That the blood would dry, and we could pretend none of it happened."

Her voice cracked.

"But the Spiral...it doesn't forget. It grows. It grew inside us. Inside me. I watched good people break. I let it happen. I let them take what they wanted erase what they needed to erase. I told myself it wasn't my hands doing it. That I wasn't the one pulling the strings."

She dropped her hands from her face, looking at Ellie with eyes gone flat with shame.

"But silence is its own kind of violence. And I chose it. Over and over."

She pulled something from her pocket. A folded page—creased and worn. It was part of the Merge Room checklist, but a section had been circled in pencil.

Post-Merge Clinical Addendum

- Subject 1C: Residual reflexive instability detected.

- Recursion viable. Monitor for delayed naming bleed.

- Do not reassign until mirror confirms integration.

Hazel's voice dropped. "The mirror cracked while I was in there. No impact. No heat. Just… split. From the center out."

She shook her head. "I thought that meant it was over. But now I think it meant she wasn't gone."

Ellie reached for the paper with a shaking hand.

Hazel didn't let go right away. "If you go back down there, Nurse Hale… don't go alone."

Ellie said nothing. The words hung between them, thick and suffocating, heavier than the stench of blood and bleach curling down the hallways. Only the hum of the vents and the flicker of one dim light at the end of the hall.

Hazel stepped back. "I'm sorry. I didn't know who you were."

Ellie's voice was thin but certain this time. "Neither did I. Until now."

CHAPTER: THIRTEEN

Mirror Calibration

Dr. Weatherly sat alone in his office, spine rigid, hands folded like a man performing surgery on thought. The room was quiet—but not still. The lamplight pooled across his desk with surgical clarity, illuminating the clutter of open files, requisition slips, and a half-drained mug of chicory coffee turned cold. The air tasted metallic.

He clicked through the facility's internal access log, fingers steady on the ivory keys of the terminal. The screen refreshed in pulses, not scrolls—each line appearing like a breath exhaled too late.

ACCESS RECORD – SEPTEMBER 10, 1947

HALE, E.J.

08:47 — PHASE ONE ROSTER FILE: OPENED

09:02 — WARD C ARCHIVE DOOR: KEYED ENTRY (LEVEL 2)

19:12 — MIRRORLINE ANNEX – UNAUTHORIZED ENTRY

21:09 — ARCHIVE ROOM 4B – ACCESS CODE OVERRIDE DETECTED

— NON-STANDARD KEY USED —He stopped. Stared.

The cursor blinked. Waiting.

His eyes moved back to the previous entries. Cross-referencing. Matching timestamps. He scrolled slower now as if giving the machine time to lie. Too much curiosity. Too fast.

He exhaled through his nose, then reached for the drawer on his left—one only he could open. The brass key fit with a quiet click. Inside: a thin folder labeled in red grease pencil.

SUBJECT OBSERVATION – 1C (REACTIVATION)

He flipped it open.

Status: Passive. Dormant. Intake integration stable.

His pen hovered. Then, with mechanical calm, he drew a line through the word Passive.

Correction: ACTIVE. INVERTED. UNFOLDING.

He paused, then wrote again—fainter:

Self-locating. Sketch-based retrieval suspected. Drift echo present. Spiral response confirmed.

He leaned back just slightly, eyes flicking to the door as if expecting someone to knock. No one did. But the walls felt tighter.

Weatherly pulled the red-ribboned typewriter closer, its mechanical hum dormant until he engaged the carriage. With practiced motion, he inserted a blank slip and began to type in perfect block caps.

SPIRAL CONTAINMENT MEMO – INTERNAL DISTRIBUTION ONLY

SUBJECT: Hale, Eleanor J. (SUBJECT 1C – REACTIVATED)

AUTHORIZED UNDER U.S. PUBLIC HEALTH SERVICE – CIRCULAR 17-B (1946), NEUROPSYCHIATRIC RESEARCH ACT.

PROTOCOL BREACH: Recursive Drift Behavior

RISK LEVEL: Moderate–Elevating

RECOMMENDED ACTIONS:

– Restrict unsupervised access to all Orchard Archive sectors

– Revoke clearance for Mirrorline Annex pending Phase III review

– Reinforce mirror obfuscation protocols in Rooms 2B–9

– Block Room 9 archival code requests (internal AI response redirect)

– Implement verbal containment protocol; suppress unsanctioned use of 'Clara' nomenclature outside C-Wing.

– Increase dosage for Patient Reeve (S.R.) – observation overlap noted

Escalation Directive:

If mirror-phase fixation persists beyond 48 hours, initiate Phase III Merge Review. Do not disclose prior subject designation. Do not engage emotionally.

Weaver believed recursion was containment. I believe it's contagion. He saw memory as mirror. I see it as virus. He trusted the system to forget. I'm betting it won't.

SIGNED: M.A. Weatherly

CLINICAL DIRECTOR – SPIRAL PROTOCOL

He rolled the memo free, inserted it into a plain envelope, and sealed it with the embossed Spiral press.

Then he returned the 1C folder to the drawer. Locked it. Turned off the desk lamp. The darkness that followed wasn't empty. It hummed. Not in sound—but sensation. A low resonance behind his eyes, like something awakening at the edge of protocol. His gaze drifted to the mirror mounted above the coat hook on the far wall.

For a moment, the glass rippled—not visually, but atmospherically. The pressure in the room shifted. And his reflection blinked before he did. His throat tightened. For a second—a terrible second—he thought he saw the spiral burned into the whites of his own eyes. He blinked it away, but the afterimage held. Just once. He did not move. Only spoke beneath his breath.

"She wasn't supposed to survive reentry."

Ellie stood before the door to Archive Room 3C with the key already in her hand. Her grip was firm—out of habit, not confidence. The brass edge pressed a faint crescent into her gloved palm, an indentation that had become familiar. She inserted the key.

Click. The lock turned, but the door didn't move. She frowned.

Tried again—this time angling slightly left, the way it always caught just before releasing.

Click. Nothing.

Her stomach twisted—not sharply, but low and slow like heat rising from beneath cold stone.

She tried a third time.

Click. Denied.

There was no sound, no mechanical jam. No resistance, even. Just refusal. Like the door was choosing.

Her hand stayed on the knob. But something in her spine already knew what the lock was saying:

Access revoked.

She took a step back. The hallway lights overhead flickered—not violently, but in pulse. One. Then three in succession. Then steady. Her breath fogged faintly, though the air didn't feel cold.

She turned slowly, forcing herself to walk—measured, calm, clinical. The sound of her shoes was wrong. Half a beat behind her movement. Echoes arriving late.

Just past the stairwell, an unattended records cart leaned against the wall. It hadn't been there earlier. Or maybe it had, and she hadn't seen it because it hadn't mattered yet.

The top folder was pristine. Placed. Waiting. She scanned the corridor. No one. No footsteps. Just that strange, static silence Arlington Hills wore like a second skin. Ellie reached for the folder.

PROJECT MIRRORLINE

SUBJECT DRIFT STUDY – INTAKE DRAFT

Designation: C.M. (approx. age 9)

Trial Phase: Mirror Calibration — Room 9 (Simulated Domestic Environment)

Observation: Subject identifies reflection before own name. Exhibits emotional fixation on sibling unaccounted for in historical record.

Displays mirror dissociation and naming delay.

RECOMMENDATION: Repeat Room 9 calibration. Introduce proxy overlay. Suppress sibling construct. Ensure naming delay persists.

Initialed: W.

Her blood turned cold. Room 9.

That number. That door. It had appeared in her dreams before she had a reason to remember it. It shouldn't mean anything. But it did. The Drift had begun again.

Ellie's hand went to her coat pocket, drawing out the spiral sketch Silas had given her. But it wasn't the same. Room 9 had been added. A square room. Two beds. One figure drawn in full. The other—sketched halfway, then erased. The name beneath it scribbled out so many times the paper had begun to tear.

Just above the tear: "ME" —written in a child's hand.

Her breath cowered inside her lungs. Not from fear. From recognition. The lights overhead buzzed again. This time, the hum didn't fade—it settled. Low, constant, like tinnitus behind the air.

A nurse passed the hallway junction ahead of her—but didn't look her way. She didn't seem to see Ellie at all. Ellie looked back at the sketch. The erasure on the page had transferred faint graphite onto her glove. She wiped it against her coat—but it didn't come off. The pencil dust had sunk into the grain of the leather.

Permanent.

She turned to walk. She didn't know where. Just… away from the door that wouldn't open. And toward the one that had never needed a key to let her in.

That night, Ellie couldn't sleep. Not fully. She drifted—light and slow, like breath across old glass. Her body lay in bed, but her mind paced elsewhere. The dormitory walls felt thinner. The radiator hissed irregularly like something caught behind it was trying to breathe. At 2:11 AM, the mirror fogged. She hadn't run the water. She sat up, heartbeat heavy. Her gloves were still on, though she didn't remember putting them back after dinner.

The mirror above the basin was small. Meant for checking bandage wraps. Routine things. But tonight, it was larger. Or the room was smaller. Or her own reflection had moved too far forward. She stood. Walked to it. Slowly. The fog hadn't lifted. Instead, it began to shift— from breath to writing. One line, traced in condensation from the inside:

"I don't want to be a vessel."

The words bled downward—slow, syrupy—as if carved into the glass by a fingertip older than hers. She pressed her palm to the mirror. It radiated not warmth, but the slow fever of breath trapped too long—heat that had forgotten its body.

She whispered, "Clara?"

The glass rippled—not physically, but optically. Her reflection blinked. Then blinked again. Out of sync.

A second image emerged—overlaid, ghosted just behind her own. A younger girl. The same face. Wider eyes. Lips parted but stitched faintly with shadow lines. Mute—but moving. And in the mirror, her mouth moved faster than Ellie's own.

A whisper came—not aloud, but in her thoughts, layered under her heartbeat:

"They kept me for you." The words peeled across her bones. Ellie stumbled back, her ribs aching as if someone had reached through her and rattled the spaces memory lived in. She pressed a shaking hand to her chest—her heartbeat still there, but muffled, like it was echoing from further away than it should. Not gone. Not hers alone anymore.

The mirror cracked—not from impact, but from memory. A slow, crawling fracture spiraled outward from the reflection's lips, webbing the glass in jagged lines.

Ellie stumbled back. Behind her, the spiral sketch—the one she had folded into the front page of her logbook—slid from the nightstand and landed face-up on the floor. It had changed again. This time, the name Clara was written twice. Once beneath a child. Once beneath Ellie. No Hale. No initials. Just Clara. Overwritten. Unsplit. The radiator stopped hissing. The mirror unfogged—but the girl was still there. Silent now. Just watching. Just waiting.

A man stood in shadow. "Stability is not healing," he said. "It is silence." Ellie woke on the floor, breath ragged. Her spiral sketch beside her. Different again. One name written. One erased. She stared at it, pulse hammering. Neither was hers anymore. The Spiral kept what names could not.

CHAPTER: FOURTEEN

The System Remembers:

Ellie didn't make it to morning rounds.

She walked the eastern corridor with her clipboard held high like a shield—half camouflage, half confession. Her steps were brisk, her spine straight, her mind anything but.

She wasn't sure why she came this way again. She hadn't planned it. She hadn't planned anything since finding the chalk spiral behind her mirror.

The floorplan on the wall stopped her cold. No Room 9. Not misnumbered. Not mislabeled. Just… never printed. Like it had never existed except in a memory no one wanted. Her feet, however, remembered the path.

Turn right past Ward B. Down the hallway where the light always flickered. Past the linen closet with the doorknob that always turned twice.

And then—

Nothing.

Just wall. Seamless. Whitewashed. Breathless. But the wall wasn't still. Not to her. It watched. She laid her palm against it. Warm. Slightly pliant. As if something once pulsed behind the plaster and might again.

A voice behind her.

"Looking for something, Nurse Hale?"

Ellie turned too fast.

Dr. Asher.

He stood at the end of the corridor, perfectly composed. Too composed.

"I saw an intake note referencing Room 9," she said, clipboard tight to her chest. "Why isn't it listed?"

"Drafted but never constructed," he replied too quickly. "Mirrorline's earliest schematics included excess simulation units. Standard practice," Asher added absently, "for wartime neuropsychiatric labs. Redundant capacity in case of patient influx. They were discarded. Hypotheticals."

"Then why did Weatherly's note describe it as a 'simulated domestic space'?"

His jaw tensed. "Hypotheticals get creative."

"You're sure Room 9 never existed?"

Asher's gaze darkened.

"Rooms don't exist unless someone remembers them."

And she did, not in words—but in weight. In the way, her boots always slowed at that turn. In the way her spine straightened, unbidden, before the wall that now bore no door.

Room 9 hadn't vanished. It had rehearsed its absence.

And then he walked away.

Gretchen – Office Log

Gretchen stared at the monitor, the glow of the archive terminal casting a sickly green sheen across her face. Her office was dark, but for that flickering light, the shadows clinging to the corners like ash that hadn't settled. The screen blinked—rhythmic, clinical, unaware of what it had just revealed.

HALE, E.J. – UNAUTHORIZED CORRIDOR ACTIVITY LOGGED

Location: East Wing, Hall B

Notes: WALL CONTACT FLAGGED. DOOR 9 PING NOT FOUND.

Her fingers hovered above the keyboard, trembling slightly. The cursor blinked with silent authority.

REVIEW

IGNORE

ESCALATE

It wasn't the log that made her hesitate. It was the image frozen on the side screen. Surveillance still, low resolution—grainy and gray—but unmistakable.

Ellie. Standing before the wall that didn't exist anymore. The place Room 9 used to be—before it was sealed, renamed, or... forgotten. Not knocking. Not pushing. Not even looking confused. Just... remembering. And that—that—was the danger.

Gretchen's throat tightened. Her breath caught halfway to her chest like her body had finally realized the past wasn't past at all. A whisper escaped her, barely louder than the static hum of the machine.

"She wasn't supposed to remember that hallway. I buried it."

But the system didn't care what was buried.

Because the file hadn't been retrieved by mistake.

The Room 9 log—the one Gretchen had folded, misfiled, mislabeled, and flagged as obsolete under Mirrorline Failures—had resurfaced. Not because it was accessed. But because it had reasserted itself. Just like the orchard drawings. Just like Subject 1C's recursion logs that wouldn't stay sealed.

She reached toward the screen, intending to shut it off. Her hand stopped an inch above the power button, hovering like she might press down—or might just keep shaking. On-screen, Ellie didn't move.

She simply stood there. One hand at her side. The other lightly grazing the tile where a door once was. Not curious. Not frantic. Still. Composed. As if she'd been there before. Because she had.

A sound echoed in Gretchen's ears—not from the monitor. Not from the ward. From the hallway outside her office. Soft. Haunting. A child's hum. The Spiral tune. Slow. Measured. Repeating. Gretchen stiffened.

Across the ward, Ellie Hale was humming the melody that hadn't been taught to her. That no one had spoken aloud since Clara's recursion breach. Not even Silas dared hum it anymore.

Gretchen turned slowly toward the window. The corridor beyond shimmered faintly beneath the emergency lighting—empty but not still.

The hum echoed again. Only this time, it wasn't a child's voice. It was Ellie's. Layered. Out of sync. Like two versions of her humming at once.

Her hand dropped from the terminal. She couldn't click Review. Couldn't Ignore. And to Escalate meant surrendering to a chain of command that had long since collapsed under its own recursion.

She sat back in her chair. The monitor still blinked. The terminal still pulsed. But she didn't move. She simply stared. And listened.

As the past began humming through Ellie's lungs like it had found its voice again—through the one girl Gretchen had promised never to lose. And already had. Twice.

Ellie scrubbed her hands at the infirmary sink, though they were already clean.

She wasn't even supposed to be in here. Not officially. No rounds. No scheduled check-ins. She'd walked here without thinking—pulled by something quieter than instinct, deeper than memory.

The soap foamed in her palms, chalk-white and too thin, the kind that never fully rinsed away. It smelled off—too antiseptic. Overcompensating. Like a lie wearing a lab coat. Like guilt.

She turned the water hotter, though her skin was already raw. The faucet hissed as steam rose in thin plumes—but none clung to the glass above the sink. She kept her eyes down. Avoided the mirror at first. But it was there. She didn't need to see it to feel it. Watching her. Or waiting.

The air shifted. Heavier now. Denser near the glass, like the mirror had weight—breath, even. Not a surface but a presence. She looked up. Her reflection stared back. And blinked—late. Half a second too slow. It wasn't the delay that chilled her. It was the intent behind it. Like the mirror was deciding to catch up. Then it began to fog. No steam. No heat. Just condensation from nothing, blooming across the glass in slow, deliberate curves. Ellie stepped back instinctively, her spine touching the medicine cabinet behind her.

And then the words came. Etched not in breath but from within the mirror itself—traced by an invisible hand on the other side of the glass.

YOU'RE CLOSE.

Her pulse stuttered. A dry panic rose in her throat. Not full, not screaming—but recognition. As if her body knew something her mind hadn't caught up to yet.

And then the hum began. Not from the walls. Not from any machine. From inside her. A vibration low and deep behind her molars, threading down her spine like a tuning fork struck in her blood. Her teeth itched. Her ears rang. The mirror buzzed in sympathy.

And then—a voice. Not aloud. Not hers. But inside. Smooth. Familiar. Layered with static.

"It's not the orchard you remember.

It's the one you drew."

Ellie's hands began to shake. Her gloves were still damp. The scent of soap—bitter and medicinal—clung to her fingers like disinfectant on memory.

"Clara?" she whispered.

The word cracked as it left her lips. It didn't feel like a name anymore. It felt like a door. And when the door opened, she wasn't the one who stepped through.

There was no answer. Only the tune. The Spiral lullaby. Slower now. Like a cradle-song sung by someone long dead, barely remembered, echoing across a room made of mirrors and breath.

She turned from the sink, reaching for the paper towels—but froze. Because her reflection hadn't moved. It stood perfectly still. Hands folded at its waist. Chin tilted up slightly. Smiling. But not kindly. Like it knew something Ellie didn't. Or maybe something Ellie had once known—and buried.

The fog on the mirror shifted again. The smile widened. And the reflection mouthed a single word. Ellie's stomach dropped.

"Run."

She staggered back from the sink, the edge of the counter catching her hip.

The hum rose again—like the room exhaled. Her reflection remained still. And behind the mirror, just for an instant, she saw it—her own face, younger. Braided. Ribbon tied too tightly around one wrist. Eyes wide. And watching. Not from fear. From recognition. From inside the glass.

Ellie backed out of the infirmary, breath ragged, gloves wet, her coat too tight in the sleeves. The hallway beyond was silent—but it felt different now. Bent. Like a hallway drawn by someone who had only ever dreamed corridors and never walked them.

And behind her, the mirror slowly faded. Leaving no fog. No trace. Only a faint spiral at the center—pressed into the glass like a fingerprint. She turned the corner too fast—shoulder grazing the tile, breath caught halfway in her chest—still reeling from what hadn't followed her out of the infirmary mirror.

And slammed nearly into Dr. Weatherly. He was standing there, still and certain, as though he had been waiting—not by coincidence, but appointment. One hand held a clipboard. Not hers. The other adjusted his cuff with mechanical precision like even his sleeves obeyed institutional decorum.

"Careful," he said mildly, like he was commenting on a misplaced file.

Ellie froze. Her skin still crawled from the sink. She didn't speak. Weatherly's eyes swept her face with practiced calm. He flipped the clipboard up against his chest and tilted his head just slightly.

"You've looked tired lately," he said.

Ellie blinked. Her voice felt distant. "I'm fine."

His tone didn't change. "Your route says otherwise."

Her throat tightened. He wasn't accusing her of anything. He was recording her.

"Sorry," she said too quickly. "It's just… the dreams. They're bleeding into the day."

Weatherly's lips curved upward. Not a smile—just the outline of one. Like he knew the word's shape but had forgotten its use.

"Dreams that feel like memory," he said, "are the most dangerous kind."

Her stomach dropped. She hadn't said anything about memory. Not to him. Not yet. She straightened, pulse beginning to rise beneath her collar. "I didn't mention memory."

"Didn't you?" he asked, eyebrows lifting with artificial surprise. "Strange. I must've heard it somewhere."

He took a step closer—not invasive, but strategic. The kind of distance that suggested authority by removal of space.

Ellie held her ground. Just barely. His voice dropped a half-register—quiet but precise.

" "If a voice calls you by your name—and it sounds like yours— Do not answer. That's how the Spiral reclaims its own."

Ellie's jaw locked. It wasn't a warning. It was a directive. She felt the hallway tilt around them. The floor didn't move, but the certainty in her balance shifted—like a thought misfiled behind her ribs. Weatherly looked at her a moment longer.

Then—without ceremony—he turned and walked away, the clipboard tucked neatly beneath one arm. His footsteps echoed softly, deliberately, too measured for the tension they left behind.

Ellie didn't move until he turned the next corner. And even then—The corridor still felt full. Not of people. Of observation. She glanced down the direction he'd gone.

And knew, without knowing how, that he wasn't watching what she did. He was watching when she remembered it.

She didn't remember deciding to go. Only the walking.

Only the sound of gravel beneath her boots, softer than it should've been. Only the way the cold didn't bite anymore. Not like weather. Not like wind. It simply was—settling into her skin like something that belonged there.

The Spiral wasn't in the air. It was beneath it. Underfoot. In the soil. In the tension of her muscles as they moved with a memory that hadn't yet revealed itself. In the way, her breath fell into a rhythm she didn't recognize but had followed before. The orchard was listening.

She felt it in the hush between footfalls. In the stretch of silence that bent too long between tree groans. In the narrowing of the path behind her—not because the trail had shifted, but because she had.

She didn't bring a drawing this time. She was the drawing. Every step inked into the earth by some unseen hand. Every turn, a stroke from a pencil she'd once held. Every breath echoing the tune of a memory drawn in spirals, not words.

She passed the last row of trees. The spiral clearing opened before her—not vacant, but expectant. The soil had changed again. Turned. Softened. Not rain. Not runoff. Something had moved. Something had been buried. She knelt. Not out of intention. But recognition. The soil felt warm, but the air bit cold. Like the ground was remembering what the sky forgot. Her gloves slipped from her hands before she realized she'd removed them. She dug with her bare fingers—into cold dirt that gave too easily. As if the orchard had been waiting for her touch. As if it remembered the shape of her hands.

First, the corner of wood—grain swollen, warped from years of silence. The box. She lifted it with care.

Then, pressed against the underside, curled like it had been hiding—The satchel. Child-sized. Frayed. Leather once red, now browned with time and earth. A ribbon still tied to one strap—nearly dissolved but intact. The initials were still visible.

C.M.

Ellie's breath caught—not in her throat, but behind her ribs. Like a breath drawn years ago had never been released. She opened the flap.

Inside: a sketchbook.

Pages clumped together by moisture and mold. Others torn with near-surgical precision as if someone had taken care to erase—but not all of it. Some drawings remained. Her fingers trembled as she turned the first page.

The orchard—seen from above. Spiral rows, identical to what Silas had drawn. Only this version included figures in the spaces between trees. Watching.

The next page: Room 9.

Drawn in perfect lines. Windowless. Two beds. No door. Just a mirror.

Another: herself.

Drawn with a child's uneven hand, but unmistakably her. Standing in a corridor that didn't appear on any map—but she'd walked it. Recently.

The lines were tight. Pressed deep. As though the pencil had trembled. Or the hand had. She turned to the last page. No image. Just words. Written in sharp, decisive strokes, darker than the rest.

YOU'RE NEXT.

Ellie flinched—though the wind hadn't stirred. And then it did. A gust, sudden and direct, sheared across the clearing—not cold, not natural. It carried a scent: chalk. Sharp on her tongue, dry as regret, tasting faintly of something unfinished.

From above, fragments of white flaked down—not snow. Not ash. Chalk dust. Drifting from the trees. She stood slowly, sketchbook pressed to her chest like something living. Her hands were coated in dirt, but her fingers didn't feel dirty. They felt claimed.

She turned in place, scanning the trunks of the nearest trees. And then she saw it.

A spiral. Not drawn. Carved. Etched deep into the bark of a tree she hadn't touched—but that had touched her once. It bent slightly in the center, just enough to draw her gaze down to the base.

And there, beneath the spiral:

E.H.

Her initials. Not written. Inscribed. She didn't scream. She didn't collapse. Because the Spiral was not asking for fear. It was asking for memory. And Ellie understood now—too clearly to deny it—This place was not where the story ended.

It was where she had begun. And the Spiral had never stopped spinning. Not for her. Not for Clara. Not for anyone. Only now, it was watching again. And it had remembered her name.

Ellie's quarters were too quiet when she returned. Not the kind of silence that invited rest, but the kind that sat in the corners like something left unfinished.

The overhead light flickered once—then again. A long pause between. Not random. Rhythmic. Spiral timing. She didn't take off her coat. Didn't set down the satchel still pressed beneath her arm. Because there, laid perfectly centered on her bed like a gift or a threat, was the manila file.

HALE, ELEANOR J. — SUBJECT 1C

Stamped in institutional red. Dated four years ago. A hand-drawn spiral had been sketched beneath the title, so faint it could've been missed unless you were already looking for it.

Ellie didn't sit. She stood beside the bed, heart beginning to beat in a syncopated rhythm, a half-beat delayed from what it should've been. She opened the folder slowly as if it might bleed.

Inside:

A grainy intake photograph. Her face—only younger. Unsure. Slightly unfocused, like she hadn't been looking at the camera but through it. She was wearing the same style coat she now had on. The same initials etched faintly into the collar tag.

A spiral cognition chart came next. Hand-marked in graphite, looping tighter with each iteration until the outermost ring began again from the inside. And then—the memo.

Typed. Clinical. Stark:

REACTIVATION MEMO – PROTOCOL 1C

"Monitor closely if memory bleed occurs.

If subject repeats the name Clara, initiate suppression protocol."

There was no signature. Just the spiral. Faint, watermarked into the paper like a shadow that could only be seen when held at the right angle. Ellie's hands trembled, but she didn't set the file down. Because suddenly, the lights didn't flicker—they hummed. Low. Electric. Familiar. Like the sound behind the mirrors. Like the echo of her own voice before she spoke. And then—a knock. Not loud. Just… certain.

Three precise taps against the doorframe, like punctuation marks. Ellie turned. Opened the door. Gretchen stood on the other side, not composed this time. Not clinical. Her hair was slightly damp, eyes red-rimmed. She wasn't holding a clipboard. Just herself. Barely.

"We need to talk," she said.

Ellie didn't move. "You left this," she said, lifting the folder slightly.

Gretchen shook her head. "No. I didn't."

Ellie narrowed her eyes. "Then who did?"

But Gretchen didn't answer right away. She just stared at the folder—as if seeing it again rewound something in her chest.

"I locked that file six floors underground," Gretchen whispered. "Before you ever came back."

Ellie felt the floor tilt. Just slightly. "So why was it in my room?"

Gretchen finally looked her in the eye. Her voice was softer now. Tired.

"Because you've always been the one who remembers, Ellie. Even when we tried to forget you."

Ellie stepped aside. Let her in. And behind them both, the lights steadied. But the Spiral hummed. Waiting. Watching. Ready.

CHAPTER: FIFTEEN

The Original Sketch

The morning light came through the east wing in fractured lines—warped by old window glass, softened by fog. It wasn't the warmth of spring, not yet, but it held the breath of something thawing. Ellie walked the corridor slowly, clipboard under her arm, the soles of her shoes whispering across the waxed floor.

Inside Ward C, the silence wasn't stillness. It was reverence. Like the building knew something she hadn't yet named. Silas was already sketching when she entered. He didn't look up. The chalk moved like it remembered its purpose better than he did. The image on the floor was not the orchard. Not this time.

A man in a black suit. One hand rested on a child's shoulder. The other child stood beside her, arms crossed, gaze low. A door behind them bore a triangular emblem. A mirror loomed above a fireplace, its glass smudged to black.

Ellie's heart stuttered. She recognized the posture. The stance. The presence. Dr. Marcus Weaver.

She stepped closer, voice trembling. "Who is that?"

Silas didn't look up. "He used to stand like that. Like he owned the room. But it wasn't his house."

She stared—and the breath caught sharp in her throat. "One of the girls stood exactly like she did when she was afraid—same tilt, same crossed arms, same foot turned inward, seeking escape that never came. The other stood just close enough in posture to feel familiar, but off by a beat. Like an echo drawn imperfectly." The same tilt of the head. The same crossed arms. One foot turned in.

"Is this a memory?" she asked.

Silas answered with silence.

She knelt. "Who are the girls?"

"You were the one they kept. She was the one they erased."

Her chest tightened. "Who?"

Silas pointed to the figure on the right. "Subject 9C."

She recoiled. "Do you know her name?"

"She had one. Once."

Later that evening, Ellie found Gretchen alone in the east wing.

"He drew a man in a house with two girls. One looked like me. The other..." Her voice lowered. "He called her 9C."

Gretchen stiffened—too fast. Her eyes flicked to the hallway before she spoke. "Silas's drawings are projections. They don't reflect real memories. Not reliably."

"But the man looked like Marcus Weaver."

"That's impossible."

Ellie didn't blink. "Is it?" The pause said more than Gretchen would.

"Weaver's work... predates Arlington,' Gretchen said too quickly. 'He wasn't Spiral. He never... not here."

Ellie watched her closely. "You're sure of that?"

"You're letting hallucinations drive your thinking," Gretchen said. And then she turned away.

Back in Room 3C, Silas was at the small table, charcoal in hand. The spiral was already forming—but it was off-center, spilling toward the margins. At the center: a tree. Twisted. Dead. Roots reaching up like they were trying to pull down the sky.

And beneath it, a figure.

Ellie.

She knew her own outline. The braid over one shoulder. The pleated skirt. But her eyes were blotted outcrossed in black.

"Silas," she whispered. "Did you dream again?"

He kept drawing. A second figure appeared beneath the tree. Small. A child. Hands folded. Head tilted.

She stepped closer. "Is that supposed to be me?"

"You blinked first," he said.

Her skin prickled. "What?"

"She isn't me," he said. Then, softer: "The one you remember being. That's not you anymore."

Ellie sat across from him, heart pounding. "What do you see?"

He blinked. "The orchard. Before the burn. The name in the dirt. I see you digging. But your hands are too small to be yours now."

"Before the burn?"

He nodded. "Only the part you left behind."

Behind the figure in the spiral, a faint shadow had been added. A mirror. A reflection. Screaming.

Ellie whispered, "I don't remember this dream."

Silas looked at her. Too clearly. "It's not yours. You just kept it alive."

She wanted to argue. But the words felt foreign. Rented. Like the echo of something Clara might have said.

What if she hadn't survived Clara's memory? What if she was the echo left behind?

"What do you mean?"

Silas leaned in. "You were the first name the Spiral couldn't forget."

Fog thinned outside the window. Her reflection shimmered. And behind her—the girl with stitched eyes. Watching. Ellie rose too fast. Her chair scraped. She couldn't speak.

The drawing between them still expanded. Bottom right corner: "Verified: W.W." Her stomach flipped. Weatherly had signed it—not as a witness, but as a warden.

Weatherly had signed it. But the date predated her transfer. Or her return. The next sketch had already begun. His hand moved as if guided. A mirror. A girl. The spiral behind her eyes.

That night, Ellie returned to her room and found the light already on. And waiting on her bed: A manila file. She knew what it would say before she touched it.

HALE, ELEANOR J. — SUBJECT 1C

Stamped in red. Dated four years earlier. A spiral sketched in graphite across the bottom edge. She sat. Slowly.

Inside:

An intake photo—her face, younger, frightened. A recursion chart. And a final memo:

REACTIVATED.

Ellie didn't sleep. She remembered instead. In the morning, she found spiral dust on her fingertips. But the pencil was still in Silas's room. She hadn't drawn. But her hands remembered.

She'd thought memory was something you carried. But this— this felt like memory carrying her. And the Spiral wasn't chasing her anymore. It was calling her back to where she'd never truly left.

163

CHAPTER: SIXTEEN

The Merge

The door to the observation room creaked on hinges that didn't belong in a government-funded hospital—not unless they wanted you to hear them coming. Ellie stood just outside, heart-catching rhythm against her ribs, as if unsure whether to step forward or retreat into the safety of unknowing.

Inside, Clara sat still. Her back to the door. Her shoulders hunched in the too-small chair. Her hair had been brushed, but not by her. Ellie knew the difference. There was order but no care.

She stepped into the room. Clara didn't turn at first, but her head tilted. As if she'd heard something beneath the floorboards. A vibration. A whisper.

"I wasn't supposed to be awake," Clara murmured.

Ellie paused, clipboard pressed to her chest. "What do you mean?"

Clara lifted her hand slowly, fingers brushing the wooden grain of the table like she was reading it for the first time. "The last one didn't speak," Clara said, fingers ghosting across the table. "They said that meant it took. That it was done."

Ellie sat. "The last what?"

But Clara only smiled, distant and wrong.

The mirror across from them—double-pane, meant for observation—bowed outward, buzzing faintly at the seams, as if the glass itself was bracing for something to break through, as if something on the other side had started to remember. Ellie tried to focus on the girl, not her own reflection, which stuttered slightly, lagging behind her movements.

"You drew this," Ellie said, placing a charcoal sketch on the table. A spiral orchard. A girl in the middle. But there was a second figure now. Unlabeled. Watching.

Clara stared at it. "She's been there longer than me."

"Who is she?"

Clara turned her gaze to the mirror. "She told me not to remember."

For one heartbeat, the lights above them flickered—not out, but inward, like a pulse in reverse. Ellie glanced at the mirror again. Her own face. Then Clara's. Then a third—childlike, stitched eyes, fading fast.

Ellie stood. "Clara, how long have you been here?"

Clara's expression didn't change. "I don't know. They changed the name so many times. First, I was Patient 9. Then I was Subject C. Then I was nobody."

"What's your name now?"

Clara tilted her head again. "You'll remember when it's safe."

The mirror buzzed louder now. She turned toward the glass. Her reflection blinked late, like a thought misfiled behind her eyes. The figure beside her wore her face—but not her stance. It leaned in close whispered something she didn't hear.

When she turned back to Clara—The girl was drawing again.

This time, it was Ellie's name. But not signed. Carved. In spiral loops. Until the letters bled into each other. Until the name wasn't Ellie anymore.

Ellie's hands trembled, not from fear but from a recognition she couldn't explain. She wanted to ask what Clara meant—but the question caught in her throat, strangled by the truth trying to surface. What name did she think belonged to her? What name had never stopped echoing beneath her own?

Ellie didn't realize her hand was shaking until the fountain pen scratched sideways across the paper. The nurse's station was quiet—too quiet for a room that was never truly empty. Even the clocks felt muted. As if time itself was waiting.

She flipped open the file labeled: Retained Subjects. Not Clara. Not 9C. This one had no photo. Just a designation: 1C | The Retained.

Under status: Active | Recurring.

No date of intake. No date of discharge. She turned the page. It wasn't just Clara. There were others. Silas. Lewis. Even the boy who'd hummed the Spiral Tune.

Each one marked with symbols Ellie didn't recognize—spirals, triangles, mirrored numerals. Notes in the margins read like a language of ghosts:

"Subject retained partial pre-merge consciousness."

"Recursion triggered by orchard geometry."

"Do not reassign to reflective environments."

Her own name—Eleanor J. Hale—appeared three pages in.

But beside it, written in different ink, was a line that made her breath seize:

Transferred: See Merge Ledger | Subject 1C

She looked again at the initials on the page. Below her name: Clara M. (archived 1943)

Archived. Not deceased.

She flipped another page tucked behind the roster—thinner stock, printed in red carbon type. Across the top:

FILE 1C–THETA

SPIRAL COGNITION MODEL – INTERNAL MEMO

Dr. Marcus A. Weaver | Date: January 1943

Clearance: ALPHA | Eyes Only

Her eyes skimmed the first line. Then froze.

"Stability is not healing. It is silence."

The text below was denser—clinical coded. But the intention pulsed through the page like static:

"Mirror-phase exposure accelerates recursive imprinting. Identity can be looped if trauma anchors are preserved but disassociated. Retention protocols must minimize narrative coherence."

In the margin, a handwritten note:

"She reflects what she is told to forget. That is the shape of recursion."

The signature: M.A.W.

The lights buzzed. Behind her, the mirror cabinet reflected the edge of her form. Then, not her form. Someone else stood in her place. In the same uniform. But the eyes—stitched. Ellie turned—nothing.

The record book in her hands flipped on its own. Back to the beginning. To the first entry ever logged in this wing. A drawing. Crude. Charcoal. A spiral. A mirror. And at the center: a child-sized chair marked with the letters:

E. H.

Her pen dropped. And somewhere in the archive, a file drawer creaked open. But no one else was there. Only the names. The ones they planted. And the one that stayed.

The Whisper Room never appeared on any floorplan. But Ellie

found it the way you remember a scar you can't see—by instinct, by ache.

The corridor outside it had changed. Narrower. Damp. The plaster blistered with forgotten condensation. Her shoes stuck slightly as she moved, each step echoing in syncopated rhythm—her breath and the hallway out of step.

She paused at the door. There was no placard this time. No etched letters. Just the shape of something that had been erased. Ellie turned the handle. It yielded.

Inside, the room was as she remembered—except more of it existed now. Where once the chair had been only reflection, it now stood in the center of the floor. Real. Child-sized. Wood worn smooth with use. A stitched cushion at the seat's center had been split, faint stuffing curling from its seam.

The mirrors surrounded her again, edge to edge, from floor to ceiling. But they shimmered now—not like glass, but like water straining to stay still. She moved, and so did her reflection—but slower, a fraction behind.

She reached toward the chair. It didn't vanish. Her hand touched it. Warm. The mirrors pulsed. A girl appeared. Not behind her—not anywhere in the room—but within the mirror. Eyes stitched. Head tilted. The same apparition from before.

Only this time, her lips moved.

"Ellie."

The sound didn't reach her ears, but her name echoed in her spine. Ellie stumbled backward, breathcatching. Her reflection didn't follow. Instead, it stood—hands at its sides—and then... it blinked first.

Her reflection spoke before she did.

"Clara."

The name slid from the mirror like a sliver of ice down her throat. A scream coiled in her chest, but it caught somewhere between ribs.

The girl in the mirror vanished.

In her place: Ellie's face. Then Clara's. Then both—superimposed, flickering in and out like a failing reel of film.

She clutched her coat, heartbeat in her ears. Behind her, the door had closed. There was no handle now.

Flashbacks hit like strobe light:

- Clara whispering, "You came from the mirror."

- Weatherly's voice: "Stabilization requires the sacrifice of the primary thread."

- A child's scream, stitched shut.

- Silas's painting of her before she arrived.

- Two spirals in the orchard. One for her. One for the one who stayed.

Ellie reached out to the mirror. The glass re-formed around her wrist—not trapping her, but wrapping tight, like muscle remembering a wound.

The glass re-formed around her wrist, sealing her reflection in place—but not the one she remembered. A voice surfaced—not aloud, but like an annotation bleeding through from old paper:

"Integration cannot proceed if the host believes herself whole."

Ellie's knees gave. The girl in the mirror smiled. And Ellie realized: the merge wasn't something that had happened. It was happening now. The chair behind her scraped. Her scream finally came. But only the mirror heard it.

She backed away from the glass—but the air behind her had changed. The Whisper Room was gone. Not locked. Not dark. Just… replaced. As if she'd stepped into a version that remembered everything she tried to forget.

CHAPTER: SEVENTEEN

The Vessel

The corridor beyond the records room felt compressed like the walls had leaned in while no one was looking. Ellie stepped lightly, but every footfall thudded too loudly—like her shoes struck something beneath the floor, not on it. Her breath came thin and fast. There was no reason to be afraid.

But the hallway didn't agree. The archive door groaned as she pushed through. Dim lighting filtered down through frosted ceiling panels, gray and suffocating. The air smelled like paper, ink, and something beneath it—salt? Metal? Memory?

At the far end, a file cabinet stood with its top drawer slightly open. Not enough to call attention. Just enough to be an invitation. Her fingers hovered over the brass handle. She expected cold. But it was warm. A key was already in the lock—thin, brass, etched with a spiral. Waiting. She turned it. The drawer creaked open.

Inside: a single folder beneath a cracked pane of protective glass.

ARCHIVE FILE 1C–THETA

CLASSIFIED – DOCTRINE (UNPUBLISHED)

Author: Dr. M. Weaver

Subject: Cognitive Recursion Stability Model

Ellie hesitated. Then lifted it. The paper was brittle at the edges, yellowed with containment. She scanned the opening line:

"The mind does not heal through absence. It rewrites to survive."

Her eyes caught a line circled in red pencil:

"Early child subjects exposed to mirrored reentry conditions display increased recursion compatibility. Familial anchors increase compliance. Emotional volatility can be erased, but emotional fidelity cannot."

Beneath it:

"Subject 1C retained core affect post-Merge. Refuses to respond under test conditions but exhibits layered memory anchors. Prototype not viable for re-release."

Then—scrawled by hand:

"Stability is not healing. It is silence."

Ellie froze. The sentence vibrated through her chest like a tuning fork. A doctrine. A confession. She turned the page—but the rest of the file was gone.

Torn out. Removed. Only the faintest ink imprint remained, bleeding through like memory pressed too hard to disappear. She backed away. Another drawer below rattled softly. Unlocked. She pulled it open. Labeled files. Military order. Typewritten tabs. Her hand stilled over one marked:

1C | THE RETAINED

Not Hale, E.J., Not Clara M. Just 1C. She pulled the folder slowly.

The first page bore her photo. But faded. Slightly blurred—like time had tried to erode it and failed. A watermark overlayed the hospital insignia: the Spiral, inked so faintly it could be mistaken for dust.

Beneath it:

NO INTAKE DATE. NO DISCHARGE DATE. NOT TO BE CLEARED.

Her fingers trembled. She flipped to the second page. Handwritten notes clustered the margins:

Subject exhibits recursion-resistant traits. Marked for long-term monitoring. Do not reassign to reflective environments.

Then, a final line:

The subject who could not forget.

Two years early… or two years late? Her brain stuttered, trying to anchor itself to a beginning that no longer held.

Had she started here? Or had she been brought back here to end?

A crackle behind her. She turned. A tape recorder sat just inside the cabinet door—one she hadn't noticed. A cassette already slotted in.

The label: CLARA – SESSION 1

She pressed play. A breath. Static. Then, a voice—small, worn down, familiar in the way a dream tastes after waking. Hers. But warped. Slowed. As if echoing from deeper inside her than her own throat ever dared reach.

"I don't want to be the vessel."

Silence. Then:

"They said I had to be. That she wouldn't survive the overwrite without me."

Click. The tape stopped on its own. Ellie stood motionless, the folder still clutched to her chest.

Her thoughts fractured—not like glass, but like loops folding into themselves. The air shifted. A drawer beside her creaked open. Inside: another folder. Older. Warped. She opened it.

Subject: 7C | SILAS

A memo dated November 1946: early visual exposure trials using chemical Drift. Hallucinations. Disordered recall. Mirror instability.

"Subject stated: 'She draws the orchard from memory because it was planted in her.'"

A photograph. Silas. Bound to the spiral chair. A mirror tilted to his face. He was screaming. But the photo didn't show sound. Only his reflection—and behind it...

Ellie. She gasped.

The Spiral in the folder seemed to inhale, its loops thickening, stretching outward—like a lung pulling in air through brittle paper, swelling until the edges blurred. No longer an image. A mouth. No longer contained to the page. The lines stretched to the edges, looping endlessly. At the corner: a faint red signature stitched into the drawing like thread.

E.H.

Her hands trembled. She reached for the file—and froze. A shadow curled beneath her left wrist—no bruise, no ink. A spiral, surfacing. Not drawn, but risen, as if her skin had been holding its breath and now exhaled the shape. It was warm to the touch—then pulsed, faint but insistent—before fading. The phantom of it lingered, like memory etched into bone. It pulsed once—then faded. But the skin still tingled, like the shape remained beneath.

A memory not hers slid down her spine, borrowing her voice:

"You were there when it was drawn."

She stumbled back, shoulder slamming into the cabinet. Folders dropped like bones. One caught her coat pocket. She reached in. A second sketch. The same Spiral. Drawn by her. Or drawn of her.

"You weren't supposed to come back," the voice whispered again, layered and low. "But you always do." From the grate above her, a whisper filtered through—not loud, not clear. Just a breath: "...a-lar-C..." Her name—spoken backward.

She turned—and the corridor exhaled, releasing her like breath that had been held too long.

The hallway ahead twisted—not literally, but rhythmically. Lights blinked in a pattern she'd seen once before, on the margins of a mirror.

Her boots scuffed the floor, her clipboard now forgotten under one arm.

A child's hum threaded through the vents.

"Don't forget. Don't forget..."

She followed it past the observation wing, past the window where the orchard should've been. Frost curled into a Spiral on the glass.

She turned a corner—and Room 12-C stood open.

A patient sat upright, waxen, unmoving.

"Private?" Ellie asked. "Do you need—?"

He turned. His face too calm.

"You used to be louder."

Ellie froze. "What?"

"In the other wing. With the other name."

Her mouth dried. "I think you're—"

"Ellie. Clara. Hale."

His voice split across syllables. One part broken. The other rehearsed.

The lights flickered. Behind him, in the window glass, her reflection didn't move with her. When the light returned—he was asleep. Or pretending. She stepped back. Too fast. The clipboard slipped from her hand. A paper fluttered loose. A note. Written in a child's hand:

The spiral remembers. But it doesn't forgive.

She stared. In the mirrored supply cabinet beside her—her reflection mouthed something. A name. Not Ellie. She ran. Back to the archives. To the doctrine. To the folder that now felt heavier than anything she'd carried since arriving. Ellie dropped to the floor beside the file shelf. She clutched it to her chest—not to protect it. But to keep something from getting out. Her memory? Or someone else's?

"I wasn't there," she whispered.

But her hands were stained with charcoal. And the drawing in her coat pocket...matched the one on the floor. Line for line. As if she'd drawn both. And maybe—she had.

Meanwhile, Dr. Weatherly sat alone in the dark, the only light coming from the glow of the playback terminal embedded in the archive wall. The tape had stopped minutes ago, but its echo still clung to the speakers.

"I don't want to be the vessel."

The girl's voice had faltered—not with fear, but fatigue. A resignation more dangerous than rebellion.

He leaned back, fingers steepled beneath his chin. The Spiral emblem flickered faintly on the edge of the monitor, pulsing once per second—heartbeat pacing. He hated that feature. Weaver had insisted on it. "Biological familiarity accelerates compliance," he'd said. Weatherly didn't care for poetry. He reached for the adjacent console and keyed into the access log.

HALE, E.J. – UNAUTHORIZED VIEWING – TAPE 1C-BETA/CLARA M.

A soft chime confirmed what he already knew. She'd found the tape. And the file. And the chair, he presumed. Spiral Phase III was never meant to be a closed loop—but it had become one anyway. Not because of the protocol. Because of her.

Weatherly opened the cabinet drawer beneath the console. Inside: a folder stamped SPIRAL STABILITY MODEL – THETA VARIANT. One page in particular was dog-eared. Weaver's doctrine. Ellie stepped back from the stack. Her fingers itched—not from dust, but from overwhelm. The files weren't meant to inform. They were meant to exhaust. Beneath the pile, one envelope was handwritten. Faint ink. A child's blocky scrawl:

"This one is real."

"Stability is not healing. It is silence."

Poetry, he'd called it. Marcus had always mistaken confession for theory. But Weatherly preferred numbers. Even guilt was quantifiable if you asked the right formula.

He'd fought the inclusion of that line in the original report. Said it read more like guilt than science. But Weaver had signed off on it in red ink, margin noted in his precise script: "They won't believe the science until it hurts enough to feel like poetry."

Weatherly didn't believe in poetry. But he believed in the numbers. And Ellie's pattern had shifted beyond threshold.

Her name hadn't been marked for reactivation. It had marked itself.

He pulled the microphone closer and clicked the red light to record.

STAFF MEMO – INTERNAL / NOT FOR FILE INCLUSION

Subject 1C drift breach confirmed. Recursive integration progressing along unpredictable lines. Mirror-phase instability now exhibits active transference across multiple patients. Clara M. signature no longer isolated. Recommend forced stabilization or—He hesitated. Then typed:

—termination of merged construct if spiral retention reaches contagion threshold.

He sat back, breath thin. The Spiral hummed on the monitor. It had never looked like a symbol to him. It looked like a fingerprint—a

CHAPTER: EIGHTEEN

The Unmade

By morning, the air was too clear—like the ward had been chemically scrubbed, not cleaned. As if clarity itself had been an antiseptic. Ellie stood beside the window, her pulse thrumming low and erratic, like a wire stretched between two towers that had forgotten their foundations. Outside, the orchard shimmered—reflected through a window that shouldn't face it at all. Not from this angle. Not from this floor. Like memory breaching walls where physics failed.

Yet, the trees were there. Still and skeletal. Their limbs didn't sway—but they moved. Subtle twists against the sky like antennae searching for signal. Or memory. Her breath fogged the pane, and for a moment, her own reflection blinked half a second too late—like it was waiting for permission.

Then she saw her. A girl—standing just beyond the edge of the spiral clearing. Back turned. Head tilted slightly to one side. Blurred, like a memory fixed too long in exposure.

"Clara?" Ellie whispered.

The name hadn't come from conscious memory, but her voice gave it shape anyway. The syllables hung in the air, fragile and unfinished.

A knock behind her pulled her away from the glass. She turned. Silas stood in the doorway of the rec room, one hand pressed to the frame like it hurt to stand without leaning. Ink-stained fingers. A smear of charcoal across his collar. His eyes were too sharp.

"I saw the part of you that walked ahead."

Ellie's throat tightened. "You mean—you dreamt—?"

"No." His voice dropped a register. "Not a dream. I saw your shadow move through the orchard. It went first. Like it remembered the path before your feet could follow."

Her body remembered how to stand still, even when her mind forgot how to move.

Silas stepped further inside, each footfall deliberate, like pacing in memory. "They never told us the spirals would keep watching after the merge. Just that they'd help us forget."

Ellie's spine stiffened. "The what?"

"Merge. Protocol Nine-C. Not a therapy. A severance. A reclassification." He looked at her then, "That's what it was called when they tried it on us."

She didn't ask how he knew. The answer lived somewhere beneath her skin. Instead, she stepped closer. "What do you remember, Silas?"

He opened his sketchbook and flipped to the latest page. A spiral tree, yes. But this one was wrong. Not symmetrical. Not orderly. Roots clawing upward, desperate, like veins searching for a pulse. At its base stood a figure split in two. One side reached toward the spiral, the other recoiled. Ellie's outline unmistakable. Her braid. Her uniform. But the eyes were crossed out in thick charcoal slashes. A second figure mirrored her. Smaller. Wearing Clara's ribbon.

Silas tapped the page. "I think I'm remembering you from someone else's memory."

She looked up sharply.

He didn't blink. "I think you were planted in all of us. Pieces stitched in until we stopped knowing the seams."

A crash echoed down the corridor. Then a scream—shattered and raw, cut short like a snapped wire. Ellie bolted into the hallway. Silas didn't follow. At the junction between the wards, a soldier was kneeling on the tile, trembling hands clenched around something sharp. A mirror shard. Slick with reflection, not blood—though his palms were torn open, the glass seemed to bleed more than he did.

Ellie crouched beside him. His eyes were wide, fixed on something only he could see. Blood welled at the creases of his fingers.

"Help," he whispered. "It's stuck in me."

"What is?" she asked.

He turned to her, tears spilling down his face. "Her name."

She reached for the emergency call switch. But behind her, every mirror in the hallway caught her reflection. Except they didn't.

In each one, she wasn't alone. A stitched-eyed girl stood just behind her. No pupils. Spiral carved into her brow.

Ellie turned. Empty. She wasn't sure which version of her had moved.

The rec room was quieter than usual. Quieter than it should've been. The windows were still rimmed with frost, but the orchard was gone from view again—as if the morning had taken it back.

Silas sat hunched at the table. He didn't look up when Ellie entered.

"I remember," he said before she spoke.

Ellie moved to the other side of the table and sat careful. His sketchpad was open again, the lines more frantic now. Frayed. A new drawing: a man strapped to a gurney, eyes sewn shut, spiral shadows carved under him.

"Who is this?" she asked.

Silas didn't answer.

Instead, he reached into his coat and unfolded another page. The drawing was simpler—brutal. A soldier crouched in the orchard clearing. Spirals stitched into his sleeves. The caption, written in her own handwriting:

"He remembers what he was made to forget."

Her hand remembered writing it. Her mind didn't. But the penstroke was hers. Ellie's voice cracked.

"Silas… how long have you seen these?"

He met her eyes. "Since they told me I wasn't Silas. Since they made me answer to someone else's name."

"They tried to rewrite you."

"They rewrote me," Silas said, voice almost tender. "Spackled over the fracture lines and called it healing. But some cracks run too deep to hold." He leaned closer. "You bled through, too. You just don't remember where you started bleeding."

She stared at her gloved hands.

"They said I retained too much," he murmured. "Called me 'bleed-prone.' Said some of us were more receptive to… drift. That's what they called it when memory re-looped. When the name didn't hold."

Ellie flinched. "And what happens when it doesn't hold?"

He didn't answer. Just looked toward the mirror. The reflection wavered first—before Ellie even moved. Her image blinked out for half a heartbeat, replaced by a stitched-eyed girl. By the time Ellie turned, her own face had returned—too late to trust.

"They told me I was a mirror," Silas whispered. "That she bent. I fractured."

Dr. Weatherly stood in the admin hall above Ward C, hands folded behind his back, watching Ellie remember herself through the glass that couldn't quite contain her. She couldn't see him. But she mirrored him anyway. The reflection echoed faintly through the pane—one version reaching for her notes, the other pausing just before contact. Her reflection hesitated. His didn't.

He turned from the glass stepped into the observation alcove. Beside him, a newly unsealed folder: SUBJECT FILE 1C – RECURSION STABILITY REEVALUATION.

He flipped it open.

Inside: test results. Spiral exposure tolerances. Drift probability charts. Her latest sketches not by her hand.

The final memo was typed in Weaver's old machine. Still smelled faintly of graphite ink and ozone.

File 1C–THETA

"The mind does not heal through absence. It rewrites to survive."

"Emotional fidelity is the final barrier to overwrite. If it persists, recursion collapses into echo."

"Stability is not healing. It is silence."

Weatherly's pen hovered above the margin.

He wrote, in clean block script:

Recommended action: Reactivation complete. Observe silently. Then closed the file.

Ellie found Hazel near the east stairwell, wiping the baseboards with a rag that looked older than the hallway itself. The mop bucket beside her sloshed with gray water.

"You were with Clara," Ellie said, voice trembling. "Weren't you?"

Hazel didn't look up. "I sanitized everything." Hazel's fingers moved on the tile as she spoke—tracing slow spirals into the dust, over and over, deeper each time. She didn't seem to notice. "You saw what they did to her."

Hazel nodded once. "She was too good at remembering. That's why they had to put her somewhere else."

"Where?"

The old woman's hands traced slow circles on the tile. Not wiping. Drawing. A spiral.

"They said it was containment," Hazel whispered. "B It was a prettier word for losing someone twice."

Ellie backed away.

"You're the one who came back," Hazel added.

"No—I'm not—"

"You don't have to remember it all at once," she said gently. "But it remembers you." The spiral darkened beneath her hand.

And then Hazel began to hum. The Spiral Tune. Soft. Circular. Wordless.

Later, alone in the supply room, Ellie rolled up her sleeve. The spiral was still there. Faint. Raised. Like memory trying to surface. She touched it. Heat flared. The mirror rippled—like breath trapped on the wrong side. Her reflection didn't respond. Then it mouthed the words: Subject One-C.

Ellie's pulse faltered. Her breath hitched. She took a step back from the mirror—but it didn't release her. Inside the glass, her reflection's lips moved again.

"You remember backward. That's why they couldn't erase you."

The spiral beneath her skin pulsed. This time, the heat was sharp—like recognition. Like a fuse reigniting. She stumbled to the file shelf. Pulled a random drawer. Scanned for anything familiar. But the first folder that caught her eye wasn't random.

It was labeled in red: SUBJECT 1C – DRIFT BREAKPOINT – DO NOT RESUME

She opened it with shaking hands. Inside, faded notes on induced identity recursion. Scrawled annotations:

"Retains pre-symbolic memory under spiral immersion."

"Fails containment during reflection exposure."

"Risk: Echo contagion across non-subject staff."

Then, a sketch. The orchard. The chair. A child sitting beneath the tree—head down, spiral carved into the dirt beside her. But the figure wasn't labeled Clara. It was signed: E.H.

Ellie's breath came fast now, irregular. Her hands gripped the desk to steady herself, but the paper still fluttered beneath her fingers like it wanted to fly away.

On the back of the last page: a message in faint pencil.

"She was the first they kept. The others… they only mirrored."

A sound bloomed behind her—wet, soft. Like someone breathing into a room that hadn't held breath in decades.

She turned. The mirror. This time, her reflection was gone entirely. But the chair was there. Not drawn. Not reflected. Placed. Directly behind her.

The stitched girl sat there—patient, certain, as if waiting for Ellie to remember her name. Head tilted. Ellie's mouth opened—but no scream came. Only the brittle crack of her own breath, shattering inside her chest. Just the rustle of paper falling from her hands like shed skin. The child raised one hand slowly. Then pointed. To Ellie. To herself.

And then the lights snapped off. In the dark, only the spiral remained—etched in faint afterimage, hovering like a memory behind her eyes.

Back in her quarters, Ellie peeled off her coat with fingers that wouldn't stop trembling. The mark on her chest glowed faintly beneath her skin as though some part of her had always carried it—waiting.

The bed was untouched. The room too neat. As if it had just been prepared. For someone else. She reached into the pocket of her coat. A scrap of paper met her fingers. She didn't remember placing it there. Unfolded, it was a note. Familiar looping script.

"She didn't forget. She just became."

Ellie crumpled it. Threw it. Then froze.

Because she remembered writing those words. In a different room. In a different life. For a girl, she hadn't met yet. Outside, the orchard was beginning to move again.

The orchard didn't grow. It inhaled—pulling the world inward, winding memory tight around its heart. Toward its center. Toward her.

CHAPTER: NINETEEN

The Unerasable

At dusk, the orchard didn't darken. It folded—limbs crossing at angles no tree should hold, their silhouettes knotting together like bone healing wrong. Ellie stood just beyond the sagging fence line where the hospital grounds surrendered to the woods—no longer manicured, no longer pretending. The rows of trees beyond leaned together in the half-light like conspirators, their branches entwined at impossible angles—too sharp, too deliberate—like bone knitting back wrong. Even from here, the geometry felt wrong. Not just overgrown. Warped. Tilted inward toward a center that didn't want to be found.

She moved slowly past the frostbitten hedgerow, boots crunching brittle grass. Her breath lingered too long in the air, fogging backward against a wind she couldn't feel. No birds called. No breath of wind stirred. But still the branches creaked—bending not with weather, but with something deeper. Something remembering. Her body remembered the coordinates before her mind could assemble the map.

The clearing waited at the orchard's center, a dark spiral of churned soil, as if something had spun there and refused to stop. Ellie crouched, brushing away a patch of wet leaves. Beneath them: brass. A small tag, corroded but legible.

A single digit, punched into tarnished brass: 9. Not just a number. A scar pressed into metal—the same mark stamped on memory where no one was supposed to look. Her heart kicked in her chest. The same number from the Whisper Room's baseboard. The number she'd seen in the margins of her folder—beneath her name, crossed out. She reached for the soil beside the marker. Her glove met something soft. Not roots. Cloth.

She dug gently, slowly pulling free a small, dirt-darkened sketchbook—its cover warped, leather peeling from age and moisture. A child's initials had been scratched faintly into the back corner: C.M.

Her breath caught. She sat back on her heels. The sketchbook fell open in her lap. The first page was a spiral orchard, inked from memory. At the bottom: Room 9—boxed in, sketched from above. No door. Two beds.

One figure was labeled ME.

The other: THE NAME THEY GAVE HER.

Ellie turned the page. Another drawing—this one a mirrored hallway. But every mirror had a girl inside it, stitched eyes and spirals carved into their foreheads. One stood outside the mirror. Ellie. Watching them. Watching herself. She flipped again. Spiral geometry mapped like veins through the hospital floor plan. Dots marked key locations: the Whisper Room, the east stairwell, the orchard.

Next to the archive room: a scrawled note. "Drift begins here."

Her pulse skittered. The sketchbook trembled in her hands. It was never about forgetting. It was about making sure no one else remembered. A rustle. She turned sharply. A figure emerged from the edge of the trees.

Silas.

He moved like smoke—formed but untouchable—drifting through the orchard clearing, coatless despite the frost clinging to every blade of grass. No notebook. No drawing. Just his breath fogging in rhythm with hers.

"You shouldn't be here," Ellie said, rising.

"I always am," Silas answered. His voice was low, even. Steady in a way that unnerved her more than panic would've.

"You remember it wrong," he said. "But the dirt doesn't."

She stepped toward him. "Tell me what this place was."

He crouched beside her, palm pressed to the spiral's center.

"They stitched the orchard into us," he whispered. "Drew it into our dreams until it rooted under the skin. You bled in this dirt same as me."

Her stomach twisted.

"I wasn't supposed to remember," she said.

"But you did," Silas said, standing. "They called it Drift. You know what it really was."

She nodded, barely. "Return."

He pointed behind her. Ellie turned. The clearing answered. Without sound. Without motion. Just the mirror—standing where nothing had been seconds ago. Curved glass already fogging like it breathed. Etched across its surface in backward script:

You remembered too well.

It cracked. And the orchard fell still.

Back inside, the staff corridor twisted at its edges. Not physically. But perceptually. Like the world had been reassembled one heartbeat too late—close enough to recognize, wrong enough to trap. Ellie pressed her back to the wall, the sketchbook clutched tightly under her arm. Her glove was still damp with orchard soil. She could feel it seeping through like the memory of something she hadn't meant to carry.

Gretchen stood near the exam room, arms crossed over her coat like armor. Her face unreadable. But her eyes—they had the look of someone who already knew.

"You're late," she said.

Ellie's voice came out low. "I found the spiral."

Gretchen's jaw tensed.

"You shouldn't have been in the orchard."

"It's not the orchard," Ellie replied. "It's the burial ground. You knew that."

Silas's voice carried from behind them. He appeared from the east hall like fog slipping under a doorframe. Calm. Unhurried.

"Funny thing about dirt," he said. "Doesn't keep secrets long."

Gretchen turned toward him, composure fracturing. "You're not supposed to be out of rec."

"Neither is she," Silas said, gesturing to Ellie. "But here we are."

He passed between them, heading deeper into the corridor.

"The orchard doesn't grow us," Silas murmured. "It remembers what it buried." Ellie froze.

Gretchen whispered, "He shouldn't be able to know that."

Ellie looked her dead in the eye. "But he does."

The hallway outside Silas's room was silent. Too silent. Ellie passed the staff mirror and paused. Her reflection moved first—turning sideways before she had. When she followed, too late, Clara's face stared back.

She copied the movement. Slowly. Her reflection turned. Clara's face stared back. No stitches. No distortion. Just recognition. Ellie stumbled back. The clipboard slipped from her hands.

A folder fell open. One page landed face-up:

A photograph.

Her own body—curled beneath the orchard tree. Spiral carved into the dirt beside her shoulder. A name scrawled in the margin:

CLARA M.

She burst into the archive, hands trembling. Moved to the last cabinet on the left—the one with the spiral etched faintly into the handle. She opened it.

Inside: a manila folder.

SUBJECT 1C.

No intake date. No discharge. No photo. Just a single handwritten line:

The girl who couldn't be erased. She stared until a shadow moved across the floor behind her.

Hazel stood in the doorway. Janitorial uniform. Mop in hand. Eyes too clear.

"You shouldn't have opened that," Hazel said.

"You were there," Ellie said. "During the merge."

Hazel nodded once.

"I cleaned the floor afterward."

"And me?" Ellie asked.

Hazel blinked. "You stayed."

In the solarium, Gretchen poured tea with shaking hands. She didn't offer Ellie a cup.

"They told us Drift was stable. That a mirror can't reflect what's yet to take form. That recursion dies if the narrative stays incomplete. But narrative is an organism."

Ellie dropped the file on the table.

"They were wrong."

A long silence. Then:

"You're the only one who made it through intact. But you weren't supposed to remember."

"I didn't," Ellie said quietly. A beat.

"Until I did."

That night, alone in her room, Ellie sat on the floor, coat still on, the sketchbook open in her lap. Her fingers traced the last drawing: The spiral tree. Two girls. One facing out. One already gone. On her collarbone, beneath the layers, the faint spiral beneath her skin pulsed. Not memory. Not warning. Return. The mirror cracked—not clean, but spiderwebbed—fractures curving inwards as if the glass was folding back into itself.

CHAPTER: TWENTY

The Broken Mirror

The chill crawling down Ellie's spine wasn't from temperature. It was architectural. The walls curved inward—not to shelter, but to erase. This building hadn't been built to contain. It had been designed to unmake.

She gripped the rusted handrail hard enough to whiten her knuckles through the wool of her gloves. Her boots landed heavy on each step, but her mind floated somewhere above them—detached, observant, braced. Her name was still echoing in three voices: Ellie. Clara. Subject 1C.

The door at the top resisted her first push, then gave with a groan so low it felt less like metal and more like breath. It opened into a corridor that reeked of antiseptic—and something older beneath it. Not blood. Not rust. The smell of preservation. Of containment.

She passed linen carts, shuttered treatment rooms, a shattered mirror above a defunct intercom box. The ceiling hung lower here. The buzz of fluorescent lights didn't just flicker—they muttered. Each bulb hummed at a different pitch—a chorus out of tune, warning not with words but with vibration.

At the end of the hallway, Gretchen sat at her desk like a portrait posed in profile—her spine too straight, her hands folded like a gate she refused to open. The window beside her was fogged with breath. On the desk, half-obscured by the lamplight, sat a black-and-white photograph. Two girls. Barefoot. One smiling, eyes turned directly into the lens like she knew it would be important. The other stood beside her, unsmiling. Tilted. A mirror fragment.

Ellie stopped in the doorway, her breath caught mid-throat, tightening like a noose pulled from the inside out. She stepped forward. "What is this?"

Gretchen's voice came slow. "I found it in the basement archive.

Folded into a file marked 'Retained Subjects.'"

Ellie's gaze fell to the bottom corner of the photo.

A name.

E. Hale.

Her own. On a child, she didn't remember being. Her voice cracked before the question left her lips. "Is that Clara?"

Gretchen's eyes lifted. "Clara was the second."

Ellie blinked. "Second?"

"There was one before her." Gretchen spoke like she was reciting scripture she had sworn to forget. "A match. A mirror. Subject 1C."

The room narrowed. Ellie looked again at the photo. Both girls wore ribbons—hers red, Clara's white. Not decoration. Identification. Like flags pinned to vessels.

"I don't remember this," Ellie said.

"You're not supposed to."

Wind pushed against the pane. Not rattling, but pressing. Like the building itself exhaled alongside the conversation. Then Ellie said it. The memory surfaced half-formed but undeniable.

"There was a chair under the tree."

Gretchen's mouth opened, but no sound came. Just a nod. And the flicker of something terrible behind her eyes.

"You remember," she whispered.

Ellie sank slowly into the chair across from her, hands still trembling from something older than adrenaline. She clutched the photograph like a map made of mirrors.

"We weren't two girls," Ellie said, the words dredged from somewhere older than memory. "We were one... broken in half."

A pause.

"Split."

Gretchen exhaled like the word had cracked something inside her. She reached for the drawer slowly as if afraid the wood itself might scream. A slim file emerged—creased, brittle. She unfolded it with reverence.

A schematic. Not architectural. Neurological. Spiral-based. Mirrored. Labeled with two sets of initials.

C.M. E.H.

At the center, handwritten in red: MERGE ATTEMPT ABANDONED — SUBJECT 1C RESIDUAL TRACE PRESENT

Ellie stared. "They tried to pull Clara out of me."

Gretchen's lips parted. "And when she wouldn't separate cleanly... they renamed you."

"I was never assigned here."

"No," Gretchen said. "You were returned."

The room shifted on its axis. Ellie gripped the desk. "You knew."

"I remembered too late."

She looked toward the sink. Toward the mirror above it.

Ellie stood slowly. Crossed the room. The reflection moved first—an instant before she could. It blinked. It smiled. And whispered—not to her ears, but straight into her bones. It blinked first. Then smiled. Then whispered—Clara's voice, unmistakable.

"You're the next recursion."

Ellie stumbled back. The mirror shimmered. The reflection layered. Her face, then Clara's, then both—flickering, out of sync. And then: the stitched-eyed girl, surfacing only in the corners where the light refused to reach.

Gretchen's voice behind her broke. "You weren't supposed to survive it."

The attic groaned beneath Ellie's boots. Dust filtered down in slow spirals, like memories unraveling themselves without permission.

She climbed each step with care—each one softer than it should've been like the wood forgot its purpose.

Inside: silence. Dense. Heavy. Not stale, but saturated.

One open crate.

She approached. And the moment her hand touched the edge, a whisper surfaced.

A sketchbook.

Drawings.

Room 9. Spiral maps. Mirror configurations. Two figures repeated across pages—one labeled ME, the other: THE NAME THEY GAVE HER.

Ellie flipped faster.

In the center: a RETURN SCHEMA. Red pencil. A spiral with initials at each layer. The core labeled 1C. The outer rim: Clara. Lines pointed inward. One word written at the center:

STAYED.

Ellie's mouth went dry. She whispered, "What… what is this?"

The words hit the dust-heavy air—and then hit again.

"What… what is this?"

The second echo wasn't hers.

It came an instant after—same pitch, same breath, same voice.

Ellie froze, throat tight. Her lips didn't move a second time. But the sound had.

The attic absorbed it like old wood swallowing a secret.

She clutched the sketchbook tighter. "That was—I didn't—" Her voice caught, fracturing.

Then, a voice behind her.

Asher.

"I didn't mean to startle you."

Ellie didn't turn. "You knew."

"I suspected," he said. "But not like this."

She held up the sketchbook. "Was I Clara?"

"No, you were the reason they stopped using children," Asher said. "They kept trying—but it never worked again."

She turned. "But I hear her voice."

"You always will," Asher said. Not unkind. Just certain.

Ellie stood in front of the Whisper Room door. She stepped inside. The mirrors shimmered. Her reflection didn't match. And then it moved first. "Clara?" she whispered. No reply. Only a voice—Clara's—

whispering again:

"You're the next recursion."

Ellie reached for the glass. It pulsed beneath her fingers. Not cold. Warm. Alive.

Later, in the burned-out lounge, Ellie knelt before the cabinet that once held the Spiral tapes. Ash. Charred reels. And one salvageable. Asher placed it in her palm.

SUBJECT 1C – POST-MERGE OBSERVATION STATUS: ACTIVE

"You said it wasn't meant to hold," Ellie whispered. He nodded. "But you did."

Back in the corridor, Ellie stood before the final mirror. The mirror shimmered. The reflection blinked first. Then smiled—a slow, deliberate thing that didn't belong to Ellie anymore. "They made room for the wrong girl," it said. And the Spiral pulsed behind her eyes. Waiting. Watching. Beginning again.

CHAPTER: TWENTY-ONE

Patient Zero

Outside the eastern wing, trees shivered in the wind, their bare limbs tapping against the frost-dulled windows—bone on bone, patient and insistent, like they were keeping count of the hours lost inside. Inside Arlington Hills, the heat clanked inconsistently—radiators coughing in fits, as if the building itself were choking on the memories it had tried too long to swallow.

Ellie stood in the stairwell's half-shadow, one gloved hand resting on the banister. She hadn't meant to stop—but her body had other plans, halting mid-step as if obeying a map her mind no longer remembered. Below, the corridor twisted right—toward the observation chambers. Above, silence waited on the landing.

She turned upward. Her hand reached before the choice had even formed, fingers curling around the rail like they'd been waiting for this exact moment to happen again. She'd stood on this landing before— hadn't she? Her feet knew where the third step creaked. Her fingers reached for the rail like they remembered the texture of the brass. But Ellie didn't. Not in words. Not yet. Her breath quickened, though nothing had changed.

The unused upper level of the administration wing had once served as a convalescent library, she'd been told. Quiet. Discarded. Forgotten. But someone had been there. The dust patterns didn't match. Too many prints. A trail that broke into a spiral, almost as if whoever left it had begun to pace—then hadn't finished.

Ellie followed it. The air grew colder the farther she stepped into the attic-level hallway. A single bulb flickered behind frosted glass, its buzz low and glitching. Beyond it, a door stood slightly ajar. It wasn't labeled. The frame had been recently painted over. But Ellie could still make out an outline where a plaque once hung.

She stepped inside. The room was lined with filing cabinets and old equipment—dusty dictation machines, reel-to-reel recorders, half-labeled boxes marked WARD D EXPERIMENTAL and 7C/ BETA RESULTS. At the center of the room sat a desk with a mirror bolted to the wall behind it. Not a decorative mirror. A two-way one. Observation glass.

Ellie froze. Her stomach twisted. Her reflection didn't match her stance—it held too still, like it was waiting for her to catch up. She whispered, "What… what is this place?"

But her voice buckled. It came out staggered, the second what landing just a fraction too late—as though an echo had slipped free from her throat, not the room.

Her breath seized. Not a stutter. A doubling.

The mirror's surface quivered, not visibly—but atmospherically, as if the glass had heard something she hadn't meant to say twice.

Part of her wanted to retreat. The other part leaned forward. Curious. Familiar. Like she was seeing the room not for the first time—but for the first time again.

Something had been written in the condensation.

SPIRALWATCHER

Below it, a charcoal sketch lay abandoned on the desk. A girl with stitched eyes stared outward, her hands held up like she was mimicking the reflection of someone who wasn't her. And in the background— trees. Bent inward. Spiraling toward her.

Ellie exhaled sharply. "This isn't the archive." She didn't recognize the drawing. But her fingers curled around it instinctively, gripping it the way you hold something you've lost and just found again. The paper felt right in her grip, the way childhood drawings did—bent at the corners where you always touched them too often. Her breath caught. This was new. But her muscles knew it wasn't.

A whisper echoed from the vent above her.

"They watch through what we leave behind."

Ellie backed out of the room, her pulse hammering. The Spiral Watcher wasn't a myth. It was an instruction. A role. A warning. And someone had assigned it to her.

The sky outside the archive wing had turned the color of old ash, heavy with an unfallen storm. Inside, the records room breathed cold—despite the radiator ticking like a nervous clock. Ellie stepped carefully across the polished tile, the echo of her footsteps too sharp as if the room were still deciding whether to welcome her.

She pulled open the ledger drawer marked CLASSIFIED: CYCLE/ PHASE I–III. The folder she'd come to find had no name on the tab. Only a spiral. She lifted it like it might unravel in her hands.

Inside, rows of names stretched across yellowing paper, typed neatly in black ink. Soldiers. Civilians. Children. Each marked with a project number, intake, and outdate. Many had a stamp: TRANSFERRED or ERASED.

Ellie's breath caught. She flipped the page. At the bottom of the next sheet, a name had been scratched in by hand. Not typed. Written in dark ink that feathered at the edges.

HALE, ELEANOR J. – Subject 1C

No intake date. No discharge. Just a single, handwritten note beneath it:

"The subject who could not forget."

Her chest ached—not from panic, but from the pressure of remembering something her mind still refused to name.

She turned to the last page. A sketch was taped to the back cover. A child's drawing. It showed the spiral orchard, viewed from above. At its center, a small chair. A figure sat in it, but the face was missing. Torn off. And beneath the drawing, written in the same hand:

"They planted the names here."

Suddenly, from somewhere in the corridor behind her, a voice murmured. Not loud—but unmistakably real.

"They stitched the orchard into us. You bled in that dirt same as me."

She turned. Silas stood in the doorway, charcoal smudged to the bone, eyes red-rimmed and too bright—like he'd been crying, or hadn't slept in days, or both.

"You were grown here, Ellie," he said. "Not brought. Not assigned. They seeded you. And now you're blooming through the cracks."

Ellie clutched the folder like it might fall open and speak. "I wasn't supposed to be here."

"Then why does the building know your name?"

Drift Beyond Ward C

She hadn't meant to return to Ward A. But something pulled her there. The nurse's station radio crackled mid-song, skipping briefly on a single syllable. Ellie paused, clipboard in hand, and turned toward Room A-14.

Inside, a patient who had never been flagged for recursion—Private Lucien Bell, post-op trauma, minimal speaking history—sat upright in bed, his hands folded neatly in his lap.

He was humming. Not loud. Not tuneful. Just... consistent. The Spiral lullaby.

Ellie stepped in. "Private Bell?"

He didn't look at her. But his mouth moved. Not with a song now, but with a name. Over and over. Soft. Disconnected.

"Clara. Clara. Clara…"

She moved closer. "Do you know someone named Clara?"

His gaze didn't lift, but his eyes flicked—just once—toward the small sink mirror mounted above the bedside table.

Ellie followed his glance—and caught her own reflection. Alone. But blurred. Breathing too fast.

This time, the voice cracked—not from age or pain, but recognition:

"She left her name in the mirror."

Ellie froze.

Private Bell had never been exposed to Spiral patients. He hadn't even left this wing in weeks. Ellie backed out slowly. The radio resumed its song without skipping again. And from down the hall, another patient in Room A-11 began to hum the same tune.

Gretchen stood in the east corridor outside the infirmary, staring at the flickering overhead light. Her arms were wrapped around herself, her posture rigid. She didn't speak as Ellie approached.

"You heard it too," Ellie said.

Gretchen nodded. "They weren't supposed to be able to remember names that were never theirs."

Ellie looked back toward Ward A. "Drift isn't contained to C anymore."

"It never was," Gretchen murmured. "But now it's loud enough for even the quiet patients to start repeating."

Ellie clenched her fists. The Spiral wasn't a pattern anymore. It was a contagion. And she was patient zero.

Behind her, the infirmary lights flickered once—then settled. But the humming didn't stop.

1C: The Retained

The rain had finally broken, but Arlington Hills didn't breathe easier. The storm had cleared without cleansing, leaving behind an unnatural stillness. Ellie stood beneath the archway leading into the east observation wing, coat still damp from her walk to the archive. The file she'd uncovered was clutched under one arm, the Spiral mark beneath her skin pulsing in time with her thoughts.

Each hallway felt more narrow than the last. The floors gleamed too cleanly like they'd just been scrubbed of something that refused to lift. Silence reigned between footfalls. Even the walls seemed to strain to hear.

A voice drifted faintly from somewhere above—a soft hum threading down through the ventilation grates. Ellie paused, heart-pinching in her chest. Not a melody. A name.

"Clara."

She spun. No one. But the grate above her head continued to whisper.

"Clara... Clara... Clara."

The voice was male. Soft. Not Silas. She turned and ran. Down the hall, through the emergency access double doors, and into the junction near Ward A. The moment she entered, the atmosphere shifted. This wing had always felt safer. More clinical. Less distorted. Not anymore.

A nurse in white stood frozen outside Patient Room 4. She turned as Ellie approached, her face pale. "He was just humming a minute ago," the nurse said quietly. "Then he said the name."

Ellie moved past her and stepped into the room. Private Bell sat upright in bed, hands folded in his lap. He stared out the barred window at nothing. His lips were moving.

"Clara. Clara. Clara."

Ellie approached slowly. "Private Bell..."

He didn't blink. His voice dropped to a whisper. "She sang the orchard open. I heard her. Inside the mirror."

Ellie froze. Bell turned his head slowly. His eyes were wrong. Not glazed. Not vacant. Intent.

"She said your name like it was hers."

Ellie backed away. The nurse crossed herself. She left the room without speaking, heart hammering. The Drift had crossed the ward boundary.

In the breakroom off Ward B, Gretchen stood at the sink, staring into a porcelain cup that had long since gone cold. Her reflection in the metal cabinet across from her stared back—but didn't raise the cup when she did. She blinked. The reflection didn't. Her grip slipped. The cup shattered in the sink.

Gretchen didn't react. She just watched the reflection. And the reflection smiled.

"Not again," she whispered. "Not again."

Later, Ellie sat cross-legged on the floor of her quarters. The sketchbook lay open before her, spine cracked, its pages spreading like wings of confession. Each image more familiar than the last—and yet she remembered drawing none of them.

A girl beneath the orchard tree. A child in the spiral chair. A body stitched from fragments. And then the final page:

A mirror. In its surface: a spiral. Inside the spiral: the name Ellie Hale. But in the margin, smeared in black graphite, another word emerged beneath the erasure lines.

Clara.

The two names had begun to merge. Her fingers traced the page. The reflection in her wardrobe mirror did the same—but her hand moved first. Ellie stood. The room tilted. In the hallway, she heard it again.

"Clara…"

But this time, it came from two vents at once. Two voices. One hers. One not. A spiral carved into the frost on her window pulsed. And Ellie knew:

She had become the signal. The Drift wasn't spreading. It was remembering.

The archive room was colder than it should've been. Ellie stepped inside with her arms wrapped tightly around her ribcage—more from instinct than from temperature. The lights hummed a half-second behind her movements, flickering once before settling into a dim, jaundiced glow. Somewhere behind her, a pipe clanked—sharp, metallic, like the echo of a scream trying to wedge itself into the bones of the building.

She had come for one folder. But the table held two. One marked SUBJECT 9C. The other no label at all. She moved slowly, like someone approaching the final frame of a reel she didn't remember shooting. Her fingers hovered first over the blank one, drawn by the silence it seemed to emit. It wasn't emptiness. It was restraint.

Inside, a single sheet: a black-and-white photograph of a girl with her back to the camera. Spirals painted onto the mirror she faced. In the lower corner, a name. CLARA M. Ellie blinked. She turned the page over. Same photo. But now the name was different. ELEANOR J. HALE.

Her breath caught. She turned the paper back. The name reverted. Not possible. But there it was. The mirror in the photo distorted slightly—as though it had remembered something the photo had not.

A throb of memory struck like static—Gretchen's voice, quiet and brittle: "You were never assigned here. You were recovered."

Her hand trembled as she reached for the second folder. A smear of rust—or dried blood—darkened the corner. Her fingers recoiled instinctively. Then the smell hit her: graphite and old glue like a schoolhouse grave. The paper was warm. But she hadn't touched it long. SUBJECT 9C. The report was clinical. Sparse. No medical history. No intake documentation. Only directives:

BEGIN PHASE THREE PREPARATION. MERGE CANDIDATE IDENTIFIED. MONITOR RESIDUAL IDENTITIES FOR BLEED.

Across the top: REPLACEMENT PENDING.

A sealed document was stapled to the back. Label: MERGE TRANSCRIPT: Subject 1C / Subject 9C – Trial Phase III

Ellie opened it.

[REDACTED AUDIO TRANSCRIPT - MERGE SESSION

1C/9C - DATE: 12 JAN 1943]

OBSERVER 2: "Subject 9C is destabilizing. Requesting emotional anchor."

TECHNICIAN: "Initiate mirror loop."

OBSERVER 1: "Subject 1C displaying eye-blink desynchronization. Recursion onset. Graft incomplete."

[LONG PAUSE]

SUBJECT 9C (whispered): "I don't want to be her."

TECHNICIAN: "Pulse spike. Pulling visual thread. Increase containment."

OBSERVER 2: "She's reasserting."

Stamped across the bottom in red:

Subject 1C reasserted. Merge rejected. Spiral contamination irreversible.

Ellie clutched the edge of the table as the floor tilted—not physically, but psychically. Like time had taken a wrong turn and was now struggling to find its footing. Behind her, the mirror warped. She turned. Her reflection was Clara.

Not mimicking. Not delayed. Staring. Then, the mouth in the glass moved first.

"You're the one they kept. But I'm the one who stayed."

Ellie staggered backward. The reflection did not follow. A whisper followed, not from the mirror, but from somewhere deep beneath her ribs:

They didn't erase you. They used you to overwrite me. The fluorescent overhead popped, casting the room into flickering shadow.

Ellie backed into the table. The folders scattered to the floor. One opened, revealing a sketch:

Two girls. One seated, the other behind her. Both faces blurred—one by charcoal, the other by flame. A spiral in the corner, drawn over and over again until the page had buckled beneath the graphite.

A final file had slid beneath the cabinet. She reached for it.

Label: Mirrorline Blue – RESTRICTED

Inside: a memorandum.

CONFIDENTIAL – PROJECT SPIRAL

Subject Classification: 1C – The Retained

Author: Dr. M. Weaver

"In all Phase II Drift Trials, no subject demonstrated recursive memory retention post-merge to the degree observed in Subject 1C. Mirror-phase overwrite failed. Core identity signature persists. Instability is not mental. It is ontological."

"Key Observation: She did not forget. She split."

At the bottom, handwritten in red:

Do not allow Subject 1C near orchard sketches. Do not speak the name Clara. Do not permit mirrored environments beyond 3 minutes.

Tucked behind the folder: a folded note. Gretchen's handwriting.

PERSONAL NOTE – DO NOT FILE

They told us it was healing. It was holding. Clara drifted because she remembered too many versions of herself. Ellie held because she never knew which one she was.

We called it stability. It was fracture all along.

When she remembers—don't let them turn on the mirrors.

One final photo. Ellie. Younger. A spiral carved into her forearm. Below it, in Gretchen's handwriting: Clara? No. She came after. This one was the first.

Ellie reeled. The drawer slammed shut behind her. A nearby frame cracked. She turned. Her reflection stood straight. She didn't. It blinked. She didn't. And just as fast, it was gone. Only her face remained. Drawn. Pale. A single word rose inside her:

Retained. She backed out of the room without filing the folder. And behind her, unseen, the mirror remembered a different name.

CHAPTER: TWENTY-THREE

The Rehearsal

After the blackout in the archive, Ellie said nothing. She moved through corridors that seemed narrower now, as if the walls themselves remembered her. The file clutched to her chest pulsed—insistent, alive, like a second heart. Without intending to, her feet turned toward the west wing.

The corridor to Mirrorline Blue had changed—not in layout or shape, but the way scar tissue remembers what split it. The walls looked unchanged. But Ellie felt the difference: it remembered her.

She walked it alone, each footstep falling heavier than the last. The lights above flickered in syncopated rhythm, and the pale blue walls looked washed through with a diluted gray, like the color had given up pretending. Her coat clung damply to her arms, the rain long gone, but its weight still stitched into the fabric. Underneath, her skin pulsed faintly where the spiral had begun to rise. Like a memory being pushed to the surface. Like something trying to come back.

The secured door at the end waited. Not locked. Not open. Expectant. She slid Gretchen's clearance card into the reader. The click was soft but final. The door eased inward.

Mirrorline Blue was colder than she remembered. Not freezing. Just empty. Intentionally emptied. Twelve mirrors lined the far wall, edge to edge, seamless. The chairs, once positioned before them, were gone. So were the desks, the clipboards, the nurses. Only the mirrors remained. Watching.

No reflections moved. Not at first. Ellie stepped inside. The floor held the faint scuff of a spiral—walked into existence, not drawn. Her boots found its edge. Her muscles remembered the motion. Her eyes did not.

She moved toward the middle mirror. Her reflection approached. It blinked first. Then it smiled. Ellie froze. Her heart thudded twice—

hard, fast—and then settled into a quieter rhythm. One that didn't feel like hers. The reflection tilted its head to the left. Ellie remained still.

"This is where they rehearsed you," said a voice behind her.

She turned. Silas stood just past the threshold, one hand on the doorframe. His shoes scuffed softly across the tile—barely louder than breath, but enough to make the mirrors quiver, as if presence itself disturbed them.

His shirt was wrinkled, sleeves damp from orchard soil. His eyes, however, were clear.

"Rehearsed?" Ellie asked.

"Memory doesn't survive on its own," he said, stepping in. "They had to teach it to you. Make it stick. So they made you mirror it. Until the shape of who you were became who they said you were."

He stopped near the spiral mark etched into the tile.

"I painted you here once. Before I ever met you. But not your face. Just the feeling."

Ellie didn't answer. Her eyes returned to the glass. Her reflection no longer mirrored her.

Ellie's breath caught, throat tightening around a sudden spike of dread. Her heartbeat surged, erratic and hard, pounding her ribs like fists against a locked door. A chill danced along the nape of her neck. Her knees stiffened, muscles locking without permission. She didn't move. Couldn't. Not when the thing staring back from the glass had her face—but none of her hesitation.

Instead, it turned. And behind her mirrored self stood a second figure: a child in a pale dress, the hem stained with dirt. Eyes stitched. Mouth parted, mid-breath. Mid-scream.

Clara.

Ellie took a step back. The mirror exhaled. The word bloomed across its center in fogged breath:

RE-ENTRY

Silas moved to her side. He didn't look at the mirror.

"You know what this is," he said. "The recursion broke. You didn't just remember. You crossed back."

Ellie's voice frayed. "Am I the memory... or the host?"

Silas's mouth twitched.

"You were the first. Clara came later. They tried to overwrite you with her."

Ellie looked at him. "And what happened?"

He pointed at the mirror. "You rejected her. But the Spiral remembered both."

Behind the glass, the spiral began to turn. Not a drawing. Not a symbol. A motion. A fracture opening inward.

Ellie clutched her coat.

"There was a transcript," she murmured. "Merge 1C/9C."

Her voice barely rose above the flickering hum of the lights.

"It said the identity graft failed." She swallowed. "Subject 1C reasserted."

She opened her coat, the file tucked inside now visible. From it, she drew a worn page, creased at the corners. In faded typewriter font, a line had been underlined twice:

Subject 1C did not comply with overwrite parameters. Core identity signatures remained stable despite protocol. Merge rejected. Spiral contamination is irreversible.

Silas nodded.

"They thought they could contain memory. But memory isn't passive. It chooses who it stays with."

The spiral on the mirror expanded. Ellie reached out. Her hand met glass. It didn't feel cold. It felt like water holding its breath. The stitched girl behind her reflection blinked. And Ellie heard her own voice from inside the mirror:

"You're not remembering. You're returning." Her lips moved. Not Ellie's. Clara's. But the mouth was hers. She'd been overwritten, yes. But not erased.

Clara was not the origin. She was the second imprint that wouldn't seal.

And Ellie—Ellie had been the one they drafted because she didn't break. She bent until they mistook the shape for compliance.

The lights flickered. The mirror cracked. Not shattered. Split. A spiral fracture radiating from where her palm had touched. Twelve lines. Twelve mirrors. All humming now. All reflecting her.

Except one. One showed Clara. One showed the orchard. One showed nothing at all.

She turned to Silas. "What happens now?"

He stepped back into the threshold.

"You walk it back," he said. "All the way to where you were split."

"And then?"

He didn't answer. The mirrors did. In her reflection, Ellie watched herself mouth a word. Merge. She wasn't afraid. Not anymore. She stepped toward the spiral.

And this time, the reflection didn't wait.

It stepped forward—slight, precise—and Ellie felt the Spiral mark on her arm flare, hot beneath the skin, as if answering a command she hadn't heard but had always obeyed. A faint hum rose in the room, not from the lights but from the mirror itself. From memory.

Somewhere deep behind the glass, a name echoed. Not loud. Not spoken. Just known. Clara. It moved first.

CHAPTER: TWENTY-FOUR

The Drift Resumes

The wind had shifted. Ellie felt it the moment she stepped through the side gate, still reeling from the mirror's last word. Merge. It didn't echo—it rewrote. Under her skin. Beneath her ribs. Already hers before she heard it. The cold air hit her differently now—brighter, sharper. Not a chill from the storm, but something more intimate. The orchard was no longer just a place; it was a memory. A waiting thing.

The gate behind the east stairwell hadn't squeaked this time. It opened as if it had been expecting her.

The orchard breathed differently in the early light. Its limbs no longer clawed but hung heavy, sagging like they knew what had been unearthed. The silence wasn't resting. It was listening—hoarding more than frost. The scent of old bark and damp leaves clung to her coat, and the shadows cast by the bare trees had thickened, braided into patterns that looked almost deliberate. As if the Spiral had begun etching itself into nature.

Each step through the brittle grass brought her closer to the spiral clearing. The path, though unmarked, opened before her. As if it, too, remembered. Her boots found the old trail, packed not with footsteps but with weight—as if grief had bruised the earth itself, deep enough to pulse memory back through her boots. As if a hundred silent regressions had carved it deep enough to welcome her back.

She passed Tree Nine. The brass tag had oxidized green, the number nearly illegible now. Her hand brushed the bark out of habit. The touch sent something flaring under her skin—a response. A pulse answered from beneath her sleeve. The Spiral mark. It warmed against her wrist like it knew it had come home.

The clearing gaped like a wound. The chair stood exposed—no longer hidden, no longer patient. Just waiting.

It sat in the center of the spiral. Roots pushed up through the soil around it like fingers trying to reclaim it. The cushion was split. The wood darkened by time and weather. But Ellie knew it. Her memory didn't need prompting. Her breath hitched, and Her knees buckled halfway. You were here. Not as Ellie. The thought wasn't hers. It landed fully formed. Embedded. A memory without an origin.

The air buzzed low, electrical. Not sound—a pressure. The way your ears feel just before thunder. Or revelation. Her hair lifted slightly as if the orchard had inhaled and was waiting to speak.

She moved closer. Each step peeled away a layer of silence. The spiral beneath her boots pulsed faintly—not glowing, but warm. Remembered. Burned into the earth like an afterimage. A map she'd walked before.

This is where they put the first one, something whispered inside her. This is where she stayed.

She reached the chair. There, beneath the seat, was the sketchbook. Not the one from the archive. A smaller one. Clothbound. Children's. Pages stuck together from moisture and age. Her hands shook as she lifted it, the fabric cold and swollen from years in the dirt.

She knelt and opened it. Drawings. Spirals. Trees. Two girls. In one, they held hands. In another, one girl sat in the chair. The other stood behind her, blurred in graphite. Ellie's breath snagged. The pages smelled like graphite, rot, and regret. On the last page:

ROOM 9

Two beds. One labeled E.H. The other blank.

Her name. Carved in pencil. The other girl unnamed. Or forgotten. Ellie looked up. Across the clearing, snow began to fall. A figure waited at the tree line—small, still, pale-dressed. No sound. No breath.

Clara. But this time, she didn't vanish. She turned. And walked toward Room 9. Ellie followed.

Room 9 was not where it had been. Not since Weatherly issued the suppression directive—scrambled maps, sealed hallways, reassigned rooms. But Ellie felt the pull regardless, a muscle-deep knowing that the door would still find her. Even now, a page from his directive flickered in her mind:

"Contain identity contagion. Isolate Subject 1C. Eliminate reflective triggers."

The hallway had shifted. The floor dipped where it hadn't before. Numbers fell out of sequence. The walls wept condensation at the seams, as if the building itself sweated under a weight it could no longer contain. The lights didn't flicker. They blinked on purpose.

But the door waited. She pressed her palm to it. The lock clicked like it knew her print by memory. Like it had been waiting. Inside: two beds. The one on the left was unmade—creases in the sheet still pressed into the mattress like a figure had risen from it only seconds before. The right bed was a lie of neatness. A placeholder for someone not yet—or no longer—there. Pillow undented. Sheets untouched. Except—they were still warm. A photograph sat on the desk.

E.H. written on the back.

The girl in the picture wore Ellie's face. But the eyes were wrong: too wide, too knowing. She stared past the lens—as if already watching a reflection of herself that hadn't yet been born. The spiral mark glowed faintly beneath her skin. She sat on the left bed. The lights dimmed. The mirror over the sink rippled. Clara didn't appear. She arrived. Like she'd always had a key.

She reached for Ellie's hand. Their fingers touched. And the Spiral remembered them both. In the records room, just beyond the intake bay of Ward A, the vent above the ceiling tiles whispered. It wasn't air. It was a name.

"Clara..."

Private Bell had never been part of the Spiral protocol. That's what the records said. That's what Weatherly had insisted. But now he sat upright in bed, eyes vacant, lips moving.

"Clara. Clara. Clara."

His voice had dropped to a low hum, barely audible, threading the Spiral tune beneath his breath like it had been encoded. Outside the room, a nurse froze mid-charting. Her pen hovered in the air. She turned—slowly—toward the sound.

"Private Bell?"

No answer. Just the humming.

She called for help. Two doors down, another patient began to murmur. Across the hall, someone cried out in their sleep. "Don't let her draw the spiral. She draws it backwards." At the observation desk, Gretchen's hand spasmed before the pen fell—as if the Spiral jostled her memory loose. It clattered against the tile like a shard of memory. She looked up. Her reflection in the stainless cabinet door looked back at her—but it turned too slowly. Then smiled.

"Not again," she whispered. "Not again."

Her hands shook. She reached for the intercom to call Dr. Weatherly—but the line buzzed before she touched it. A message blinked on the screen:

PROTOCOL SIGMA-RED. LOCKDOWN INITIATED. SUBJECT 1C – ACTIVE.

In the west wing, far below, Weatherly stared at the flickering light on the terminal. He didn't blink. Then he reached for the file he'd buried deepest.

SUBJECT ** 0B – DECOMMISSIONED**

His hand trembled as he opened it. But the page wasn't inert anymore. It remembered. And it wrote him out first. And the Drift resumed its course. Not outward. Inward. Back to where it began.

CHAPTER: TWENTY-FIVE

The One Who Stayed

The corridor behind the eastern ward had narrowed—compressed by shadows that didn't belong to afternoon. Ellie moved slowly, her breath snagged between two thoughts she couldn't separate. Each step echoed twice: once from her heels—and once from somewhere memory-shaped but bodyless, just ahead.

She reached the archival wing, where patient records were housed in drawer after drawer of misremembered truths. There was a room she hadn't entered before— not because it was locked. Because some small, intact part of her had known she wasn't ready to remember.

But today, the door was open.

Inside, the light hung too low, a single bulb suspended from a frayed cord. Dust shimmered like breath made visible. A long metal shelf divided the room, lined with reels of film, manila folders, and stamped index cards that bore no names, only numbers. Ellie passed her hand along the shelves until one card slipped free.

9C – PROXY MERGE INCOMPLETE. SECOND TRANSFER PENDING.

She froze. The number pulsed—familiar, forbidden, like a stitch pulled from an old scar. Her fingers tightened on the edge of the drawer.

Behind her, a rustle. She turned—Silas. He stood at the threshold, eyes unfocused but steady. "This is where memory rots," Silas said. "But it doesn't die. It ferments."

Ellie looked at him. "You knew about the Proxies?"

Her voice caught. "I saw the drawing. A girl in the spiral. She had my face."

Silas's eyes flicked to the shelves. "It wasn't your face then. But it wanted to be."

Ellie moved past him to the last file drawer—marked OBSOLETE SUBJECTS. Her hand hovered over the handle, but Silas stepped forward and opened it for her.

A single folder inside.

SUBJECT 1C — THE RETAINED

The word Proxy appeared six times in the margins—each time followed by a different patient number. But next to 1C, there was no Proxy designation.

Just a note, circled twice: Origin Node.

Her own intake photo stared back at her, paperclipped to the file. But the name on the form wasn't Ellie Hale. It wasn't Clara M. either.

Just:

THE ONE WHO STAYED

Below that, one line:

"Does not dissolve. Suggest long-term recursion control or archival containment."

Her vision blurred—not from tears, but from a pressure blooming behind her eyes. Her fingers twitched before she understood why. Her hands remembered the file. Her pulse spiked like it had found a predator.

I've read this. I wrote this. No. That couldn't be true. But the thought came faster than doubt.

Her hands twitched like a reflex buried too deep to unlearn. "This… this means I was never assigned here."

"You weren't," Silas whispered. "You returned."

She looked at him, her voice raw. "Then who was Clara?"

He met her gaze. "A reflection you tried to bury. But mirrors don't forget."

The bulb above them flickered, casting two shadows instead of one.

And from somewhere behind the wall, the sound of a chair scraping across the floor—a sound Ellie had never heard in this room but had always known. The file in her hand went cold.

In the chapel, Hazel sat beneath the stained-glass eye of Saint Dymphna, locked inside with the janitor's keys and silence. The altar candles were unlit. Her mop had been abandoned by the confessional. On the back of the pew in front of her, she'd carved the words with a letter opener:

WE BURIED HER WRONG.

Splinters clung to her fingernails. Blood had stained the hem of her smock. She did not pray. She watched her reflection hesitate—then move before she did. She whispered, "Not again." Then once more, quieter: "Not again."

Ellie sat across from Silas, the sketchbook open between them. He hadn't drawn yet. Just stared. She pointed to the page.

"Do you remember anything from before the orchard?" she asked softly. "Before Clara?"

His eyes twitched almost imperceptibly.

"Before?" he echoed.

"Yes. From when you were younger."

Silas slowly picked up a crayon—red, as always.

"Not from then," he murmured. "But from before you came back."

She blinked. "Silas… what do you mean?"

He tilted his head, gaze hooked somewhere just past her shoulder.

"I remember you from before."

"From before I worked here?"

He didn't nod. He didn't blink.

"Not as Ellie," he said. "As the one they called 1C."

He didn't choose to draw. The crayon moved like it had found its own hand—obedient, automatic. Not the orchard. Not the spiral. Her. Seated. Still. Eyes sewn shut. Her name carved into the chair. And beneath the image, in unsteady scrawl:

She was the one who watched too long.

Back in the records room, Ellie moved with hesitation. Each step echoed too loudly. The smell of iodine and old paper clung to the floor tiles, mingling with the sting of rubbing alcohol. A folder lay open. Not by her hand. At the top:

A photo of two girls. One looked straight into the lens. The other—half a step behind—looked away. Blue ribbon. Pale dress. Eyes wide.

Ellie turned it over.

Clara M. & Subject 1C – Pre-Phase.

Her breath caught. She didn't recognize the second girl. Her bones didn't just know. They recoiled. She felt it ripple backward through her spine like déjà vu. A voice echoed from a memory—her own or someone else's: Don't write it down. They'll erase it from you.

Silas appeared behind her. "It found you," Silas said. "It always does."

"I don't know what I've found," she whispered.

"You do," he said. "Because I remember you screaming before I ever knew your name."

He laid a spiral drawing on the table. Inside it: Ellie Hale.

"You already have," he said. "You just don't remember what it took."

In the abandoned archive corridor, Ellie reached the final drawer.

PROJECT: PROXY

Inside: a reel-to-reel recorder. Canisters. A photograph of a child in the Merge Chair. She flipped it.

Subject 1C. The Retained.

She didn't need to read further. The recorder clicked. From the speaker:

"Please… not me again."

The mirror didn't shimmer. It breathed. It wasn't her. The posture was hers. The eyes were Clara's. In the margin of the final document:

Protocol Addendum – 1C: Memory overwrite unsuccessful. Identity persistence beyond thresholds. Recommend recursion or mirroring termination.

One word circled in red:

Rewrite. A girl appeared at the end of the hallway—dress too thin, feet bare.

"I remember it wrong… but I still remember."

She turned into Room 9C. Ellie followed. She looked at the drawing in her hand. Not Ellie. Not Clara.

1C. The Retained. And in the distance, the mirrors began to hum.

CHAPTER: TWENTY-SIX

The Archive Breathes

The archive wing hadn't been abandoned. It had been sealed. Left to starve on silence. Dust clung to the molding like moss. The light above the door sputtered every thirteen seconds—Ellie had counted on the way in. The flicker counted something. Not seconds. Heartbeats.

She pressed the brass key Weatherly had once given her into the rusted lock. The spiral was still etched into its head, dulled by time and friction, and it clicked into place with a sound that felt older than the hospital itself.

Inside, the air was colder than it should've been. Filing cabinets lined both walls, and along the back, a row of wooden drawers labeled in block lettering: PROJECT DRIFT / PATIENT FILES / AUDIO / INTAKE IMPRINTS.

A reel-to-reel machine sat like a relic on the table's edge, its twin spools inert. Ellie crossed the room slowly, trailing a gloved hand over the metal drawers. Each breath fogged the air with something that didn't quite belong to her. She didn't speak. The room expected silence. She paused. Clipboard in hand. The label on the first drawer "PHASE ONE – SUBJECT FILES A–E" glitched in her vision. A folded newspaper clipping peeked out beneath the clipboard—VETERANS AFFAIRS CONSIDERS NEW PHASE IN BEHAVIORAL EVALUATION, WASHINGTON POST, AUG. 1947. Ellie slid it back in without reading more. The date was enough. For a moment, the "E" shimmered into "H." Her pulse spiked. Then, gone.

She found it in the third cabinet: SUBJECT 1C. A folder thick with copied charts, trial logs, and something else. Audio reels. She fed the tape into the machine. It caught, stuttered, then began to play. A voice filled the room—young, unsteady. Female.

"I don't remember when it began. But I remember who they said I was."

Ellie didn't freeze. She folded—her own voice bending her spine like a splinter worked loose from the past. Her own voice. A younger version. Maybe fifteen. Maybe sixteen. Soft with the edges of trauma, but clear.

"I didn't want to be Clara. Not really. But they said she forgot better than I did."

Her throat constricted. She should've recoiled, denied it—should've felt outrage or fear. But her body didn't flinch. It recognized the voice. Like muscle memory. Like blood memory. Silence on the tape. Then, a second voice—clinical, male.

"Can you recall the orchard now?"

Ellie's breath caught. The real orchard—bare trees and frost-scabbed soil—flashed across her mind. The sketch in her pocket. The ribbon beneath the root.

On the recording, she—the girl—began to hum. The Spiral Tune. A low, circling melody. Not words. Not melody in the traditional sense. Just… spiral. Ellie backed away from the recorder, the table edge pressing into her hips. Then the tape crackled again.

"The subject shows retention atypical of implanted identities. Recommend classification: THE RETAINED."

Another silence. Then, the sound of a chair scraping.

"Erase the orchard. Cut the roots. Burn the soil. I bloom anyway," the voice whispered.

"You weren't supposed to wake up this far along. They didn't stitch you. They sowed you."

The tape clicked off.

Ellie staggered back into the cabinet, her hand flying to her mouth. The hum remained in the air. But the machine had stopped. The spiral etched on the side of the reel shimmered faintly. Just a trick of light. Or memory. She turned slowly toward the glass pane in the door. Her reflection had been peeled away, like skin, leaving only the orchard beneath. Branches tangled like nerves. Soil turned and clawed. And in the center, the spiral chair.

Empty. Then, not. A girl sat in it. Face hidden. Hair damp with soil. She wore Ellie's coat. And when she looked up—she didn't blink.

The door behind Ellie slammed shut. And she remembered the last thing she'd drawn as a child. Not the spiral. Not the orchard. Her own face. But she had written the name beneath it:

Clara.

The walls of the archive room were lined with steel cabinets, each labeled in precise, block-letter type: PHASE ONE – SUBJECT FILES A–E, PHASE TWO – SUBJECT FILES F–K. Rows upon rows. Silent. Unmoving. Too perfect.

Ellie's fingers shook as she turned the dial of the reel-to-reel recorder, the metal cold against her skin. The audio file Weatherly had tried to bury was spliced together from two decades of experiments— proof layered like a spiral of its own. The tape hissed.

Then a voice, younger than she expected. Quieter. A girl.

"My name is Clara. No—I mean... it used to be. They told me to forget it."

Another click. The tape advanced.

"I drew the chair before they showed it to me. They said that meant the Spiral took."

Ellie sat down hard on the edge of a forgotten cot. Her hands went numb. The tape crackled again. Then, another voice. Older. Measured. Male.

"Subject 1C has demonstrated recurrent spatial distortion, pre-incident memory access, and successful transference signature. (Audio distortion.) "Subject 1C shows premature recursive bleed. Mirror Lock may stabilize the primary thread—or splinter it permanently."

Her throat burned. Mirror Lock. The term from the files Gretchen had hidden. The one Weatherly never used in front of the others. Another click. This time—her own voice.

"I'm not Clara. You told me not to say that name anymore."

Then silence. Ellie pressed pause. Her heart rattled like a loose drawer. Her pulse thudded between her ears in a rhythm not quite her own. She rewound the tape. Played the last line again.

"I'm not Clara. You told me not to say that name anymore."

She hadn't remembered saying it. In the metal edge of the tape reel, her reflection stared back. Too still. Too calm. And when she blinked, the reflection didn't. A new voice cut through the static. Faint. Off-mic.

"Erase the identification number. Let the memory hold the shape. She'll stay contained if she believes she chose it."

Ellie remembered Asher's eyes—always too calm. As if watching a machine perform exactly as it was built to. I was never his patient. I was his product. Ellie staggered back from the recorder.

That voice—Dr. Asher. Not calm. Empty. Like someone reading an obituary from memory.

"Subject 1C demonstrates unusually high resistance to overwrite. She may be a candidate for recursive memory application."

The chair behind her scraped across the floor—by itself. Ellie turned to run but stopped short. The hallway had dissolved.

Instead, the mirrors had returned. Not hung. Grown. Curved glass rising from floor to ceiling, each pane catching a different version of her—one crying, one laughing, one frozen in a scream. The reflections flickered through griefs she hadn't lived yet.

In the left reflection, the reel-to-reel kept turning, though she'd shut it off. In the one to her right, a girl stood behind her. Stitched eyes. Spiral in her palm. In the center mirror, Ellie's name tag peeled from her chest and fluttered to the floor. But it didn't read Ellie. It read:

1C | THE RETAINED

She bent to retrieve it. The laminate was warm. Not dirt—a smudge of ink, bleeding up beneath the plastic. Another name: Clara. Half-erased. She touched the glass. Warm.

She touched the glass. It was warm. And the archive began to breathe. She bent to retrieve it. The laminate was warm. Her fingers recoiled. The ID had a smudge beneath the number. Not dirt. Ink. Another name—Clara—half-erased. She touched the glass. It was warm.

Behind her, a cabinet drawer burst open. Files erupted—not chaotically, but with eerie precision, fluttering through the air like birds released from memory. Pages reassembled themselves in midair, rewriting, retyping.

She watched, horrified, as one file labeled SUBJECT 7C opened. A photograph fell. Not Silas. A girl. Young. Pale. Her mouth sewn shut. The margin note scrawled in red:

FAILED OVERWRITE / TRANSFERENCE INCOMPLETE.

Clara wasn't first. Wasn't final. Just another mirror trying to catch the original shape before it broke. Ellie stumbled back toward the corridor. The Spiral was never a symptom. It was the system. And it had just woken up.

CHAPTER: TWENTY-SEVEN

The Archive Rewrites

The ledger room hadn't cooled. It had calcified. Memory frozen mid-breath, refusing to thaw. The light flickered—steady, stutter, steady—casting bars of shadow across the walls. Paper rustled without wind. Somewhere deep in the drawers, the years kept breathing.

Dr. Asher stood beside the open drawer like a surgeon about to pull something diseased into the light. His fingers hovered over a thick, water-stained file. The pages were edged in rust—not blood, but close. The stink of institutional rot. Whatever had been filed here had aged before its time.

Ellie remained silent as he pulled out the folder. Her breath caught as her fingertips tingled—like the file recognized her.

"Subject 1C," Asher murmured as if saying it aloud summoned something from the walls.

Asher didn't look at her yet. "There were thirteen subjects in the initial Merge phase. We recovered six. Two were… transferred."

He tapped the folder. "And one—stayed."

The Spiral was stamped on the corner of the first page, a triangle folded inside it. Her initials—E.H.—appeared faintly beneath.

"You kept this hidden," Ellie said.

"We didn't hide it," he said softly. "We buried it. That's different."

"Burying's for bodies, Asher. Not the truth."

Asher's mouth twisted—not quite guilt, not quite remorse. "You're not wrong."

"I remember the orchard," she whispered. "But not like a memory. Like a warning."

He closed the file gently. "You asked me once if names could hold trauma. If being called something long enough makes it true. You remember that?"

"No."

"You did. In the early sessions. When you were still... yourself."

"And who exactly was that?"

He didn't answer. Just handed her the folder.

She took it with trembling fingers. Inside, the pages were uneven and misaligned. On one, a photograph—not of her, not exactly. A younger girl. Spiral drawn beneath her eyes. The name blacked out. But beneath the black bar, faintly scratched into the paper:

Clara.

And in the bottom corner—shaky, unmistakable—her own handwriting:

Don't forget what they took to make you forget.

Her fingers gripped the folder. The air seemed to pause. Asher exhaled, running a hand through his graying hair.

"Ellie... If we knew what it would do to you, we never would've—"

"Don't lie," she snapped. "Not here. Not now."

"I didn't lie," he said, quieter. "I chose to forget."

Ellie turned away. His final words followed.

"You were the only one who begged not to forget."

The light above them flickered once more. A single pulse. Then stillness.

The stairs remembered her weight. They groaned in greeting, not resistance. One hand trailing the wall, the other gripping the file. The lower levels of Arlington Hills were colder—not from temperature, but from abandonment. These rooms were never meant for return.

The sconce at the hallway's end blinked once—an eyelid closing over a memory she hadn't earned yet. She entered anyway.

The archive room's door resisted. Inside: mildew, ink, formaldehyde. A second smell, sharper—like film dissolving. Drawers stretched wall to wall, labeled by year and designation. Her fingers skimmed until she found it: not a date. A symbol. Spiral. She pulled the drawer. Inside: thick folders, mismatched. Codes only. 9A. 5B. 3D. 1C.

She drew out the 1C file, wrapped in wax paper and stamped with the Spiral-Triangle insignia. Inside: a hand-drawn map of the orchard. Spiral formation. Each tree labeled—A1, B2, C3…

At the center: a chair. Instead of a label, a stamped number: 1C. She turned the page. A list. Merged subjects. Most REDACTED. A few marked RELEASED. Only one marked RETAINED.

Symptoms: Involuntary recall. Memory bleed. Dual-phase identity stability. Spiral sensitivity extreme.

A final note in handwriting she recognized—Dr. Weaver's:

Do not reassign. Subject shows recursion, not regression. The orchard stayed with her. She never left. Ellie stumbled back. Her elbow hit a shelf. A folder fell. She bent to gather the papers—and froze. A child's sketch—shaky, desperate. Her own hand. Younger. Jagged with fear.

Shaky handwriting: ELLIE. "I buried the wrong one," the scrawl accused, the graphite already smudged by time or desperate erasure.

A typed tag hung half-attached:

Reassigned to Spiral Research Wing – per Dr. M. Weaver. Merge viability undetermined.

Behind her: a voice.

"Clara?"

Silas.

He stood in the doorway, eyes steady. "It's not just what they called you," Silas said. "It's what they planted."

She didn't answer. Silas knelt beside her. Picked up the sketch. Turned it.

April 12, 1937.

"I saw you," he said. "You didn't cry. You just… stared. Like you knew what was coming."

"Dr. Weatherly said you were stable. That's how they kept you."

Ellie's blood turned to ice. Stable. Like a word carved into bone.

"I was just a child," she whispered.

Silas's voice cracked. "You were a mirror."

She tried to stand. The room spun. The Spiral map pulsed once—recognition, not light. She turned. The mirror had returned. No bolts. No frame. Her reflection smiled first—before she even thought of it. Her timeline split—just slightly, just enough to slip. Only the mirror moved first.

Her voice didn't echo. It threaded. She hummed—not the melody, but the pattern. That Spiral tune Ellie had only ever heard in silence. And when she blinked, the girl's mouth moved—but the mirror whispered first: "She hums before she remembers."

Behind the reflection, Clara. Lips moved: "You forgot the name. But the mirror kept it."

A knock, but not against wood—against memory. She turned. No one. Back at the glass: her reflection now wrote in reverse:

1C IS NOT CLARA.

She remembered first. Ellie backed into the chair. At its base—a nameplate.

HALE, E.

Beneath it, carved by a child:

Return to Sender.

Her reflection fell back into sync. But its fingertips still dripped with a memory Ellie hadn't yet allowed herself to claim.____In the vault, Ellie opened a secondary drawer. Files rewritten. Names erased. The Subject 3D report now listed as 7C—no mention of Silas. A handwritten line scrawled across the margin:

"7C was a girl. Clara was not the first."

Another folder—Subject 4A. Merge failed. Identity fragmented.

A note from Dr. Asher:

Subject 4A exhibited early Spiral symptoms but failed to overwrite Clara. Memory bleed residual. Merge unsustainable.

They weren't experimenting on Clara. Clara was an experiment.

The file drawer slammed shut on its own. A flicker of lights. A shelf groaned. Then, collapse. Ellie spun. Behind her, one wall of files began to contort—not fall, but fold. Pages twisted, letters rearranged themselves mid-sentence. A label on the 1C drawer now read:

"ORIGIN UNKNOWN – LOCK ENABLED."

The archive wasn't falling apart. It was shedding its skin. Reconstructing memory faster than she could unlearn it.

Observation Log: Subject 7C — Night Record, 03:00 Hours

Location: Ward C, Room 14 Status: Stable / Active Recall Phase Authorization: Spiral Clearance Only

Subject remained silent through scheduled lights-out. At 03:00, subject stood and faced the east window. Duration: thirteen minutes. No motion. Eye tracking: focused inward.

Subject whispered:

"They stitched the orchard into us." "You bled in that dirt same as me."

Subject then traced a spiral on the window. Pattern reversed mid-motion.

No staff present. Surveillance confirms: subject did not speak to her reflection. The reflection spoke first. Possibly to Nurse Hale. Unconfirmed.

Recommend immediate review. Spiral motif recurrence in both Subject 7C and 1C. Identity entanglement confirmed.

—Filed by Dr. A. Weatherly ARCHIVE LOCK ENABLED

CHAPTER: TWENTY-EIGHT

The Echo Room

The orchard had frozen deeper than frost. Memory had gripped the trees, not winter. The air carried no birdsong, no wind—only the creak of silence hardening to ice. Beneath Ellie's boots, the snow sagged in uneven patches—disturbed not by time, but by return. Someone—or something—had been back here. Often.

Her fingers clutched the sketch Clara once gave her: a spiral orchard viewed from above, the geometry too precise, too familiar. She'd memorized every angle. What unnerved her now was the realization that the trees had grown to match the drawing, as if memory had dictated their roots.

A low wind stirred the snow. Ellie stepped onto the path. It spiraled inward, not like a maze, but like a ritual—one meant to bind, not lose. At the center clearing, she stopped.

There it was. A ledger. Half-buried beneath a flat stone and a braid of roots that hadn't been there last week—as if the orchard had tried to bury it alive.

She knelt. Her gloved fingers brushed the snow away, then the dirt. The leather cover cracked beneath her touch—old, water-damaged, and warped like it had soaked up years of names.

She opened it near the center. Instinct.

1C — Retained

The words blurred at the edges. No intake date. No discharge. No medical summary. Just that word: Retained. She flipped back. Earlier entries listed men by rank, initials, trauma tags. One name jumped.

S. Durney – Recurring spiral hallucination.

Another:

Clara M. — Memory displacement via mirror recursion.

Then—

E. Hale — Cross-referenced.

But it was crossed out in faded ink.

Beneath it: Clara. Not her full name. Just Clara. In a different hand.

Ellie closed her eyes. Her pulse drummed in her temples. It was her writing. She turned to the last page. Blank. At first.

Then, as if waiting for warmth, charcoal markings bloomed: a spiral drawn in thick strokes—and beneath it:

They didn't plant trees here. They planted names.

She looked up. The fog had gathered again, but only around her. The trees at the orchard's edge were still. Beyond the clearing, the reflection pool had frozen. And within the ice— A girl. Eyes stitched shut. Standing not where Ellie had been—but where Ellie was supposed to have stayed. The reflection pointed. Not at Ellie. At the ledger. She had seen that face before. Not just in mirrors. In dreams. In drawings. In memories that didn't belong to her—except they did. She wanted to scream. But she didn't know which name would come out.

Ellie stepped back. Her boot caught on a root. She stumbled. When she looked again, the girl was gone—but her stitched smile lingered in the ice like a scar. The whisper didn't travel through air. It rose through Ellie's ribs like smoke through a broken chimney. It bloomed inside her, old as breath: You didn't come here to remember. You came to return.

The spiral beneath her feet pulsed as if lit from beneath. Ellie clutched the ledger to her chest, turned, and ran. But part of her stayed behind—just a breath, a flicker, a name written in dirt. And it wasn't Ellie's.

The corridor leading to the Echo Room had always been colder, but tonight, it was frigid in a way that felt deliberate. Not a broken radiator. Not a draft.

Something deeper. Ellie wrapped her arms tighter around the ledger. She shouldn't have brought it. The cover seemed to hum faintly against her coat, like it was remembering itself too loudly.

The Echo Room had no official designation. No nurses posted. No files logged. But Clara had spoken of it once. "The place where the walls remember what we forgot."

Now, Ellie stood at the door. It wasn't marked. It never had been.

Her hand found the knob without hesitation—as if muscle memory she didn't remember earning had guided it.

She turned it. The door opened without a creak. The room was small—circular. The walls were smooth, painted a color that might've once been white but now held a tint closer to bone. There was no furniture except a small stool in the center and a cracked mirror leaning against the far wall. Not hung. Not mounted. Just... propped.

Ellie stepped inside. The door sighed shut behind her—without a hand, without a hinge groan, as if memory itself sealed it. No sound. No click. But the air changed. Grew heavier.

She crossed to the mirror slowly, the leather-bound ledger pressed flat to her chest. Her breath ghosted the glass. Then the reflection blinked. Not hers. Clara's.

Ellie didn't move. The figure in the mirror did. It stepped forward. Another layered behind it—Silas. And then—Ellie again, younger. Blood at her collarbone. Hands stained with chalk and something darker. They spiraled over each other—ghost images stacking faster than she could breathe. Spiraling. She stumbled backward. The mirror didn't show her falling. It showed her kneeling. Digging. Her hands digging not for survival—but for retrieval.

Something that screamed. She gasped—but the scream echoed only from the glass. Behind her, the door opened again. A footstep. She turned.

Silas stood in the threshold, pale and wide-eyed. His fingers were trembling, but his voice was clear.

"They use the Echo Room to trace back the ones who won't let go."

Ellie couldn't speak. Couldn't breathe. Silas stepped closer, his gaze fixed on the mirror.

"Do you see it now?" he whispered.

She turned slowly, facing the glass once more. The mirror had changed again. It was showing the ledger. Open to a blank page. No—it was writing. A name.

1C – Subject retained. Identity drift unstable. Memory echo escalating. Then, beneath it, three names in different hands. Clara.

Ellie.

E. Hale.

She reached forward to touch the glass.

Her reflection didn't move. It only mourned with a look she couldn't name—like pity sharpened to a needlepoint.

Behind her, Silas spoke. No louder than a thought.

"They think memory is a disease. But it's not. It's a mirror. And some of us were never meant to reflect."

The mirror flickered once. The writing unraveled in reverse. And in the hush that followed, Ellie felt the first drop of blood slide from her nose.

The ink wouldn't dry.

Ellie stood in the ward's back archive, the broken bulb overhead casting thin shadows across the ledgers stacked around her like gravestones. Her hand trembled as she lifted the old registry again— the one she had found in the Echo Room but couldn't seem to let go of.

Every time she turned the page, the spiral deepened—growing darker, carving deeper, as if her reading it helped it burrow. Not drawn. Not printed. Burned into the fibers like a memory refusing to fade. The symbol swirled inward. Always inward. She traced it with her fingertip.

Halfway through, her vision tilted. Like the floor itself shifted beneath her boots. She gripped the edge of the filing cabinet until the dizziness passed, but the sensation left something behind: not nausea.

Recognition.

There, in the margins of the ledger, was a date. January 9th, 1940.

Seven years ago. She flipped the page.

"1C — SUBJECT RETAINED"

No date of discharge. No family listed.

Status: Unresolved Recursion.

And beneath that, in smaller print:

"If the subject returns, do not engage. The name cannot be reissued."

Her pulse fluttered like a bird caught between ribs. Because she had seen her own name listed in this very file three days ago—Eleanor Hale.

Now it was gone.

In its place:

C.M. – Status: Retired.

E.H. – See Subject 1C.

Subject: Incomplete Separation.

Her mouth went dry. A photograph paperclipped to the back fell loose into her palm. It was a girl. Clara. No—Ellie. Younger. Eyes wide. But the symmetry was wrong, off just enough to unnerve—as if someone had mirrored the left side twice.

Uncanny. Almost familiar, almost foreign. The back of the photograph was stamped in red:

SPIRAL CONTAINMENT PROTOCOL – PHASE THREE INITIATED

She dropped the ledger. It thudded to the floor with a sound that felt louder than it should've been—like a verdict. The lights above her flickered and stuttered. One popped.

Ellie sank to her knees, pages fluttering open around her like a flock disturbed from rest. From behind a rusted filing drawer came a child's whisper:

"You were the first one, remember? You chose it."

She turned, but the room was empty. Only dust. And a spiral sketched onto the floor in charcoal—mirrored perfectly by a water stain on the ceiling above. She blinked, and it was gone. But she knew what it meant now.

They hadn't tried to heal her. They had tried to hollow her. They had tried to keep her from remembering what they made her do. What she volunteered for. What they told her she had to forget.

She gathered the fallen pages with numb hands. Not to organize them—there was no order left. Only the illusion of it, tucked between hospital lines and ink that refused to stay where it was written.

As she reached for the last page, her fingertips grazed the spiral again—this one smaller, more deliberate, etched into the edge of the cabinet in a child's handwriting.

Beneath it, faintly penciled:

"She was the test before the orchard took root."

Ellie's breath caught. Because she had written that line once before. She didn't know when. Or why. But the graphite smudge on her fingertip was hers. A click sounded from behind her. She turned.

The lights in the hallway were blinking one by one, as if someone— or something—was walking toward her and flipping the switch behind each step.

Ellie stood slowly, the spiral still burned into the page clenched in her fist. She didn't run. She didn't hide. She walked toward the hum. Toward the place where the Spiral wasn't drawn. It was born.

Because if she was Subject 1C, then it was time to find out what the C had always stood for.

Clara. Or Containment. Or maybe, just maybe—Choice.

CHAPTER: TWENTY-NINE

What It Left Behind

The corridor to the eastern wing wasn't on any map Ellie had ever seen. Not in the nurse schematics. Not the emergency layouts. But she followed it now with an ache—not in her bones, but deeper, as if the Spiral had already redrawn her from the inside out.

She passed the old intake alcove, the glass fractured into spiderwebs that froze her reflection into a thousand hollowed silhouettes, each one blinking just a breath too late.

The air thickened. Not with dust or mildew—but with memory. Beneath her palm, the faded wallpaper pulsed with ghost names: S. Marlin. T. Leclair. 1C.

At the end of the hall stood a door. No knob. No lock. Just a fingerprint plate, rusted and forgotten. Ellie didn't touch it. She waited. The light above flickered once. The door opened.

Inside: a room she hadn't seen since before the erasure, but her body remembered—the low metal chair, the arched mirror, the faint circle of chalk etched into the floor like a closed wound.

The chair faced the mirror. There were no restraints. Ellie sat anyway. Her breath ghosted the glass. Her reflection did not. Across the mirror, in slow-bleeding letters, one word emerged:

WELCOME BACK.

Below it, a spiral. Drawn with the precision of someone who knew exactly how many loops it would take to make a person forget. Ellie didn't flinch. The reflection smiled first—white-eyed, stitched at the edges like a marionette pulled by unseen strings.

The chair behind her was empty. The mirror was no longer a reflection. It was a recording. A trap. It showed her younger—hair longer, pinned in a style she didn't wear. A darker uniform. A badge not marked E. Hale but C. Martin.

Clara.

She reached out, her fingertips grazing the glass. The reflected hand moved too—but it was bandaged, red leaking through the gauze. The recording rewound.

The mirror now showed her sitting in the chair—while she watched from behind the glass. Not a reflection. A window. A memory.

The floor beneath her tilted slightly, like the building had decided it was done pretending. Her hand brushed the wall—cool, ceramic-tiled—and found a seam. She pulled free a faded scrap of paper wedged there.

A medical chart.

SUBJECT 1C — MARTIN, C. (ALIAS: HALE, E.)

No intake. No discharge. Only the Spiral stamped across the corner, sharp and final.

Beneath it, handwritten:

Retained across phase thresholds. Memory bleed increasing. Name must hold. Identity must fracture.

Ellie staggered back and the paper blurred.

"I didn't choose this," she whispered.

The mirror answered by showing her again—small hands sketching the Spiral into the wall, the chalk breaking under pressure.

Her voice, a child's voice, whispered from nowhere:

"Don't remember. Don't forget. Don't remember…"

She dropped to her knees. The light shifted. The reflection turned its head—and for the first time, looked directly at her.

"Ellie," it said. Calm. Certain. "It's your turn to stay."

Then it smiled. The spiral beneath her began to turn—not a drawing, not an illusion—moving.

They told him time bent after trauma. Silas knew better.

Time bled.

He sat cross-legged on the tile floor, palms pressed flat. Listening.

The hum was faint now, buried beneath layers of lies and linoleum, but he could still hear it: a child's voice looping through the walls:

"Don't remember. Don't forget. Don't remember..."

He scratched another spiral under the bench leg. Fifth one today. Paint couldn't hide a wound—it could only delay the bleeding. Above the far door, the light flickered on the fourth count. Always the fourth. Not electrical. Orchard rhythm. He whispered to the darkness:

"She's remembering out of order."

The spiral deepened at his feet. He hadn't drawn it. This one drew itself. Silas stood. The corridor pulsed. Behind his eyelids: not dreams.

Not nightmares.

Archives.

A name pulsed there.

1C. The Retained.

"She's almost back," he said.

"And when she is, we'll both know which memory was ours."

CONFIDENTIAL – EYES ONLY

SUBJECT ID: 1C

CODE: "The Retained"

Patient History Fragmentation Report:

Subject continues to display high-stability recursion patterns, consistent with prior 9C exposure events.

Emotional anchoring incomplete; memory bleed elevated.

Observed behaviors:

– Mirror lag confirmed.

– Spiral sketching initiated without external cue.

– Spontaneous verbal recall: "They planted the names here."

Critical Risk:

Subject may be misidentifying herself. Re: HAYES / M. / Clara.

If Subject 1C continues to remember against design, containment failure projected. Immediate contingency recommended.

Signed,

Dr. Thomas Asher

11.02.47

Ellie woke folded tight, hands crossed against her chest like a body laid for burial. The ceiling pulsed faintly overhead, plaster curling at the corners like skin peeling from bone. The cot beneath her felt unfamiliar. Too soft in the wrong places. She couldn't remember lying down.

She moved on stockinged feet, careful not to disturb the floorboards that remembered her weight.

On the dresser: her badge.

E. Hale.

The bloodstain at the corner was dry. Still, the metallic scent of iron clung to the air. The mirror across the room caught her halfway across. Her reflection hesitated—blinking too late. Moving too slow. She turned to leave. The reflection stayed a beat longer before reluctantly following.

In Ward C, the air had thickened. It didn't buzz anymore. It waited.

Silas's door opened for her before she knocked.

Inside: blank paper. Blank walls. Blank faces. Silas sat at the table, unmoving, his fingers trembling only slightly.

"You're here," he said.

Not a greeting. A recognition.

Ellie stepped closer. "Did you sleep?"

Silas smiled without humor. "I don't think I've ever stopped dreaming."

She sat opposite him.

"I found the ledger," she said. "My name wasn't there."

He didn't look at her. "That's because they didn't give it to you. They took it from someone else."

Ellie gripped the spiral-backed chair. "Who was I?"

Silas's jaw locked.

"You were the first," he whispered. "You remembered. And they hated that."

The fluorescent light overhead snapped. The bulb burst with a pop that smelled faintly of singed hair. In the mirror behind him, her reflection knelt—not standing. Not resisting. Digging. Bleeding. In her ears, a child's voice whispered:

"Don't write it down. They'll see it too."

The blank page between them was no longer blank. The Spiral had burned itself into the fibers. And when Ellie reached out, the burn fit the shape of her fingertips exactly.

She hadn't survived the recursion.

She'd only been what it left behind.

CHAPTER: THIRTY

The Spiral's Design

The staircase to the lower archives curved like the underside of a ribcage, each step groaning beneath Ellie's weight—as if the bones themselves were bracing. The electric sconces flickered just out of rhythm, casting long, quivering shadows along the concrete walls. They didn't just shake—they pulsed, as if trying to sync to something breathing below. Ellie kept one hand on the cold rail, the other clutching the folded page tucked into her sleeve—the spiral Silas had burned into the paper.

You've already been here, she thought. Not in body. In echo.

The hallway leading to the archive was too silent. No machinery. No flutter of papers. Just the thick, stale air—sour with mildew and the scorched-paper smell of memory collapsing into itself. Every breath tasted like dust left behind by someone else's forgetting. At the corridor's end, a brass-plated door waited—riveted like a submarine hatch. On the facility maps, it had been labeled "Condemned." But the lock was clean. Recently turned.

Ellie slid the spiral-marked key into the lock. It turned without resistance. Inside, the archive breathed. Not literally. But it felt that way. Shelves spiraled inward, curling like a labyrinth built by something that didn't believe in straight lines. File cabinets hummed low with static, their metal seams vibrating like breath held too long. Paper rustled without wind.

This is it, she thought. This is where they shelved the versions of us that didn't take.

The temperature dropped another degree as she stepped farther in. Her breath clouded in front of her.

In the center: a reel-to-reel machine. Spinning. Flickering.

She approached cautiously, lifting the headphones with shaking hands. They crackled with static, then voices—young, strained.

A girl, crying.

A man, whispering.

Then: Asher.

"Subject 1C retains pre-overwrite trauma. Spiral exposure incomplete. Mirror phase resisting compliance. Recommend environmental recursion escalation."

A sharp click. Then Gretchen's voice, brittle and near-breaking:

"There's too much left of her. You can erase a name, but not a scream."

Ellie dropped the headphones. They clattered against the machine, stuttering the tape. Her pulse thudded so loud it drowned out the archive's humming.

"You knew this. You've always known."

She turned toward the nearest cabinet. Its drawers were labeled with letters, not numbers.

A. B. C...

She found one marked: H.

Inside: thick folders—edges worn soft as cloth.

One stamped:

 Hale, Eleanor J.

Another beneath it:

Subject 1C | Clara.

She opened both. Laid them side by side.

The pages fluttered under her fingertips, alive.

Not just similar. Identical. Notes transposed. Observations repeated. Trauma loops mirrored. Dates scrambled. Only the signatures differed. Dr. Weatherly on one. Dr. Asher on the other. Her hand rose to her throat before she realized why.

The collar always felt tight. As if buttoned over two lives.

She stared until the words blurred together. A margin note scrawled beside Subject 1C caught her eye:

"Do not transfer again. Spiral holds. Retention necessary."

Across the room, a shoulder-height mirror hung where she hadn't noticed it before. Her reflection blinked first. Her lips moved—but not by her will.

"They named you Clara before you remembered who you were."

Ellie staggered back, heel catching a box. A sealed envelope sat on the cabinet, too clean, too expectant.

Addressed in a hand she didn't recognize:

To: Subject 1C.

From: Clara M.

Her hands shook as she opened it.

Inside:

A photograph of the orchard.

A nurse's coat, soaked at the hem.

A child crouched at the tree's base, carving spirals into the dirt. In the corner—another child. Watching. Ellie's breath caught. The spiral had always been there. And so had she. She blinked back the sting rising behind her eyes.

A second sheet slipped free—a protocol fragment:

Subject 1C demonstrates reflexive recursion under visual loops. Memory inadequate terminology. Suggest term: residual agency. Containment reliant on belief in self-authorship."

She crumpled it without reading further. It didn't matter what they called her. She knew now.

Not a subject.

Not a mistake.

A warning.

The windows in this wing reached too high, chasing light they never caught.

When it managed to break through the stained glass, it scattered across the floor fractured and thin—like light filtered through water.

Ellie's steps echoed too sharply.

The ache wasn't in her muscles anymore.

It was in her marrow.

In memory she hadn't consented to.

The portraits on the walls leered.

Dr. Margaret Weaver, cold smile pinched tight.

Dr. Asher, chalk dust smeared over spiraling diagrams on a blackboard. But it was the glass that made her stop. Reflections shimmered wrong.

Late. Delayed.

The glass blinked after she passed. Eyes staying fixed too long.

Ellie's stomach twisted. Not now, she thought.

Not yet. She reached the Mirror Archive. The chain that once bound the door hung useless.

The rusted key Asher had slipped her weeks ago fit perfectly.

Inside: Dust. Chalk.

A single desk. Files arrayed without labels.

Waiting. Four photographs.

One: Ellie.

One: Clara.

One: a stitched girl, mouth sealed by scars.

One: Silas.

Beneath Silas's photo, a chart:

S-21B | Residual Witness Phenomenon

"May retain visual data from memory overwrites not assigned to subject."

Her breath caught. She flipped the file beneath the photographs. A fragment from Weatherly to Weaver:

"Subject 21B shows drift bleed not linked to direct event exposure. Witnesses 1C recursion echoes visually. Retain proximity for containment. Do not inform Subject 1C of link."

Her chest squeezed tight.

They kept him close on purpose.

He was a buffer. A mirror they weaponized against her.

The mirror across the room caught her movement. She turned. At first, nothing.

Then—the reflection stayed seated after she stood. Her mirrored self sat in a spiral-backed chair.

Behind her: Clara, mouth moving. No sound. Only the forming shape of words on the glass:

"You forgot the name. But the mirror kept it."

A sharp knock behind her. No one. When she looked back—the reflection was writing. Scratching with bleeding fingertips. Words formed backward:

"1C IS NOT CLARA.

 She remembered first."

The spiral pulsed faintly behind the letters.

Ellie crouched.

Near the chair's base—buried under dust—she uncovered a nameplate.

HALE, E.

Stamped.

Not carved.

Not chosen. Beneath it, in a child's trembling hand:

"Return to Sender."

She staggered back.

Her reflection matched her again.

But something behind her eyes didn't return. Her hand was clean but the mirror's wasn't.

Protocol Note surfaced in her mind without warning:

"Merge integrity test failed. Subject 1C reasserted. Spiral contamination irreversible."

The light overhead stuttered once. Then silence. A silence that wasn't empty. It was watching. Waiting for her to take the next step.

CHAPTER: THIRTY-ONE

Built to Become

The morning air had turned metallic. Not cold—just sharp, like it carried the scent of something recently cut. Ellie stepped into the north corridor where the light didn't quite reach the floor, and for a moment, she wondered if she was walking through memory instead of space.

The Spiral mark beneath her skin ached faintly. It wasn't pain. It was something worse: anticipation. Gretchen stood at the end of the hallway, clipboard tight to her chest, eyes fixed on the corridor window that looked out toward the orchard. The pane was fogged. But even through it, the spiral trees seemed to lean inward.

"Has the Drift reentered?" Ellie asked, voice low.

Gretchen didn't turn. "It never left. We just got better at pretending we couldn't hear it." Ellie stepped closer, catching sight of the edge of a classified file under Gretchen's arm. "What is that?"

"Spiral Recursion Logs," Gretchen said, eyes still on the orchard. "The original files from Project Eden, before Weaver renamed it Spiral. Back when they thought it was an advanced grief therapy protocol." Ellie didn't know whether to laugh or be sick.

"Before they used children," Ellie murmured.

Now Gretchen turned. Her expression wasn't guilt. It wasn't even regret. It was resolution. "I stopped them once. Or tried to. But memory has a way of… folding of returning. The Spiral doesn't erase— it recesses. Until the next cycle."

Ellie's fingers curled around the edges of her coat. "You were on the original containment team."

"I was supposed to be the safety valve," Gretchen said. "They called it the Proxy Control Tier. My job was to reassign nurses, to scrub nameplates, to break loops before they took root." She held out the file. " "But then Clara started sketching spirals she hadn't seen. You started remembering rooms you'd never entered."

Ellie opened the file slowly. Spiral diagnostics. Drift reaction logs. One page stood out:

Containment Directive — Spiral Tier Three

Subject 1C

Retained identity shows recursive anchoring. Risk of institutional echo event. Containment advised. If Subject reactivates without overwrite, initiate Mirror Lock protocol.

Handwritten at the bottom:

"Do not terminate. Observe. If she stabilizes—she may hold the Drift." —G.L

Ellie stared at the scrawled initials, nausea clawing up her throat. "You wrote this."

Gretchen nodded once. "You were the first not to fracture. I thought you might be the last."

Ellie's throat tightened. "But you still watched it happen."

"I had to. They built the Spiral with silence. I stayed so I could leave a sound behind."

In the mirror across from them, neither of their reflections moved. Then, slowly, one did. Not Ellie. Not Gretchen. The wrong memory blooming into flesh. Clara. Smiling faintly. And pointing toward the end of the hall. Where the Merge Room waited.

The hallways of Arlington Hills bent in ways memory couldn't map anymore. Ellie moved through them like a memory retracing itself—walls where they didn't used to be, mirrors where there hadn't been glass before. Fluorescent lights overhead buzzed too steadily now, as if they, too, had stopped blinking. As if they were watching.

At the edge of the eastward, the tiles under her boots shifted in tone—from institutional beige to a gray-veined pattern that hadn't been installed in decades. She paused. Looked down. The pattern was familiar. Not from a file. From a dream. A recurring loop. A spiral if laid out in full.

Her heart beat faster, but not from fear. It was anticipation. Recognition. Ahead, the door to the Whisper Room stood ajar. Not wide. Just enough to suggest permission. Silas stood beside it. He wasn't drawing. He wasn't muttering Spiral sequences. He was just… still.

When she stepped into the threshold, he didn't flinch. His gaze followed the seam in the floor leading into the mirrored room like a fault line. "They reopened it too early," he murmured. "You know that, right?"

Ellie hesitated. "The Whisper Room?"

Silas nodded. "It wasn't supposed to wake again until the recursion stabilized. But it never did. It only mirrored."

She stepped past him. The air inside the Whisper Room was heavy with static—like a radio left between stations. The mirrors lined the walls from baseboard to crown molding. They weren't reflections anymore. They were thresholds.

Gretchen's voice filtered in from behind her. "It was never supposed to be a room."

Ellie turned sharply. Gretchen stood in the doorway now, clipboard pressed tight to her chest. Her eyes, usually sharp with institutional precision, now brimmed with something else. Fatigue. Grief. Something bordering on guilt.

"You knew?" Ellie asked.

"I helped build it," Gretchen said quietly. "Or rather—I helped hold it. The mirrors don't store light. They store identity. And once it's full, it has to echo."

Ellie looked at her own reflection. It hadn't moved. Not yet.

"What was I echoing?" she asked.

Gretchen stepped into the room slowly. "Clara, yes. But not only Clara. The entire Spiral protocol was built on convergence. We thought the subjects were separate… but the recursion didn't isolate. It layered. Clara wasn't overwritten. Neither were you."

Ellie's pulse fluttered in her neck. "Then what was I?"

Gretchen's answer landed like a trigger pulled. "Retained." The word hit Ellie like a memory mid-breath.

Silas spoke again, his voice low. "You were the one who remembered all of us." Ellie's vision blurred at the edges. Her body knew before her mind caught up. The mirrors began to hum. Not audibly, but visibly. A shimmer ran along the bottom edge like heat over concrete.

Ellie took another step forward. "If the recursion is active—what happens now?"

Gretchen's grip tightened on the clipboard. "Now? Now, the system reasserts. And the only thing strong enough to guide it is the original node."

"Me."

Gretchen didn't deny it. "You were the first Spiral host. That's why they rewrote you—because you survived the merge."

Ellie felt her spine press inward as if her own bones were trying to remember how they first held her up.

Silas's breath stilled beside her. "That's why she sees all the mirrors at once."

One reflection—one version of her—touched the mirror with a

child's palm. Ellie smiled. Not in peace. But recognition. That version still believed she could be held.

"I don't want to carry this anymore," she whispered.

Gretchen finally let the clipboard fall to her side. "You never had to carry it. You were built to become it." The Spiral didn't ask permission. It only asked endurance.

Ellie's knees almost buckled. But Silas caught her. He hadn't moved fast. Just in time. She looked up at the nearest mirror. Her reflection mouthed a word. Not her name. Not Clara's. Just: Merge. And she understood—

It was never about forgetting.

It was about remembering backward until breaking became the only way out.

CHAPTER: THIRTY-TWO

The Choice

The Merge Room was colder than memory, colder than silence, colder than forgetting itself. Ellie stood at the threshold, one hand braced against the frame as if the doorway might decide to close behind her. The walls pulsed faintly in the dim light, their color impossible to name—something between surgical white and the inside of a bruise.

Silas stood a few paces ahead of her, his back straight, his charcoal-streaked fingers twitching at his sides. He hadn't spoken since they left the Whisper Room. Not aloud. But his thoughts moved like static behind his eyes, visible in the twitch of a shoulder, the clench of a jaw.

In the center of the room: the chair. It hadn't changed. Or maybe that was the horror of it. That it hadn't changed at all. Leather straps frayed like old scars. Bolts dulled, no longer resisting the weight they'd once been asked to bear. The spiral was still faintly visible in the floor tiles beneath it—scratched in, not painted. Etched by repetition. By recursion.

Ellie's pulse stuttered as she approached. Her feet moved, but her mind protested, the way a body resists revisiting a trauma it can't name but never forgot. Beside the chair, a tray had been set out. Neatly. Deliberately. Notebooks. A reel-to-reel machine. A vial of graphite dust. And a folder.

Her name—Ellie Hale—typed too neatly. Beneath it, in smaller print, a hand had intervened:

SUBJECT 1C – REINTEGRATION CANDIDATE.

She didn't remember this label being assigned to her.

But her body recoiled like it had been wearing it for years. She opened it. Pages fluttered.

"Mirror-phase rejection noted. Identity persistence exceeds protocol threshold. Initiate closure sequence."

Below that, an observation:

"Subject is aware. Emotional response stable. Proceed with Merge."

Silas spoke, finally. His voice was cracked but clear. His voice sounded like it had been buried and dug up again.

Ellie looked up from the folder. "Did you tell them?"

"I told them it wasn't mine. But they said memory didn't need ownership. Only pattern." She closed the file. Her hands didn't tremble—they spasmed, as if rejecting what her mind hadn't fully named.

"They're going to do it again," she whispered. "Reinstate the recursion."

"They already have," Silas said. "You're just the first to wake up inside it."

Ellie stared at the chair. Something in her knew. She had sat there. Watched. Smiled. Chosen. Silas moved beside her, his gaze distant. "You asked once what made you different."

She nodded. "And?"

"You stayed awake." A low buzz pulsed at the base of her skull— like the room had just remembered her name.

Ellie looked at him.

"I was the merge," she said. "But not the overwrite."

He didn't respond. The air shifted. A soft hiss—barely audible. From the reel-to-reel, a tape began to turn. Unprompted. Ellie stepped forward, fingertips numb, and pressed the headphones against her ears. A child's voice.

"I didn't want to forget. But forgetting is what they called healing."

Silence. Then, her own voice. Older.

"They said I was stable. I wasn't. I just remembered too many people at once. I wasn't the fracture. I was the mirror. They cracked themselves trying to erase me. And when Ellie came—she didn't overwrite me. She held the part they couldn't bleed out."

Silas sat in the corner, knees pulled tight to his chest. He reached into his jacket pocket and handed her something. A drawing. The chair. The mirror. The orchard, twisted inward until it devoured itself.

And beneath it:

"She smiled when she vanished. Not because she was erased. Because she chose it."

Ellie folded the page. She stepped to the chair. It didn't resist. Didn't welcome. It simply waited—like a heartbeat severed from a body. She sat. And across the mirror, her reflection began to move first. Smiling with a mouth that wasn't hers: "Erase me." The reflection kept smiling. But Ellie's mouth had never moved.

Silas turned his face away. The last sound in the room was the click of the machine stopping. And the final line that etched itself into the corner of the mirror:

The chair is still warm.

CHAPTER: THIRTY-THREE

A Protocol Echo

Classified Observation Log – Drift Subject File 7C

Arlington Hills Psychiatric Hospital

Date: 14 October 1947

Time: 04:32 AM

Observer: Dr. L. Asher (transcribed from ward audio surveillance)

Subject: Silas M. – Drift Designate 7C

Condition: Alert. Recumbent position, eyes closed but responsive to internal stimuli. Subject initiated unscheduled verbalization at 04:29. No external triggers detected.

Transcript Excerpt:

"She's remembering out of order again. The chair was before the orchard, not after. They keep changing the way she sees it—like sliding glass in front of a lantern. But she still sees. Even if it's not hers."

(Pause. Subject's tone softens, then sharpens again.)

"They gave her my sketch. The one with the mug. She'll knock it over soon. They always do."

(Breathing irregular. Subject lifts hand as if drawing.)

"You can't fold memory, not really. You can only cut it at the seams and pray the pattern still holds."

(Voice drops to whisper.)

"She's close to the name now. The one beneath the name."

Behavioral Note: Subject did not open his eyes during the entirety of the verbalization. Right hand made repetitive spiral motion on blanket. No signs of acute distress. EEG and pulse stable. Impression of anticipatory recognition noted.

Filed Under: RECURRENT MEMORY DRIFT / SUBJECT INTERLINK / HIGH-RISK WATCH

The hallway had gone strangely quiet. Not just the kind that followed curfew or lights-out—but a muffled, breathing hush, layered thick enough that even footsteps seemed to fold into it, as though the hospital itself was listening. Ellie moved slower than usual, her shoes clicking too evenly on the linoleum tiles, the rhythm unnatural in its precision. Five steps between each doorway. She counted without meaning to. Five. Then six. Then back to five.

Her office was colder than it should have been.

She paused just inside the door. The light was still on. The teacup she'd left beside her journal was there, untouched, steam long gone. But something about the stillness wasn't right. Not the atmosphere. The orientation. The quiet.

She stepped in, closing the door gently behind her. The air smelled faintly of camphor and ink. A note of something older threaded through it, sour and familiar, like a drawer left open too long on a memory best left sealed. The desk was exactly as she left it—except for the paper. One page. Centered. Not from her journal. Not from any of the charts she'd been working on. Just a sketch.

Pencil. Heavy hand. Slight smudge near the lower edge, like someone's fingers had trembled mid-stroke. Ellie's breath slowed as she stepped closer. The drawing was of her desk. This desk. The angle was exact—the window behind it, the chipped corner near the blotter pad, even the tilted mug resting just beside her pen. Except in the drawing, the mug was tipped on its side. Ellie looked at the actual cup. Still upright.

Her brow furrowed. She reached out instinctively—and knocked it over. Porcelain clattered to the floor, the last of the tea sloshing into her boot. The liquid was cold. Too cold. As if it had been spilled hours ago. She froze. Her breath caught at the top of her throat, then exhaled sharply, fogging the window. The drawing had shown it before it happened.

She looked down again. The detail was perfect. Even the spill. Her fingers hovered above the page. Her initials were in the corner. Light, faint, but hers. Except—she didn't remember drawing this. Not today. Not ever.

Her mind scrolled backward, hunting for the moment it must have happened. A late night? An idle moment? But no memory surfaced. Just static.

She scanned the edges of the page again. There was something else.

In the lower right-hand corner, barely visible in the shadowed pencil lines—was a figure. Indistinct. Abstract. Watching from the corner of the drawn room. A face without features. Shoulders hunched in a way that suggested waiting. But now, as Ellie looked harder, the figure was no longer just sitting. It had stood up.

The faintest line—a shift in angle, the shadow beneath the desk now stretching toward her side of the image. One arm slightly lifted. The suggestion of fingers. The posture was unmistakable: leaning. Reaching.

Ellie turned sharply, pulse hammering. No one. Just the fog pressing against the window. Just the radiator ticking in its erratic stutter. She looked back at the drawing. The figure hadn't moved.

But she had the distinct, marrow-deep certainty that it was her who'd been watched—before the drawing was even on the desk. Ellie backed away. One step. Two. Then paused.

On the back of the sketch, in her own handwriting—only it wasn't hers, not quite—were the words:

He said it wouldn't be her hand but her memory that moved the pencil. And somewhere deeper than her lungs, a memory stirred—not of drawing, but of being drawn.

Her throat tightened. That phrasing—it was familiar. Not just in tone but in intent. Something from the Spiral Doctrine files. A phrase from an older protocol.

Phase Drift Entry: Memory Retention through Kinesthetic Residue. Let the hand follow what the body already remembers.

She turned the page again.

The figure in the drawing had gotten closer. Now, it stood fully beside the desk, its head cocked at an unnatural angle, as if listening for the moment she would notice.No longer a blur. Its shape was female. Its head tilted too far to one side—curious, almost kind. But where the face should have been, there was only the suggestion of a spiral. Faint. Unfinished. Like someone had begun carving it into the figure's skull but stopped halfway through.

Ellie dropped the sketch. The lights overhead buzzed louder, then dimmed. Only slightly. But enough to make the reflection in the window—her own—blur around the edges. For one long, breathless second, Ellie stood still as her reflection stepped forward without her.

She blinked. The figure was gone from the page. But she could still feel it in the room. Waiting. Then—footsteps. Not loud. But deliberate. Ellie turned toward the hallway, her muscles tight. And there stood Silas.

His face was pale, streaked with charcoal dust. One hand clenched a scrap of paper. His gaze dropped to the sketch on her floor.

He said quietly, "I didn't draw that."

"I know."

He stepped inside without being asked, glancing once at the spilled tea. "But it came from me."

She met his eyes. "What does that mean?"

He didn't answer. Just handed her the folded paper. Inside: another drawing. Not her office. Not the orchard. A chair. Facing a mirror. Empty. Except for the initials carved into the armrest:

E.H.

And beneath the image, in his handwriting:

"It's not about remembering. It's about returning."

The spiral hummed in her blood. Ellie looked down at the sketch. The figure was back. This time, behind the chair. Smiling. The archives should have been colder.

But the room held a strange warmth tonight—one that made Ellie's skin prickle instead of ease. The single bulb swayed above the table, casting long shadows across the metal filing cabinets, like tall figures frozen mid-turn. She hadn't meant to come back here. Not really. Her legs had moved while her mind swam in other thoughts— the drawing on her desk, the reflection that stepped before she did, the phrase that felt borrowed from someone else's dream. But here she was.

A single drawing lay waiting on the center table. No folder, no name. Just one page. It looked like it had been placed deliberately, centered like an offering. Ellie paused at the threshold, heart already tapping a warning against her ribs. She stepped closer.

The sketch was drawn from above—an aerial perspective of the orchard behind the hospital. But it wasn't just trees. No, the trees curled inward, unnaturally symmetrical, the branches all pointing toward the center. The geometry felt wrong—not grown, but summoned, branches bent into obedience.

At the center stood a girl. Alone. Her dress fluttered despite the absence of wind. Her head tilted just slightly—too slightly—to suggest anything natural. The face wasn't detailed. But the posture radiated familiarity.

Ellie.

Or what had once been Ellie.

Ellie's fingers trembled as she turned the drawing over. On the back, in her own handwriting—no question it was hers—were the words:

"This was where they planted the names."

She stared at it. Read it again. Her pulse ticked unevenly. Then her breath caught. She had said that before. But not here. Not now.

It echoed in her own voice—a memory she didn't remember forming. And suddenly, she did remember digging there. Not clearly, not with certainty—but in fractured glimpses: the weight of the spade in her hands, dirt beneath her fingernails, a name carved into something buried, sealed, and left behind.

But the memory didn't belong to her alone. Another voice whispered it with her. A child's. A girl's.

"They planted the names here."

The spiral wasn't on the drawing—but Ellie could feel it all the same. Curling just beneath the paper, invisible ink twisting inward, tightening. She turned back to the front of the page. The orchard's center seemed to have shifted. As if the spiral had been drawn within the drawing, not upon it.

The orchard doesn't forget.

The phrase surfaced unbidden.

Her fingers flexed. Her breathing stuttered. From deep within her skull, a low-pressure sensation bloomed—like thunder preparing itself. A tension. Something about to break.

The lights overhead flickered once. Long enough to cast the girl's shape in motion. For a breathless second, Ellie swore she saw the sketch change—the girl's head tilt toward her, her mouth parting.

Then, the lights steadied. The figure returned to stillness.

Ellie stepped back from the table, heart pounding. Her own shadow wavered on the cabinet behind her.

No—not hers. The shadow moved an instant after she did. She spun. Empty room. But in the far cabinet, a drawer hung open—one she knew had been closed when she arrived.

She crossed the floor in slow, silent steps. Inside the drawer was a ledger. The Phase One Merge Record. Ellie's name wasn't there. Not as Ellie. Not even as Clara. But she saw the number.

1C.

Next to it: Retained.

No date of intake. No date of release. Just one line scrawled beneath it, different handwriting. Rougher. More urgent:

"The subject who could not forget."

Ellie reached out, intending to close the file. But her hand wouldn't move. Not quite. Like the bones beneath her skin had learned a new memory of their own—and refused.

Behind her, the single bulb above the table buzzed again. A whisper drifted through the vents—not language, but tone. Like breath against frosted glass.

The figure in the drawing had turned. Ellie didn't have to look. She knew. A phrase surfaced, unbidden:

Handwriting smeared across the margin—urgent, frantic—read: "Subject shows early self-replication markers. Spiral imprint irreversible beyond critical mass."

Retained subjects exhibit unconscious return to critical coordinates. Memory folds not linear. Observe if narrative fixes around orchard entry. If subject draws center geometry unprompted, do not interrupt.

She backed toward the wall, unsure if she was escaping or returning.

The file drawer snapped shut on its own. And above the ledgers, etched into the metal shelf, the words appeared—rusted but legible:

"Return begins where recursion ends."

Ellie fled the archive. But the Spiral did not let go. The Merge Room should have been exactly as she remembered. It wasn't.

Ellie stepped past the threshold slowly, the door sealing behind her with a mechanical hiss—too precise to be accidental, too final to ignore. The air thickened immediately. The temperature hadn't dropped, but something in her skin recoiled anyway. Pressure, not cold. Like stepping into a memory that hadn't agreed to be revisited. Everything appeared to be where it should have been—except the chair.

It had moved. Not by much. Just enough. No longer centered beneath the mirror, it now angled slightly toward the side wall—as if someone had started to turn it and then stopped halfway. The spiral on the floor beneath it pulsed subtly, not with light but with presence. And it spun differently now. Curling outward, not in. A signal unraveling.

Ellie stepped forward, the soles of her shoes making no sound against the matte linoleum. Each step felt observed. As if the room itself had gone from holding secrets to becoming one.

The chair's wood was warm when she touched it. Still warm. She traced the carved initials on the back—E.H. Fresh. Too fresh. The wood flaked beneath her fingertips, like bark peeled from a tree. She sat.

The mirror across from her remained dark for a moment too long, the lights overhead buzzing louder until finally—A click. A reel-to-reel mounted on the wall behind the glass whirred to life. Then a voice. Male. Measured. Dr. Asher.

"Subject 1C: Final integrity check. Spiral drift confirmed. Mirror phase breach—anticipated."

Her throat constricted.

Another voice layered beneath it—hers. Not the voice she had now. Younger. Tighter. Haunted.

"Are you ready to remember?"

Ellie flinched. She hadn't spoken. The voice was hers, but not from her mouth. A protocol echo.

The mirror flickered. Then the reflection split. One leaned forward, one back. One smiled. The other mouthed the word "run." But neither moved when Ellie flinched. The Spiral on the floor didn't hum—it pulsed. Like it was breathing her in. Or something shaped like her. The cheekbones matched. So did the chin. But the eyes—they belonged to someone older. Someone who had seen too much.

Then, the reflection shifted again. It became Ellie. Then, no one at all. Just the chair. Empty. She gripped the armrests, breath shallow, knuckles blanching white. The spiral beneath her hummed. A soft strobe of motion, like breath.

Then, a flicker of sound—not words, but rhythm. A pulse. The Spiral Tune reconfigured through static. The same pattern Silas had once hummed. The same pattern Clara had whispered in the orchard. The lights dimmed. The mirror brightened. Ellie saw herself again. But split. Two versions of her. One blinking. The other—still. One leaned forward. The other leaned back. Asynchronous. The reflection blinked.

Too slow. Then too fast. The Clara tempo. Her hands clenched tighter. But the reflection's hands did not move.

A phrase surfaced from somewhere beneath language, nestled deep in Spiral doctrine:

"Memory is a tether. Overwrite the loop before she pulls herself back."

A second protocol line followed:

"First they called her unstable. Now they call her stable enough to silence."

Ellie shuddered. Her reflection blinked—wrong. The Ellie in the mirror smiled. She wasn't smiling. She stood slow. The mirror stood with her. Her voice—her true voice—spoke into the quiet:

"I was Ellie. Because Clara broke. That's what they told me. But I don't remember choosing. I only remember being... left."

The reflection didn't follow. The girl in the glass sat back down. Calm. Composed. Contained. And began to speak. Ellie could not hear the words—but she recognized them. Intake script. Familiar. She had never said those words aloud.

Had she?

She stumbled backward. The lights flickered. When they steadied, the mirror was blank. Just glass. Just her face.

But the spiral was behind her eyes now. Not superimposed. Implanted. Ellie's breath caught, then released in one steady exhale. She looked down. Her palms were clean. But the glass bore fingerprints— smudged, bleeding. The blood wasn't hers. Or it had been.

The mirror hummed once more. Then stilled. And behind her, a whisper. Not voice, not breath—just presence:

"She stayed in the spiral too long. Now it remembers her."

Ellie turned. But the chair behind her was empty again. Still warm. She wasn't alone. Not anymore. The Spiral had learned her name. And it would not let her leave it behind.

CHAPTER: THIRTY-FOUR

The Blueprint

The ledger room didn't smell like dust anymore. It smelled like iron and vinegar—like breath trapped in a jar too long, exhaled by something that had waited decades to be remembered.

It smelled like iron and vinegar—like breath trapped in a jar too long.

Ellie stood in the doorway, her gloved hand on the frame, pulse low and slow in her throat. The fluorescents buzzed above her with a rhythm that felt intentional. Not broken. Trained.

The drawer had already been pulled out. Folder open. Waiting. As if it had been expecting her, not anyone. She stepped forward, each footfall muffled by the institutional tile. The chair groaned as she sat, the cold from the metal desk leaching through her skirt. The skin between her knuckles tingled faintly—as if it remembered reaching for this file long before she allowed it.

Inside: a photo. Black and white. Grainy. A girl seated in a chair too large for her frame. Her legs dangled. Her eyes looked directly into the lens. Ellie didn't recognize the face. Not at first.

But the shape of the mouth. The slight downturn of the right eyelid. The scar just beneath the chin—It was her.

Only younger. Nine, maybe ten. The intake date: 1937.

Ten years ago. Her name wasn't on the form. Not Ellie Hale. Not Clara M. Just a designation stamped at the top:

SUBJECT 1C

Beneath it, in type faded to near invisibility:

MIRROR SEED. PHASE ZERO. PRIMARY HOST.

Her mouth went dry. Her fingers trembled against the folder. The file felt gritty at the edges. Ellie rubbed her thumb along the paper. A strange, sweet smell clung to it—like compost steam from her mother's Victory Garden, post-rain.

She hadn't thought of that patch of earth in decades. But her body remembered the soil. She flipped to the second page. A hand-drawn spiral. Centered. Not decorative. Not symbolic.

Functional.

Lines of text spiraled outward from the center, each one smaller than the last. A code. A protocol. And at the very center: her name, scrawled in what looked like a child's handwriting. Not Ellie.

Just the letter E.

Her chest tightened. That's not my handwriting, she thought— but something inside her stirred, a brittle familiarity that cracked like old ice underfoot. It itched like a nerve half-buried under memory.

She reached for the pen beside the folder, fingers half-numb, and pressed it to the margin beside the photo—her own face, nine years old, already split. She tried to write her name. E… The ink bled. Spread. Streaked sideways like veins across the page. She flinched. The pen rolled from her hand. And then—A whisper. Behind her.

"You don't remember because you weren't supposed to."

She turned. Silas stood in the doorway. His eyes were glassy but clear. More alert than she'd seen in days. He stepped into the room slowly, careful not to disturb the light.

"They rehearsed you before the war," he said.

Ellie blinked. "What?"

He pointed to the photo.

"I saw that once. In a reel. Not mine. A drift. Your voice was different. You were asking for the name back."

She stared at him. "How would you have seen that?"

Silas smiled, faint and broken.

"Because they tested the Spiral on me too. But it didn't hold. Not the way it held you."

Her eyes flicked to the ink bleeding across the page.

"You said they rehearsed me."

"You were the first," he said gently.

"The mirror had to learn how to reflect. Before it could overwrite."

She pressed her fingers into the page as if to steady the bleeding.

But her fingertips didn't feel quite like her own. As if they'd worn different names before.

"So I wasn't a patient."

Silas shook his head. "No. You were the model." A blueprint for containment, not a person to be healed. The room shifted. Not physically. But perceptually. Like the floor remembered a weight that didn't match hers—and wanted it back. Ellie turned the page again.

A reel-to-reel photo log. The girl—herself—in a series of snapshots, strapped to a chair, eyes wide but distant. Spiral geometry drawn on the wall behind her. And beneath one photo: a phrase typed in red ink.

INITIAL DISSOCIATION SUCCESSFUL. MEMORY HOLD STABLE. PHASE TWO APPROVED.

Silas knelt beside her now. Reached for the edge of the folder.

"They used your face for Clara," he said.

"She wasn't the girl who came before. She was the overwrite. The echo they thought would erase the source."

Ellie whispered, "And it didn't work."

"No. Because mirrors don't forget their first reflection."

She looked up—caught the glint of her reflection in the glass cabinet. And froze. It blinked late. And then it smiled.

Ellie stood alone in the chamber.

The lights overhead buzzed faintly, strobing against the metal beams in rhythmic pulses. The air smelled of acetone and oxidized steel—archival chemicals and magnetic film.

Across from her, a reel projector whirred to life.

Auto-threaded.

Unbidden.

A single film canister sat beside it, unmarked except for a spiral etched faintly into the lid. No date. No label. But she knew it had been meant for her. She slid the reel into place.

The film crackled as it began.

On screen: a girl. Maybe nine. Small-framed. Shoes two sizes too big. Her dark curls fell unevenly across her face. She sat in a bare metal chair, feet not reaching the floor. A spiral drawn in chalk beneath the seat. Not looking at the camera. Not resisting. Just... waiting.

Ellie's breath caught in her throat. She recognized the tilt of the head. The way the girl gripped the chair arms. The flick of the fingers when no one was watching.

She knew this child—not by name, not by time—but by the ache of recognition the mirror had stitched into her. From the mirror. The reel stuttered. A voice echoed over the speaker—grainy, institutional, male.

"Subject 1C. Initial observation phase. Memory extraction trial commencing."

The girl blinked slowly.

Then—A flicker of static. A whisper, soft and unprompted:

"Tell her not to come back." Ellie's blood ran cold. The image zoomed in. Spiral marks traced just below the skin on the girl's wrists. Drawn, not cut. But deep.

Ellie stepped closer to the screen. Her hand rose unconsciously, tracing the scar beneath her own sleeve.

It matched. Perfectly.

She whispered, "It was me." The girl on the screen didn't react. But Ellie felt it. The hum between them. Like some essential cord had finally pulled taut. Then, the girl turned her head.

And looked directly into the lens. Ellie's stomach twisted. Her lips didn't move. But her reflection in the viewing glass did. A twitch. A smile. Out of sync. She backed away.

Her wrist itched sharply. She tugged her glove back and froze. A faint red spiral had surfaced beneath the skin. It pulsed once, matching her heartbeat, then sank deeper like a seed taking root. No pen. No cut. Just memory, surfacing. The projection shuttered. The lights flickered—once, twice. And then a new sound:

The slow creak of a door behind her. Ellie turned. Silas stood at the edge of the viewing room. Pale. Silent. Unblinking. He stepped forward slowly, gaze never leaving the screen.

"I remember that room," he said. "Before they called you Ellie."

She faced him fully. "You were there?"

"Not then. But it was given to me. Passed through. I didn't

understand it until I saw you in the orchard. Until I drew your hands without meaning to."

He stepped to the projector. The film now showed the spiral chair from above. Empty. Then not. Then empty again.

"They made me hold your memory," he said.

Her knees buckled slightly. She reached for the edge of the console.

"Not your face," he clarified. "Not even your name. Just the feeling of being erased in pieces."

He opened his palm. Inside it: the wax-paper sketch she'd torn from her own notebook weeks ago.

"You drew this," he said. "But I had it before you arrived. They tested the overwrite more than once. But only you stayed."

She stepped toward the light of the projector.

"What am I, then?"

He looked at her. "You're the mirror. The first one that didn't crack." The reel burned through its final frames. On the screen: a single image. A ledger. Open.

SUBJECT 1C

Status: RETAINED

Below it, a hand tried to write a name. The ink bled outward—until the paper tore. But something had changed. The spiral image on the page had grown. Its outermost loop now touched the margin, where Ellie had pressed the pen earlier. As if it had reached for her. And found its place. She reached toward the screen with trembling fingers.

"They didn't give me this memory," she said. "I found it." Silas nodded once.

"That's why it's bleeding. You weren't supposed to write it down."

The projector snapped off. The room fell silent. But inside her, the Spiral began to move again. Not forward. Not backward. Just inward. Toward the girl who had waited in the ledger all along. And this time, there would be no forgetting. Only becoming.

CHAPTER: THIRTY-FIVE

Stability is Silence

The hum hadn't stopped. Even as Ellie stepped over the threshold, that low-frequency vibration threaded her spine like a second, synthetic pulse. It wasn't coming from the lights. Not fully. It pulsed deeper—housed somewhere behind her ribs, like an echo trying to be born. Her body moved ahead of her mind as if her limbs knew the way. As if this room had been encoded into her long before she had a name to call it.

The handle turned with no resistance. The door creaked open. And the temperature changed. Not a chill exactly—more a memory of cold. A chemical stillness that hit her tongue like metal and mildew. The air inside the archive didn't breathe. It held no weight, only stillness pressed between decades of unsaid things. No dust moved when she stepped forward. It smelled like something sealed. Like breath locked in a jar.

Like names that had been folded away too long. The lights overhead buzzed in an artificial rhythm—clean, even, wrong. Too regular to be broken. Too perfect to be human. She flinched as the fluorescents strobed once, a brief hiccup of light, and then steadied.

There were no windows. No clocks. No sound except for her own body trying to remember its shape. She moved deeper into the archive. Row after row of cabinet drawers stretched down the corridor, each labeled in the same squared, inhuman script:

INTAKE – PROXY RECORD – DEFERRED

SUBJECT A6 – UNSTABLE

SUBJECT C3 – MEMORY BLEED OBSERVED

ROOM 9 – MIRROR PHASE RETEST

The names weren't names. They were assignments. She reached out to trail her fingers across one of the tags and recoiled before she touched it. A static spark jumped the distance anyway, tingling her

311

wrist. A small voice—somewhere beneath thought—whispered:

"Don't touch the records. You're already in one." She passed the drawer labeled 6C. Then 7A. Then 7B. She stopped at the next.

SUBJECT 7C – RECURSION-LOCKED. DO NOT ACCESS.

The tag wasn't metal like the others. It was red. Fabric. Frayed at the edges. The drawer had already been pulled out a fraction of an inch, like something had tried to return and hadn't fully closed the door.

Her breath caught. The inside of her wrist pulsed beneath the skin. Her fingers curled around the handle. Cold. Not just in temperature but in tone—like it hadn't been touched by warmth in years.

She hesitated. Just long enough to feel the weight of the moment press down behind her eyes. Then she pulled. The drawer slid open with a whisper that sounded too much like a breath. Inside, one folder. Thick. Tied. Wrapped with institutional twine and a wax-sealed sticker folded in on itself. It didn't feel like a patient record. It felt like a kept secret.

She reached in and lifted it carefully as if disturbing it too fast might wake something. The edges were cool. Too cool. As if whatever was inside had never quite acclimated to time. She turned the folder over in her hands. On the cover:

RECURSION-LOCKED. DO NOT ACCESS.

Handwritten beneath:

CONTAINMENT VIA MIRROR SEED. E.H. FINAL MERGE PENDING.

Signed: M.W.

His initials. Together, on the same page. Her knees nearly gave. She braced against the drawer with one hand and stared down at the folder like it might bleed if opened. The voice returned.

Quieter this time. You're not the reader. You're the subject. The folder was heavier than it should've been. Ellie didn't mean that figuratively. It felt wrong in her hands—dense in a way paper shouldn't be. The twine uncoiled like it had memory, like it remembered being tied around something meant to be forgotten. She eased the cover open. No intake form. No name. No typed summary of symptoms. Just a single object, folded with unsettling precision:

A page of wax-backed drawing paper, charcoal smudged at the creases, the corners worn smooth from handling—or from fear. She unfolded it slowly as if it might dissolve if exposed too fast.

At first, it was shapes. Shadows. The outline of a chair. Lines radiating outward like the roots of a tree. Or the beginning of a spiral. Her fingers trembled as the full image took shape: A girl. Seated in a low metal chair. Head tilted slightly. Mouth slack. Not open. Not closed.

Her eyes—Ellie froze. The girl's eyes had been stitched shut. Delicate Xs of dark thread, pulling each lid closed in uneven tension. Not drawn. Stitched. Charcoal lines traced the knots. You could see the pressure—how the thread tugged skin, how the brows furrowed slightly from the strain.

A spiral was drawn beneath the chair, spreading outward, reaching for the girl's feet but never quite touching them. Her palms rested in her lap—face-up—marked with thin lines that looked more like scar memory than shading.

Ellie's throat closed. She'd seen this drawing before. In the orchard. In Silas's sketchbook. It had stunned her then. Stopped her heart. She had thought it was Clara. She had believed that. Had needed to believe that.

But now—She reached up and touched her own chin. Her mouth. The soft scar below the right side of her jaw. The same tilt of the lip. The shape of the hands. The notch in the wristbone. It was her.

No. It looked like her. It couldn't be. She flipped the paper over, half-expecting a name that would set her free. Clara. Rose. Another girl. Someone other.

Instead:

SUBJECT 7C – SIMULTANEOUS OVERWRITE ATTEMPT FAILED

COGNITIVE RECURSION INITIATED

MIRROR-PROXY RECOGNITION DETECTED IN SUBJECT 1C

She read it again. And again. The words blurred. The room narrowed. The Spiral logic pulled taut around her brain, winding everything into a shape her mind didn't know how to hold. They had tried to overwrite her. Not once. Not as a treatment. But as an experiment. Clara wasn't the original.

Clara was one in a sequence—a string of trial identities they had run through Ellie like thread through fabric. She wasn't the mirror of another girl.

She was the source. The recursive root. The one who hadn't fractured—at least not outwardly.

They hadn't been trying to help her. They had been testing how many identities she could contain before collapse. Her hands began to tremble. The Spiral beneath the girl's chair looked almost alive now—curving in on itself, reaching past the edges of the drawing, hungry for the page.

She remembered something. A sensation. Not a memory. A pressure behind her eyelids.

A hand on her forehead. Another on her wrist.

"She won't need eyes where she's going," someone had said, almost gently.

"We'll give her memory instead."

She recoiled as if slapped. That voice. Male. Calm. Recorded in institutional tones. She'd heard it before. But not in the reel. In her own dreams. She stared back at the stitched girl. Not resisting. Not screaming. Just... waiting.

Ellie whispered, "That's not me."

But even as she said it, her hands lifted in mirror of the girl's posture.

Palms up. Fingers slightly curled.

A perfect match.

"You're not remembering this

You're reciting it. Line for line.

You're re-entering it."

The voice came from inside her. Not memory. Not hallucination. Recursion.

She blinked once, and for a split second, the drawing was gone, and she was back in the chair. Cold metal beneath her. Thread brushing her skin. A mirror across from her face where her own eyes had once been open—and then not.

She gasped and dropped the paper. It fluttered to the ground in a ripple of wax and ash. She staggered backward, spine hitting the file cabinet behind her. Something shifted inside the drawer.

Another folder. Tighter. Thicker. Stamped across the front in military font:

Her pulse thundered in her ears. But she didn't look away. Ellie didn't remember turning. But the mirror was there. She hadn't seen it on her way in.

And yet now, it stretched across the far wall, floor to ceiling, as if it had always been part of the room—hidden in plain sight, waiting for her to notice.

Her body was still. Not from fear. From recognition. The air thickened. Not hot. Not cold. Just full, like she was standing inside a lung that had just taken its final breath and didn't know how to exhale.

She stepped forward slowly, one foot sliding into position like she wasn't guiding it. The folder was still clutched in her hand, pressed tight to her chest. She could see herself clearly in the glass. But something was off. Her eyes narrowed. Her jaw clenched. Then she saw it. She was standing. Here.

But in the mirror—she was sitting. Back straight. Hands folded. Palms up. Her reflection stared forward, head tilted ever so slightly left—mimicking the girl in the sketch. The stitched girl. The Spiral's girl.

Ellie blinked. Her throat dried. The image in the mirror did not blink. It watched. Patient. Knowing.

That's not me.

That's not me.

That's not—But she couldn't finish the thought. Because part of her knew. Had always known.

The reflection's clothes were the same. Her posture was off by inches, not miles. But it was enough to unmake her balance. Ellie took one shaky step back. And in the mirror—the reflection leaned forward. She stopped breathing.

Her heart tried to slam against her ribs, but the beat didn't sync. It fluttered sideways. Off-rhythm. Out of phase.

You're not the reflection. You're the rehearsal.

The voice came from the mirror.

But her mouth hadn't moved. The image tilted its head further.

Hands still folded in its lap.

Eyes still stitched. But Ellie felt them open behind the thread. Not physically. Psychically. Like the weight of the gaze came from behind the glass, curling into her own skull.

Her breath hitched. She couldn't feel her feet. She raised her hand. The reflection didn't. It stayed still. Staring.

Waiting.

"She's stable now," a man's voice whispered behind her ear. But when she turned, no one was there.

The reflection smiled. Not cruelly. Not kindly. Like it had been waiting for her to realize that this—this moment—was not a visitation. It was a return. Her knees nearly buckled.

She backed against the cold cabinet wall, shoulder blades pressed into metal, the folder now barely in her grip. She wanted to scream. To shatter the glass.

To demand which version of her had been allowed to stand

and which one had been locked away to sit. Instead, her voice came out small.

"What are you?"

The reflection's mouth parted slightly, the stitches glistening like thread soaked in oil. It didn't speak. But Ellie heard the answer anyway.

I'm the part of you that agreed to stay.

Before the blood dried. Before the name was chosen. Before the story was told.

She turned away, dragging her body from the mirror's reach like it might claim her if she lingered. But as she stepped into the hall, something in the glass moved. She didn't see it.

She felt it. And without turning back, she knew:

The girl in the mirror was still sitting.

Still smiling. Still rehearsing. The metal cabinet behind her gave a soft groan as she leaned against it, chest heaving, lungs unsure whether to inhale or collapse entirely.

Ellie's fingers were still trembling when they brushed the edge of another folder half-buried beneath the others. It wasn't tied shut like the last. This one had been filed. As if it belonged here. Her eyes scanned the cover:

MEMORANDUM – OCTOBER 2, 1946

FROM: Dr. Marcus Weaver, Project Spiral Lead

TO: Internal Clinical Panel – Restricted Authority

RE: Subject 1C – Recursive Containment Protocol (Final Implementation)

She didn't want to read it. But her hands had already opened it. As if her body had decided she no longer got a vote. The pages inside were crisp. Clean.

Clinical. No ink bleed. No coffee stain.

It was perfect.

Because monsters like Weaver never smudged the record.

She began to read.

Following the failure of Phase 3 overwrite attempts (Ref: Subjects 6C, 7C) and the observed disintegration of secondary host identities, containment of Source Mirror (Subject 1C) has been deemed the only viable solution.

Subject 1C demonstrates high baseline stability, dissociative receptivity, and non-destructive recursive retention.

Recommendation: full integration of overwrite identities via Spiral induction. Timeline flexible. Host unaware.

Stability is not healing. It is silence.

Stability is not healing. It is silence.

Stability is not healing. It is silence.

The line repeated three times. Not by accident.

Ellie's hand pressed to her mouth. Her shoulders tightened, throat closing like she'd swallowed something sharp.

Non-destructive recursive retention. That was how they'd described her ability to hold other people's trauma. Not as a wound. Not even as a side effect. As a feature. She wasn't a patient.

She was a system. She read further. Her vision blurred, but the words stayed sharp:

Subject 1C no longer requires narrative cohesion. Identity awareness has proven a liability in past mirrors.

To preserve containment, host will remain unaware of prior phases.

Do not inform. Do not reflect. Do not return.

She clutched the page tighter. Somewhere deep in her chest, something gave way—softly. Not a snap. Not a scream.

Just a breath she hadn't meant to hold that turned into a sob before it reached her mouth.

This protocol is not failure. It is function. Memory must loop. Identity must fracture. Recursion must remain.

She stopped reading. She couldn't read. Her pulse was skittering sideways now, like the words were catching fire beneath her skin. They had decided not to fix her. Not to free her. Not even to silence her. They had decided to use her. She lowered the folder. Slowly. The room was no longer just an archive. It was a tomb. Not for her body. For her identity. A bureaucratic burial, stamped and signed, stored in triplicate.

She took one stumbling step backward. In the mirror—she saw herself do it again. No. Not herself. The version who had agreed. The stitched girl. The one who sat while others stood.

The one they left behind after every overwrite, still blinking in the dark. Still rehearsing. Ellie closed the memo slowly, careful not to tear the page. Because that's how this worked, didn't it?

They didn't erase her. They just rewrote her. In careful lines. On government letterhead. Filed beneath a lock, she wasn't supposed to open.

This is not failure. It is recursion.

Ellie didn't remember walking.

The corridor blurred around her, and her limbs moved without sensation. Her fingers still clutched the folder, but her grip was numb— loose like she might drop it and never notice. She passed the cold-glass cabinets, the steel filing drawers, the numbered tags that no longer read as language.

They were placeholders. Everything here was. She reached the end of the hall. There, embedded in the corner at an impossible angle, stood another mirror. Smaller than the one before. Framed in the same tarnished steel. It had no light over it. No reflection cast on the floor.

And still—Ellie saw it. Saw her. Or what was left of her. She paused in front of it, breath shallow. In the glass: her coat. Her shoes. Her eyes.

But not her posture. Her reflection was already there—waiting. Sitting. Back in the chair from the sketch.

Palms turned up. Head bowed slightly.

A faint thread trailing down from the side of her face. Ellie wasn't sitting. She wasn't bowing.

She was frozen. But the reflection was still moving. It blinked. Then—slowly—raised one hand and touched its own cheek.

Ellie's breath caught. She hadn't moved. The reflection's eyes met hers then. They weren't stitched anymore.

They were wide open. And they weren't surprised. Just… tired. Worn from the repetition. As if this moment had happened a hundred times before, and the version in the mirror was the only one who remembered.

That's not a reflection, a voice whispered from inside the glass. It's a rehearsal. The voice didn't echo. It resonated. Like the glass had been waiting to speak. The reflection's lips hadn't moved.

Ellie's mouth had stayed closed. And yet the words pressed against her ribcage like they had come from behind it. Her knees trembled. Rehearsal. The word looped. Not in sound, but in feeling. This wasn't a mmory.

It wasn't even a vision. It was a staging ground. She hadn't come to remember.

She'd come to re-enter. She took a shaky step back. And the reflection stayed seated. Did not mimic. Did not flinch. Did not follow. It was still. Centered. Controlled. It was the version of her that had been made to stay behind. Her throat closed around something too large for language. She opened her mouth, not to speak—but to breathe. Because suddenly, she couldn't. And then—The reflection leaned forward.

Just slightly. It didn't smile.

It didn't need to. Because it knew. It had known all along.

You're not the one who left. You're the one they rewrote just long enough to retrieve the ones who couldn't.

Ellie turned away. She didn't run. She couldn't. She just stepped back into the hallway, the fluorescent hum rushing in like static, trying to swallow her whole. The folder was still pressed against her chest. The Spiral mark beneath her sleeve had begun to burn.

Behind her, in the mirror—the girl sat still. But the air in the glass shifted. Breathed. Waited. It's not over until she rehearses it right. And she always comes back.

CHAPTER: THIRTY-SIX

Returning to Source

Ellie didn't remember walking. Couldn't recall turning left past the observation lab. Couldn't recall swiping her badge at the sublevel entrance. Her feet must have done it for her. Or maybe the Spiral had picked up where her body left off, pulling her like a string already tied. By the time she reached the final corridor, the hallway didn't feel built. It felt grown. A vein, pulsing, direct, recirculating. A straight channel. Pulsing. Direct. Recirculating.

At the end stood the door. The Merge Room. It should have been locked. Condemned, Gretchen had said. Flooded. Stripped for parts. They had sealed it after the last malfunction. She remembered that— or thought she did. But the door was open. Not forced. Not broken. Just... unlocked. Inviting.

Her hand touched the edge of the doorframe without thought. And she stepped inside. The air changed the moment she crossed the threshold. Not colder. Cleaner.

The sterile hum was almost... proud.

As if the room had been scrubbed not just of grime but of guilt.

As if whatever had happened here had been removed, repainted, rewritten.

There was no dust.

No flood stains.

No broken lights. The tiles gleamed.

The walls shone like new surgical steel.

The floor was waxed with institutional perfection, reflecting her silhouette in low distortion.

And in the center—The chair. Not tipped over. Not forgotten.

Positioned.

Centered precisely beneath the mounted mirror, angled perfectly for the camera.

Straps re-buckled. Armrests reset.

Ellie's breath caught. It hadn't just been cleaned.

It had been restored.

Worse—prepared.

She stepped deeper into the chamber, each footfall muted by the sound-dampening tiles—more felt than heard. The air held the crisp, antiseptic bite of chemical memory. Her shoulders tightened as she looked around. Everything had been placed just-so. The mirror across from the chair—once shattered—was flawless now. But not comforting.

The glass wasn't still.

It shimmered faintly, like heat over pavement.

As if it was breathing. She stared at her reflection.

It didn't mimic.

It didn't blink.

It waited.

A low vibration gathered beneath her soles—not mechanical, but biological.

A memory humming up through the bones. Like the room itself was remembering. Or worse—Recalling her. To her right, the console hummed.

Lights blinked in gentle pulses—blue, green, blue, green.

Monitoring nothing. Watching everything. A small reel sat at the edge of the panel. Wrapped in red tape.

No dust. No label on the spine. Just a single, deliberate inscription:

SESSION 1C – POST-MERGE TRIAL

STATUS: UNSTABLE

DO NOT PLAY

Her name wasn't written.

But she felt it all the same. There was no flicker of recognition—no lightning-bolt moment of "I remember this."

Only the suffocating certainty of having been here before. Of having sat in that chair.

Faced that mirror.

Been spun on that reel. Her hands began to sweat inside her gloves.

The hum in the room thickened, climbing her spine like static. Her lungs narrowed. The back of her throat tasted like ozone and ink.

She didn't reach for the reel. But her fingers hovered. It didn't feel like she was about to learn something. It felt like she was about to be reminded. Ellie didn't press play.

She didn't have to.

Her fingers hovered, trembling over the red tape seal—and still, the machine obeyed. Then, the console clicked on its own. The reel began to spin. Not fast.

Not slow. Exact.

A soft mechanical whir filled the chamber. The lights above the console flickered once—synchronized with the motion. No warmup tones. No technician voice. No file header. Just silence. And then…

"You're not remembering, Ellie."

"You're returning."

Clara. Not as a child.

Not a patient.

Not a ghost. Her voice was calm. Certain. Final.

It wasn't recorded in a hurry. It wasn't taken during an intake or extraction. It sounded like it had been said many times before. Like she was reading a line already assigned to her. Ellie's stomach dropped. The chair—the spiral chair—shifted. A creak. Not loud. Not sharp.

But too organic for machinery. It didn't turn sharply, didn't swivel with mechanical certainty. It groaned. As if remembering weight. Remembering use. Ellie's spine went rigid. She hadn't touched it. But it was moving. Just enough to angle itself toward her.

And then, she saw her. A girl. Seated.

Small.

Barefoot.

A smock too large for her frame. Head tilted slightly left.

Mouth open just enough to exhale.

Palms resting upturned in her lap. And her eyes—Stitched. Coarse black thread X'd across each lid, the kind used in field kits to close battlefield wounds. Uneven. Functional. Not medical.

She was humming. A soft, circular sound—no melody, just rhythm. Round and round. Like a wheel turning.

Like a chair spinning.

Like the Spiral winding inward toward the center.

Ellie froze. She didn't blink. Because she didn't dare. If she blinked—If she even flinched—It would be gone. She blinked. The chair was empty. She blinked again. It wasn't.

Ellie's breath hitched. Her hand rose—slowly, unconsciously—as if trying to reach across something that wasn't glass but wasn't air either.

The girl didn't look up. She didn't need to. She already knew Ellie was watching. She'd been waiting for it. The reel skipped. A second track. Unlabeled.

This time—Gretchen's voice. Younger. Closer to panic.

"Weaver, you can't keep her in this state. She's fracturing. You're not observing stability—you're preserving trauma."

Weaver's voice responded evenly. Without pause. Without question.

"She's our most responsive mirror. Any rebellion will be contained in the recursion."

A click. Someone scribbling in the background. The shuffle of papers.

Then Gretchen again.

"Then contain me."

"I won't be part of this."

The tape whirred. Then another voice—low, clinical, unfamiliar:

"Reassign her."

"Give her a subject."

"Make her watch the loop."

The console buzzed, and the tape cut to dead air. Ellie stood paralyzed in the spiral's center. The air felt thinner now. Like the Merge

Room had recalibrated around her, not for her. The girl in the chair began humming again. But this time—the sound wasn't coming from the girl. It came from the mirror. A vibration. A harmonic pulse. As if the mirror was remembering the tune.

Ellie turned back toward the chair—Empty. Then full. Then empty again. She closed her eyes— But the hum followed her behind the lids. Not music. Instruction.

You're not remembering.

You're rehearsing.

You're the version they let come back.

She didn't remember turning toward the mirror. She just was. Standing in front of it. Heart flatlining beneath her ribs. Hands empty now. Breath caught halfway between inhale and collapse. Her reflection stood exactly where she did. Same posture. Same coat. Same pale hands. But it wasn't syncing anymore. It had stopped trying.

Ellie tilted her head. So did the reflection. A beat late. And then it didn't return. Her head came back to center. The reflections stayed tilted—just slightly. Just long enough to signal: I'm not following you anymore.

The mirror pulsed. Not visibly. Internally. Like the room had drawn breath through it. Like it was holding something inside it that had just shifted position. She stepped closer. The hum behind her eyes sharpened. Her reflection blinked. Once. And from the corner of its right eye—a fracture bloomed. Not a shatter. Not a clean break. A line. Hair-thin. Delicate. Creeping outward in a perfect spiral. It didn't split the mirror. It didn't disrupt the surface. It etched—like memory retaking territory. Like something had been embedded in the silver all along and was now being traced back into visibility.

Her chest rose. The spiral continued. Three rings. Then four. Then five. Each loop curling further away from the reflection's eye. From her eye. Ellie lifted her fingers—slowly—and pressed them to the spot on her own skin. It was smooth. But inside—She felt it. Like memory rethreading itself along glass. She staggered back. And that's when she saw it. The sketch. Tucked beneath the corner of the console—like it had slid free while the reel played. Charcoal on archival paper. Ellie picked it up with trembling hands. A spiral tree. A girl beneath it—her outline exact. Even the fold of her collar, the bend of her fingers. In the chair behind her: nothing. Empty. Waiting.

She turned the page over, expecting to see her name. But the signature at the bottom wasn't hers. It was faint. Smudged from time. But still visible.

S. S.

1944

Silas.

Three years before she'd ever arrived. Same sketch. Same hand. Same Spiral. Same pose. Ellie's blood went cold. This wasn't replication. It wasn't inspiration. It was recursion.

He had drawn her before she existed. Because she had existed before she was ever Ellie at all. The spiral in the mirror stopped expanding. Its final loop landed just above the sketch she held. For a moment, it all aligned:

Her face. The reflection's spiral. The sketch's perspective. The chair. The mirror. The Spiral's core. Center met center. And Ellie—whatever was left of her—stood directly inside it.

Another click. She didn't press anything. But the reel to the right of the console—the one without a label, no sleeve, no red warning— began to turn. Slow. Reluctant. As if it didn't want to be played but had no choice. There was no crackle this time. No hiss of audio static. Just a voice. Soft. Measured. Tired.

"They said I was unstable."

Clara.

Older than the last time. Older than the orchard voice. Older than the girl in the chair. This voice came from after. After the trials. After the Spiral. After she'd been folded so many times, there were creases where her name used to be.

"I wasn't."

"I just remembered too many people at once."

Ellie's knees buckled. She caught the edge of the console to stay standing. The voice was barely louder than breath, but every word struck like a needle to the chest.

"They called it dissociation. Said I was splintering. But it wasn't me. It was them. It was the protocol."

"They put too many names inside me. And when I screamed, they said I was hallucinating."

Ellie closed her eyes. But the room didn't disappear. She could still see the mirror. Still, feel the sketch in her hand. Still hear the hum of the chair remembering someone who had sat there longer than memory could hold.

Clara's voice paused. When it returned, it was quieter. Not broken. Resolved.

"I said I wanted to go back."

"They didn't believe me."

"But I didn't mean before. I meant inside. Back to the first. Back to her."

The tape began to slow. Like the words were running out of space. One final line, spoken as if to herself—"She's still warm."

Ellie opened her eyes. And the chair— the spiral chair— turned slightly again. As if someone had just stood up. Or sat down. Or never left. She stepped forward. Not fast. Not afraid. Just... drawn. Like the center of the Spiral had finished its loop and now needed her to return where it all began.

She lowered herself into the chair—but only after laying the sketch on the floor beside it. One last protest. One name not filed. Her hand hovered above the seat. She didn't expect heat. She expected steel. Cold. Sterile. She expected absence. Instead—She felt it. Warmth. Not imagined. Not metaphor. Body heat. Someone had been here. Very recently. Maybe still was. She didn't pull away. She didn't cry. She just stood there, hand hovering above the fabric, listening to the echo of a voice that might have once belonged to her. And behind her—in the glass—

the reflection wasn't watching anymore. It was waiting. It had always been waiting.

CHAPTER: THIRTY-SEVEN

The Doctrine

Gretchen hadn't meant to come this far back—not into the past, not into herself. She hadn't meant to be here at all. But the key turned too easily. Like it had been waiting. The lights flickered on when she stepped inside, and something about the dustless stillness of the archive annex made her breath go thin in her chest.

This room hadn't been used in years. And yet—it was clean. Organized. Waiting. The second cabinet down the row bore the initials in thick, stamped ink:

M.W. – DOCTRINE FILES

AUTHORIZED REVIEW ONLY – INTERNAL THEORY – 1C–THETA

She didn't flinch. She pulled it open with steady hands. What else could she do?

The folder inside wasn't thick.

Just three documents, typed on institutional bond paper. No redactions. No signatures. No clinical gloss. Just philosophy. Spiral-branded.

A doctrine of containment masquerading as psychology. The first page was dated with no year. The header was underlined in pen:

INTERNAL MEMO: PROXY THEORY – COGNITIVE CONTAINMENT MODEL

SPIRAL DOCTRINE – FILE 1C–THETA

Dr. Marcus Weaver, Project Lead

She lowered herself slowly into the chair beside the lamp. Her knees locked halfway down. She didn't know if it was restraint or resignation.

She began to read.

CLASSIFIED INTERNAL DOCTRINE – 1C–THETA

By Dr. Marcus Weaver

We have misunderstood the problem.

The human mind does not shatter from trauma. It shatters from isolation. From being asked to hold more memory than identity can sustain–alone.

We have attempted healing through catharsis. Through medication. Through overwriting. But the Proxy system proves a superior containment structure.

If one identity cannot carry the whole, let it be mirrored across many.

Mirror-seed subjects are unique. They retain the trauma of others. But they do not collapse.

The youngest successful recursion was eight. She re-entered clean by day five.

Stability is not healing.

It is silence.

Subject 1C did not fracture.

She became host.

The experiment is not about recovery. It is about recursion.

The Proxy is not a patient. The Proxy is the vessel. The echo. The keeper of what we dare not admit. The Spiral is not metaphor. It is architecture. Not for healing—but housing. Violence made sacred by repetition. Memory not erased, but grafted. Bent into shape. Mirrors reflect identity. The Spiral contains it. The Tree witnesses it. Together—they root. They grow. They loop.

Do not reflect. Do not return. Do not allow rupture. Contain her in silence. This is not failure. This is function.

The room around her began to warp. Not physically. But perceptually. The fluorescent hum that had always been background now felt like it was listening. As if the lights had heard the doctrine before. As if the air remembered what it had been built to hold.

Gretchen lowered the page to her lap. Her hand covered her mouth. She had been trying to help Ellie. She had fought Weatherly. She had defied Weaver. She had brought tea and sat quietly and believed that kindness could make up for everything Ellie couldn't remember. She whispered to no one: "He knew. They borrowed language from the MKULTRA boys, but sanitized it for peace. Instead of 'mind control,' they called it 'cognitive closure.'"

But now—Now she saw it in every word: Her reassignment to Ellie hadn't been an act of redemption. It had been a punishment. Or a placement. An extension of containment.

The cup on the tray beside her hadn't moved. But the tea began to shake. Gretchen stared at it, frozen. A hairline crack spidered from the base of the porcelain up the handle. Then—without tipping, without a fall—the cup split. Liquid pooled into her notes. Steam rose faintly.

No impact. No warning. Just the silent betrayal of stillness pretending to be peace.

She stood abruptly. Papers spilled across the floor. The doctrine in her hands blurred—her eyes welling too fast to stop it. She backed into the corner of the room and pressed her hand over her chest like she was trying to hold her ribs together.

Gretchen shook her head violently as if she could dislodge the memories pouring into her.

"No," she rasped, backing away, her palms slapping against the peeling walls. "They're not mine. I didn't see. I didn't know—"

The Spiral unfurled around her feet, its black threads spidering outward, reaching. She clamped her hands over her ears, squeezing her eyes shut. "You can't make me remember. I didn't..."

But the memories weren't asking permission.

They seeped through the cracks in her mind, relentless — a child's scream echoing down a corridor, the wet slap of bare feet on stone, the sour, metallic stink of fear soaking into her lungs.

Gretchen dropped to her knees, clawing at the floor as if she could anchor herself to this moment, to herself, to the fragile shell she had built.

"I didn't—" she whispered. "I wasn't—"

The memories whispered back.

"Yes, you were."

She let out a raw, broken sound — not quite a sob, not quite a scream — and let the Spiral take her. She curled in on herself, trembling, her voice so small it barely stirred the dust.

"Mama said... if you close your eyes, the monsters can't find you."

But the monsters weren't behind the door. They were inside her all along.

Now Gretchen's eyes were already closed, and the Spiral found her anyway. Ellie had only found the chapel because she followed the sound. Not footsteps. Not voices. A quiet, rhythmic scrape. Like fingernails against softened wood.

The corridor opened into what might have once been a place of worship—if worship could rot. The altar was gone. The windows boarded over.

What remained was a skeleton of reverence—bare pews, a warped floor, and cracked stone that smelled faintly of mold and rain.

At the front, Hazel sat sideways across the first pew. Her knees drawn to her chest. A shard of charcoal clutched in one hand. Her fingers were black-streaked, not from injury—but from repetition. She was carving. Ellie approached quietly. Hazel didn't look up. Didn't flinch. Her hand continued to etch letters into the side of the wood—shallow, blunt.

we buried her wrong

Again.

we buried her wrong

Again.

She wasn't crying. She wasn't speaking. She was repeating. Like something in her was still trying to warn the room. Ellie lowered herself beside her, knees creaking against the stone. She waited. Not for permission. For rhythm.

Hazel stopped carving mid-letter. Her thumb brushed the groove she'd made. Then, softly—"It wasn't supposed to be like this."

Ellie didn't ask. Hazel blinked slowly.

"Before they called it Spiral, they called it observation."

"I was good at seeing things."

"They sat me in front of the orchard. Told me to draw it."

Her voice was soft. Flat. Almost ceremonial.

"I got the branches wrong. So they gave me names."

She pointed to the far pew—where a dozen faint inscriptions were carved into the wood.

Not initials. Names. Children's names. And one row below, barely legible: military ranks. PFC. CPL. LT. Names grouped together by hand that had never been trained to separate them.

Hazel looked at Ellie then, and her eyes weren't frightened. They were hollow with knowing.

"Dr. Weaver told me I had good retention."

"Then he asked if I'd ever seen a girl forget herself backward."

Ellie's blood went cold. Hazel's gaze drifted down to her stained fingers.

"Sometimes I see her. The stitched one. She hums like a metronome. Not a melody—just time."

Ellie had heard it before—not in song, but in silence. Between each document flip in the pause before her name changed. That hum wasn't Clara's tell. It was her tether.

She turned back to her carving.

"You think it's memory that breaks you?"

"It's the silence between loops. The pause before they put someone else in your mouth."

She pressed the charcoal into the letters again.

we buried her wrong

A beat. Then quieter.

"And we'll do it again."

Ellie reached out. Not to stop her. Just to let her know she wasn't alone. Hazel didn't stop carving. But for a moment—Her hand trembled.

The orchard was quieter than usual. Not silent. Just hushed. Like it had just finished speaking and now waited for a response. Ellie walked the path slowly, her boots stirring dry grass and scattered leaves. The air carried a damp sweetness—the kind that comes before a storm. The Spiral tree stood at the heart of it, its limbs still half-bare from winter, branches unfurling like fingers too tired to make fists anymore. The orchard breathed like something ancient—not sacred, but buried.

This was not the chapel. That was where names were forgotten with prayer. Here, they were carved into bark and bled through root systems. The chapel offered mercy, but the orchard was only a memory. The chapel forgot. The orchard made them carve what they wouldn't archive.

She paused at the base. And saw them. Names. Etched into the bark with all the care of children and soldiers and fractured minds desperate not to vanish. Some were shallow—faded by time or weather. Others were deep, dug in with something sharper than a knife. There were initials and full names. Dated. Undated. Crossed out. Rewritten.

S. Silas

CPL. A. Martin – Ward C

Delani – Orchard Recursion Trial

Clara M. – Room 9

And lower down, by the roots—E. Hale – Subject 1C – UNSTABLE

She hadn't carved it. But someone had. Before she arrived. Before she was Ellie. She knelt. Pressed her hand to the trunk. The bark was rough. Grooved.

But warm. Like the Spiral tree didn't hold names.

It held memory. Behind her, a door creaked open. Not one she could see. The wind shifted.

And from the edge of the orchard fence, Dr. Weatherly stood. Clipboard in hand. Coat stiff with starch. The same expression he always wore: unreadable. Institutional.

He said nothing. He didn't come closer. But he didn't leave. He just watched her at the tree. Watched her read the names like someone visiting a graveyard he helped plant. She rose slowly. Turned to face him.

"Ward C," she said. Her voice didn't shake. "You knew they weren't recovering."

He didn't blink.

"They weren't patients," she said. "They were vessels."

No denial. No justification. Just a clipboard. Weatherly lowered it. Looked at her the way you look at someone reading your confession out loud. He didn't nod. But he didn't have to.

They buried them wrong.

They buried them in her.

And in the orchard. And in the mirror. And in the glass that keeps cracking without sound.

The Spiral tree didn't sway. It acknowledged. As if its branches had been listening the whole time.

Becoming the Spiral

The key was cold in her hand. Stamped with nothing but a spiral—no file number, no department tag—just the same unbroken loop she'd seen traced into bark, into walls, into wrists. It slid into the lock with no resistance. The door didn't creak. It exhaled—like lungs held too long beneath water.

Like the room behind it had been holding its breath for years, and only now—only now—did it believe she'd finally come back. The chamber was smaller than she'd imagined. No larger than a hospital storage closet, maybe. But it felt vast. Not in size—in consequence.

The kind of weight that made her ears ring, her breath catch, her pulse skip— And then whispered, not in words but pressure:

You've been here before.

One chair. Bolted to the floor. Padded arms. Spiral-stitched seat. A monitor hung above the glass-paneled wall—a wall that looked like a mirror but didn't reflect properly. The light bent wrong. It wasn't silvered. It wasn't honest. It was one-way memory.

Silas didn't say anything at first. He stood in the doorway, his hand clenched just inside his coat pocket. He looked older here. Not by age. By return.

He stepped inside. Stopped beside the console. His voice was low. Brittle.

"I sat in that chair once."

Ellie turned to him. He didn't look at her.

"I was nine. They called it Phase One. Told me to draw what I saw."

"But what I saw wasn't mine."

He touched the console gently. His fingertips shook.

"They showed me this room."

"They said it was a future. But it was someone else's past."

He finally looked at her then.

"I didn't draw the future, Ellie."

"I drew you."

The console was already powered.

The lights blinked green. The reel sat ready—spooled loosely, tail out as if it had been played recently and left precisely where it stopped.

Ellie reached for it. Her fingers hovered. The reel had no label. No time stamp. No initials. Nothing. It didn't need one. She felt what it was. She had asked for this. The moment her fingers brushed the reel's edge, the screen flickered. The light dimmed. And the door behind her sealed shut. Silas didn't move. He stared at the playback window like it was a casket, not a screen. Ellie sank into the bolted chair. It fit her body. Too well. Like it had been cast from her bones. The lights above dimmed to a glow. The air-cooled. The screen crackled.

"This is the part where you stop remembering," the voice would say.

But Ellie already knew—This was the part where she started returning. The screen hissed. Not loudly. Just enough to make Ellie's skin crawl

like the television static in a room that shouldn't be awake. And then it began.

PLAYBACK START

March 4, 1943

Session 1C – Consent Recording

Camera 1 – Merge Preparation Interview

The frame opened on a girl. Not strapped in.

Not struggling. Just sitting. Still. Shoes too big. Dark curls half-pulled back.

A Spiral chalked faintly beneath her chair.

No sound from the other side of the glass. She was maybe nine. And the voice—"You said I'd forget her."

Ellie's chest seized. It wasn't Clara's voice. It was hers. Younger. Thinner.

As though everything had already been pulled out of her.

"You said if I helped, you could give her back."

No tremor. No confusion. Just unbearable clarity.

"I'll do it. I'll hold her. I don't care what it costs."

The room shifted around her. Not physically. Perceptually. The walls pulled in. The chair felt heavier now. Not from weight—but recognition.

Not because she sat in it now.

Because she'd never truly left it. Because she had always been sitting in it.

From offscreen, Weaver's voice:

"Proxy consent recorded. Merge scheduled. Phase One approved."

A clipboard tapped once. Footsteps retreated. The child did not look into the camera. She looked at the mirror. Not scared. Ready.

The tape ended. But the silence didn't. Ellie couldn't speak. The air was too dense. Like the room had sealed itself from oxygen the moment it heard her again. Across from her, Silas's hand gripped the edge of the console. His knuckles white. His mouth open. But he didn't speak. Not at first. Then—"You wanted this."

Not an accusation. A heartbreak.

Ellie shook her head. "I don't remember—"

"They made sure you wouldn't."

She looked back at the screen. Frozen now. Paused on her younger face. So calm. So sure. So desperate to keep someone she loved from disappearing.

She didn't know that to keep someone, she'd have to vanish first.

The reel hadn't stopped. The screen flickered once, then resumed— Not with a slate or date. Just an image. A long corridor. Walls the color of chalk and scabbed linoleum. Low light. Windowless. At first, nothing moved. Then—hands. Reaching. Dragging. Pressing against the paint. The footage panned. Slowly. Purposefully. Every few feet, a spiral had been drawn. Not painted. Not assigned. Scratched. With fingers. With broken pencil tips. Some in ink. Some in blood. All identical. Onscreen, there it was again—the hum. Low, breathy rhythm without a tune. It always came just before Clara spoke.

Then the voice whispered, "Not this one. Not again."

Soft. From the edge of the mirror in the hallway.

"Don't let me hear her name in my voice."

Then again. From another patient's mouth. This time louder.

"Let her hold it this time."

The tape cut to a two-way mirror. Behind it: the chair.

Empty. Then not.

Then flickering. Then Clara, sat calmly, hands in her lap. No restraints. Only the Spiral under her feet. She looked into the mirror—not at herself. At Ellie. Then spoke. But the voice—Was Ellie's.

"I wasn't unstable."

"I just remembered too many people at once."

In the first loop, that line condemned her. In this one, it absolves. The Spiral didn't change. The reader did. That's what recursion hides: not repetition—but revision.

Ellie's throat closed. She whispered, "That's what I said—" The tape played on. The reflection didn't match Clara's face. It showed Ellie's mouth moving. Stitched. Then unstitched. Then smiling. The mirror began to fog. From the inside. Letters began to appear as breath condensed:

SUBJECT 1C – RETAINED

Silas stepped back, his voice low and broken.

"She was the first."

"And the last."

The footage cut again. A room full of children. Drawing spirals on their arms. On the walls. On each other. One child looked into the camera. Her mouth moved silently. Then her voice emerged from the mirror's speaker:

"Please not me again."

Ellie turned to the mirrored wall in the playback room. Something in it moved. Not light. Not form. Just presence—lurking behind the glass-like breath on the back of her neck. She stepped forward. Her own reflection met her. No delay. No distortion.

Just one difference—Her eyes were spiraled. Two curls blooming outward, just behind the iris. Subtle. Then brighter. Like they'd always been there. Like pretending not to see them had been part of the containment. Ellie didn't look away from the mirror. She couldn't. The Spiral was in her eyes now. Not as a symbol. Not as a trick of the light. It was her pupil.

Curled. Alive. Spinning so slowly it could be mistaken for stillness. The Spiral always worked this way—quiet, patient, surgical. Until your eyes forgot they had ever belonged to you.

The screen beside her hissed once more. A final frame blinked into place. It showed the Merge Room. The chair. Empty. Then Clara again. Then not. The image shifted—And it was Ellie in the chair. Not younger. Not before. Now. Same clothes. Same hands. Same breath she was holding in this moment. But her reflection didn't blink. It watched her blink. Ellie staggered backward.

Silas moved toward the console.

"Don't watch that," he said.

Too late. The tape glitched—like memory skipping a beat—then smoothed itself, as if the Spiral didn't permit interruption.

"Do you remember the girl who stood still?"

"Do you remember who sat in her place?"

Two voices. Clara's. And Ellie's. Layered. As if they'd been spliced into the same recording. Or had never been separate to begin with.

Silas reached for the off switch, hand trembling—then stopped. As if even trying to end it might be a kind of betrayal. He just looked at her. Like someone watching an eclipse swallow the sun.

"She didn't disappear," he whispered.

His voice cracked. He turned—not from the screen, not even from the Spiral blooming in her eyes. From what it meant.

"They made her…"

A breath.

"…into you."

Ellie didn't cry. There was no room left for grief. Only recognition. In the glass, her reflection smiled. Not cruelly. Not warmly. Like it finally saw what it had been waiting for—its other half.

CHAPTER: THIRTY-NINE

Contain and Commend

Ellie crossed the threshold of the orchard like stepping into the throat of something that had long since forgotten how to breathe.

It was late afternoon, but the light didn't fall right here. It came in sideways, fractured through trees that grew too close, too coiled. The branches didn't reach for the sun. They curled inward—toward center, toward collapse, toward the Spiral. This place had always felt sacred.

Now, she saw it for what it was: A design. Not wild. Not accidental. Measured. Each path, a radius.

Each tree, a spoke.

The Spiral tree—the one at the center—its roots exposed just enough to suggest symmetry, not survival.

She stepped carefully, counting.

Twelve paces. Turn.

Twelve again. Turn.

Her boots followed a pattern she hadn't realized was already inside her. The soil felt memorized. Like it had been stepped a thousand times in the same sequence by feet no longer alive. By children. By soldiers. By subjects. When she reached the clearing at the Spiral tree's base, she stopped. Something was missing. It took her a moment to name it. The chair. The wooden one, slightly tilted, always waiting—Gone. Only a depression in the earth where it had been. Four legs' worth of indentation. A faint scarring of the Spiral's innermost ring beneath it. And in the air—A voice. Faint. Childlike. But clear.

Ellie's breath caught. The words hit like a shard to the ribs—small, sharp, irreversible. The sound didn't echo. The orchard never echoed. But it repeated.

"I had a sister."

The voice was not a scream. It was a statement. A last line etched too lightly to hold onto its speaker. It came from the roots. Or the wind. Or the dirt itself. Ellie stepped forward. Kneeling. She touched the ground where the chair had stood. Her fingers pressed into the impression as if she could feel the weight of whoever had sat here last.

The dirt was warmer than it should've been. Not sun-warm. Body-warm. The Spiral tree creaked above her. Not from the wind. From age. From memory. And from being used.

Ellie looked up through its twisting branches and realized: This was not a grave. It was a conduit. This wasn't memory—it was marrow. Etched into bark. Buried in bone. The orchard didn't grow fruit. It grew echoes. And each spiral in the soil wasn't a grave. It was a womb. For names that didn't belong to just one body. They didn't bury people here. They ran them through it.

Children had sat in this clearing like mirrors, made to absorb soldiers' fragmented minds—facing the tree, facing the Spiral, facing each other in layered circuits of pain. Not to remember.

Not to heal.

But to contain.

The Spiral Protocol hadn't started in the hospital. It had started here. Under the tree. In the dirt. With the smallest subjects. The ones who could hold pain without language.

The ones they thought wouldn't be missed. A leaf fell past her ear. Its descent curved gently. Not down. Inward.

Ellie whispered, barely audible.

"What did they make me forget?"

And somewhere beyond her voice—The orchard listened. And didn't answer. Ellie didn't hear Hazel's footsteps. She only sensed her—like the orchard had shifted slightly to make room for someone who had walked this spiral before. She didn't turn. Not right away. Hazel's breath hitched—barely a sound. Then the orchard seemed to exhale with her, as if recognizing one of its own.

"You found it," she said.

Her voice wasn't accusatory. It was resigned. Like she'd known this day would come and had run out of ways to delay it. Ellie rose slowly, brushing the dirt from her skirt. Her palms still tingled from the heat of the ground beneath the vanished chair. She turned.

Hazel stood ten feet away. Arms folded tightly across her chest. A charcoal smear beneath one fingernail. Her sweater hung too loose, like something had been removed from beneath it and never put back.

Their eyes met. Ellie didn't ask. Hazel spoke anyway.

"They told me you'd be the last."

Her voice cracked on the word last.

"Said the recursion couldn't hold another version."

"That they'd let it end with you."

Ellie's throat tightened. She stepped closer. Hazel didn't move.

"I thought if I stayed quiet…"

"…if I didn't interfere…"

"…maybe it would stay buried."

She blinked rapidly.

"But the Spiral doesn't bury anything. It just loops it quieter."

Her arms dropped.

"You know that now, don't you?"

Ellie nodded. Slowly. The silence between them thickened—not from avoidance, but from too much known. Hazel took a step forward, her hand curling loosely at her side.

"I remember you," she whispered.

"From before they gave you the new name."

Ellie's breath caught.

"You had a different laugh then. Light. Quick. Like you were afraid if you stayed too long, the mirrors would catch it."

Hazel looked up at the tree.

"I should've said something. When they brought you back. When they called you Ellie instead of…"

She didn't finish the sentence. She didn't have to. Ellie's voice was barely audible.

"You were there."

Hazel nodded. A tear slipped down her cheek.

"I pressed bleach into every crack. Burned the linens. Buried the names in order of disappearance. But the Spiral still hums in my teeth." Her hands trembled. "And I still see your hands in the dirt. Not from memory. From muscle. You kept writing her name."

Her voice broke.

"Only they told me not to say it out loud."

The Spiral tree shifted in the wind. Above them, a leaf curled and fell—turning as it descended. Not down.

Inward. Hazel looked away.

"They never end it, Ellie."

"They just name someone else."

"And I thought maybe… if I didn't fight it… they'd stop choosing girls like us."

"You kept writing her name."

Her voice broke.

"Only they told me not to say it out loud."

The Spiral tree shifted in the wind. Above them, a leaf curled and fell—turning as it descended. Not down.

Inward. Hazel looked away.

"They never end it, Ellie."

"They just name someone else."

"And I thought maybe… if I didn't fight it… they'd stop choosing girls like us."

A long breath.

"I was wrong."

The chapel basement was colder than she remembered. Or maybe she just noticed it now—now that she knew what was buried here wasn't sacred but strategic. She moved behind the altar, where the floorboards dipped.

Gretchen had once whispered that the Spiral's early blueprints had been stored here—before they learned to call it therapy. Ellie pried the crate open slowly.

Inside: scorched files. Singed at the corners. Water-warped. But not destroyed.

Preserved.

Because someone wanted to forget—but not too much. She peeled back the top sheet. Typed in military header:

UNITED STATES DEPARTMENT OF VETERANS AFFAIRS

JOINT MEMORANDUM – CLASSIFIED EYES ONLY

RE: Project Spiral – Containment Protocol Outcomes and Civilian Management Strategy

Her hands didn't just tremble—they recoiled, as if touching the page made her complicit.

> *"Project Spiral has demonstrated exceptional results in trauma reallocation and post-war memory stratification."*

> *"Containment of recursion failures is proceeding without public disruption. Memory drift categorized as minor civilian noise."*

> *"Consent remains functionally obscured through intake alteration and narrative therapy."*

"Maintain protocol: CONTAIN AND COMMEND."

Ellie stared at those words. Contain and commend. As if assigning someone to disappear deserved a medal.

The next page:

"Volunteer-based merges will proceed under adjusted terminology: recovery, improvement, reentry."

"Releases classified as 'Recovered' are to be repurposed for further retention trials or neutralized as needed."

And handwritten in red ink:

"Civilian awareness negligible. Spiral containment: successful."

"All remaining identities classified as UNSTABLE."

Ellie's stomach turned. The patients had never left. They weren't released.

They weren't recovered. They were recirculated. Or erased. She shoved the memo into her coat. Then climbed the stairs. Weatherly's office was dark when she entered. He wasn't inside. But the file drawer was unlocked. Almost like he wanted her to see it now. Inside: a manila envelope labeled in small, neat handwriting:

SUBJECT RECOVERY LOG – INTERNAL REFERENCE ONLY

DO NOT FILE TO DISCHARGE

She flipped it open. Blank lines. No signatures. Dozens of names. Each followed by:

Recovered – reassigned.

Recovered – unstable.

Recovered – NULL.

Her name was there. So was Clara's. So was Silas's. None of them were marked "released." At the bottom:

SUBJECT 1C – RETAINED

STABILITY: FALSE-POSITIVE

Below that, scrawled in graphite:

"She loops clean. But she remembers crooked."

—MW

Ellie stepped back, her hands shaking. The light flickered above the desk. In the mirror across the room—Her reflection held still. But behind it—Someone moved.

The corridor bore no number. No designation. Just the polished hum of something that had been waiting without permission. Just a plain black frame. And inside—glass. The Mirror Hall was never part of the patient map. No one ever spoke about it. But Ellie had seen glimpses. In blueprints. In Weaver's margin notes.

SPIRAL ECHO ZONE: OBSERVATION REFLECTORS – HALL C

She stepped inside.

It was cold. Not from temperature. From memory. Every wall paneled in mirrored glass—edge to edge. The kind that doesn't reflect light quite right. The kind that holds things longer than it should. Ellie walked slowly. Her boots echoed faintly against the linoleum, but in the glass— Her steps had already happened. Her reflection moved a half-beat behind. Then ahead. Then, not at all.

She stopped in the center of the corridor. Faced the largest mirror. And blinked. Once. Her reflection blinked, too. But not just hers. Behind it—Layers. Dozens of faces. Some sharp. Some blurred. Children. Women. Soldiers. Staff. All behind the surface. Not reflected. Embedded.

She stared. Frozen. Their eyes weren't empty. They were heavy. Watching. Not waiting to be saved—but to be seen. One girl—barely twelve, hair matted to her cheeks—stepped forward inside the glass. Her mouth opened. No sound. But Ellie understood the words. She saw them form.

"Tell them I was here."

Another face emerged behind hers—an older man in a patient gown, eyes sunken but clear. His hand pressed to the glass, where hers had just touched. Then another. A nurse. A boy. A spiral etched on his throat. They didn't speak. They stared. Like Ellie was the first person who had ever looked back and seen them.

The air thickened. The mirrors didn't distort anymore. They clarified. And Ellie saw it: She was the hall. Not walking through it. Carrying it. Every reflection a recursion she'd been made to hold. Every face a version she'd absorbed without knowing. She whispered—not into the air, but into the glass itself.

"I see you."

And in the stillness that followed, the glass remembered how to listen. And the smallest face—the girl with the matted hair—smiled. Just slightly. Then faded.

The lights flickered. And the mirrors didn't go dark. They went still. Like memory returning to rest. Ellie stepped out of the Mirror Hall. But something in her reflection stayed behind. Waiting for the next girl. Or the next name.

CHAPTER: FORTY

The Erasure

The Merge Room Annex had always been locked. It didn't hum like the primary chamber. It didn't glow. It was still. Paper-colored. Smelled faintly of aging acetate and powdered latex. But inside—it remembered everything.

Ellie crossed the threshold like a patient stepping into her own autopsy report—already written, already filed. A single clipboard rested on the console. No blinking lights. No warnings. Just a neatly stacked folder, a pen, and the dull anticipation of something long overdue. She picked it up. The first page bore no emotion. Just purpose.

MERGE INITIATIVE: FINALIZATION NOTICE

SUBJECT 1C – STABILITY RATING: RE-APPROVED

INTENT: *REPLACEMENT RECURSION – PROXY OVERWRITE / CLARA M.*

REINTEGRATION TARGET: IDENTITY ABSORPTION / MEMORY STABILIZATION – CONTAINMENT TYPE 1C

The clinical tone made her dizzy. She gripped the edge of the console. This wasn't a protocol written about her. It was written for her.

She turned the page. A note—handwritten in Weaver's cold, slanted script:

"Loop stable. Spiral integrity maintained under subjective self-narrative."

"Subject believes restoration is healing. Result: self-containment achieved."

Her stomach turned. This was never recovery. It was performance. Another page. Older. Faded at the edges. Blueprint overlay. The Merge Chair. The earliest version. But the label said:

MIRROR SEED / 1C / ORIGIN NODE

DATE: 1943

INITIALIZATION STATUS: HELD

She pressed her fingers to the edge of the page like it might bite her. It didn't feel like schematics. It felt like birth records. Not born of body. Born of design.

She backed away. A single sentence slid through her like glass:

"They didn't heal me."

She said it aloud. Her voice made it real.

"They stabilized me."

Not to fix her. To prove she could hold. To erase Clara. To absorb others. To mimic stability long enough to quiet the system. And the final lie? Her name.

"They took my name," she whispered.

And gave her one easier to file. Easier to reassign. Easier to repeat. Ellie. Not Clara. Ellie Hale. Not Subject 1C.

A low breath left her body. Not grief. Recognition. The Spiral didn't target the fractured. It targeted the ones who remembered too well. And then it silenced them—by making them *someone else.*

Behind her, the Merge Room's main door remained closed. But inside— She knew the chair was waiting. Not for her recovery. For her return.

Ellie didn't realize he was behind her until she smelled smoke. Faint. Charcoal and old paper. She turned slowly.

Silas stood in the doorway of the annex. His coat was wrinkled. His eyes red—not just from tears, but from the kind of exhaustion that comes from watching someone be erased again and again.

He didn't speak right away. His hands were shaking. In his left: a sheet of paper, already scorched at the corner. He looked at her like she was a ruin wearing someone else's face.

"I knew before you did."

His voice was low. Raw.

"I knew what they made you."

He stepped closer.

"And I tried to draw around it. I tried to sketch *you* out of it—find something they didn't design."

He held up the page. It was one of his. Maybe the last. Charcoal lines smudged into a spiral. A girl beneath it. But the face—half-formed. Eyeless. Mouth open. Hands cupped around a flame. She looked like Clara. Or Ellie. Or both. Or neither.

"But I couldn't save her," Silas whispered.

"Because *you were built to outlive her.*"

His hand trembled. The sketch caught a stronger flicker of flame. He dropped it. It burned fast. Like it had waited years to disappear. He staggered back a step, then forward again—unsure if he wanted to collapse or scream. And then it came:

"You kept *her* alive—by forgetting *me*."

The words shattered something in the air. Ellie couldn't breathe. Not because it wasn't true—Because it was.

"They let you hold her," he hissed, "because you didn't remember what she meant."

"But I did. And they left *me* behind with it."

He crouched near the ash on the floor, shaking.

"Do you know what it's like to remember someone they won't even say out loud?"

"To be a living echo in someone else's mouth?"

Ellie knelt. Not to console him. But because her legs gave out.

"I didn't know—" she tried.

"No," he snapped.

"That's the point."

His voice softened.

"You didn't know."

"Because if you had, you wouldn't have been stable."

He looked up at her. Eyes glassy. Voice shaking.

"You weren't the cure, Ellie."

A pause. A breath like broken glass.

"You were the erasure."

Neither of them moved. The sketch had crumbled completely. Nothing left but a spiral of soot where her name might've been. The fire had died. Ash curled between them in a broken spiral—like the husk of a name no one dared to say. Silas didn't speak again. He turned toward the stairwell, shoulders hunched, and disappeared without a sound. Ellie didn't follow. She stood alone in the Merge Annex, breath shallow, hands numb. The folder Weaver had left behind was still on the shelf. She hadn't opened it before. Now, her fingers moved automatically, like they already knew what it would contain.

The pages inside were brittle. Not from age. From exposure. From being pulled too often by hands that wanted to believe the design was noble. She flipped through treatment summaries and diagram overlays until she reached the final sheet. A blueprint.

Merge Chair Schematic

Revision 0 – Original Concept Model

Date: October 1943

Initiator: Dr. Marcus Weaver

Trial Subject: [unlabeled]

But scrawled at the bottom, in ink that hadn't faded:

MIRROR SEED / 1C / ORIGIN NODE

She stared at it. The lines were delicate. Intentional. This wasn't medical equipment. It was architecture. A geometry of recursion. A frame not for healing—But for housing.

Her breath caught. All this time, she'd thought she was the outcome. The survivor. The last test. She wasn't the result. She was the beginning. The Spiral hadn't grown around her; it had grown from her.

She traced the schematic's center. The chair's seat was overlaid with a spiral drawn in tighter and tighter loops. But not toward disappearance. Toward containment.

They hadn't made the Spiral to heal. They had made it to preserve the lie. And she was the vessel. From the start.

She folded the blueprint slowly. There was no shaking. No tears. Only gravity. And the quiet knowledge that she had never been missing. She had been designed to be found.

On the blueprint's spine, beneath the Spiral core, someone had written a single word. Folded there, between ink and breath, the truth waited.

"Held."

CHAPTER: FORTY-ONE

The Final Merge

Ellie didn't knock. She didn't need a key. The Merge Room had already opened for her. The moment she turned the final corridor, the lights along the floor came to life—one by one—tracing the path like a breadcrumb trail laid by memory. The door stood ajar. Not wide. Just enough to say: You're expected.

Ellie stood frozen, her hand trembling inches from the door, the air too thick to breathe and too thin to turn back. She could leave. Pretend she hadn't found it. Pretend she hadn't seen the bloodmarks smearing the floor beneath the cracked linoleum. Pretend history could stay buried, safe and, neat, and forgotten. In the tightening silence, Hazel's voice surfaced in her mind, sharp and merciless:

"Silence is its own kind of violence."

Ellie closed her eyes. When she opened them again, she shoved the door wide. She stepped in. The air had changed. No mildew. No static discharge. It smelled like stillness now. Like a room that hadn't just been waiting—But preparing.

The Spiral chair sat at center. Upright. Polished. Not waiting. Expecting. The straps hung open at the sides like arms uncurled. The console across from it flickered softly, scrolling idle code. She hadn't spoken yet. She hadn't touched anything. But her name was already on the screen:

SUBJECT 1C – RECOGNIZED

The room exhaled. A quiet hydraulic sigh from the walls. Not mechanical failure—compliance. Every line in the tile, every whisper of light, bent toward the chair. Ellie inhaled through her nose, slow. Not afraid. Not detached. Complete.

She stepped forward. The hum beneath the floor grew stronger—not louder. Denser. Like it wasn't sound, but signal. Her boots landed with the soft thud of inevitability. At the edge of the chair's base, she paused. Not to decide. To *acknowledge*. She had feared this place once. Not anymore. Now, she understood: It hadn't been built to erase her. It had been built from her.

The console pulsed once. A soft alert:

MERGE CYCLE: PENDING

INITIATOR: [NONE ASSIGNED]

Manual override available.

She lifted her chin.

"I'll do it myself," she said, and the room seemed to exhale.

Her voice didn't echo. It didn't need to. The Merge Room had already accepted her command.

Behind the mirrored glass, the reflection shimmered faintly. Like someone had just stepped into place behind the silver.

Ellie's hand reached toward the console. She touched the corner panel—gently, like returning a piece of herself to the altar that had always been waiting.

The screen responded.

MANUAL INITIATION: CONFIRMED

SUBJECT 1C – STATUS: AWAKE

She turned to the chair. And for a moment, her fingers hovered over the armrest. Not with hesitation. With ceremony. Then she sat. Ellie settled into the chair. It didn't creak. It didn't resist. It welcomed her. The armrests curved slightly, closing in with a quiet, pneumatic seal. A small blue light at the base of the console blinked once.

SUBJECT STABILIZED. READY FOR MERGE.

The mirrored wall across from her shimmered faintly. Then—

clarified. And there she was. Clara. Not standing. Not imposed. Just… reflected. The same girl Ellie had seen in dreams, in sketchbooks, in orchard soil. But now her face was still. Composed. As though the Spiral had paused long enough for her to speak. And this time—it did.

"You're the last one left."

The voice didn't echo from the speaker. It came through the glass. Soft. Measured. Too calm to be haunting. It wasn't a ghost. It was residual identity. A line of code. A saved breath. A thread left behind.

"You're the one they'll remember."

A beat of breathless quiet.

"So they can forget the rest of us."

Ellie blinked. Not in fear. But in understanding. She had never been chosen to survive. She had been chosen to contain. To appear whole. So, no one asked what had been taken.

"That's what the loop needs," Clara said.

"One face to remember. So all the others can be forgotten."

The reflection did not mimic Ellie. It watched her. Like someone saying goodbye. Or handing off a burden too heavy for the dead.

Ellie leaned forward slightly. She spoke without thinking. The words came from somewhere behind her ribs, where names once lived.

"Erase me."

Clara smiled. Just slightly.

The mirrored surface rippled. Then stilled. Ellie sat back in the chair. The hum beneath her bones deepened. Not loud. Just… final. The Spiral initiated without sound. No alarms. No countdown. No clinical voices from behind glass. Just a subtle shift in the hum beneath the floor. Like something old and infinite had just turned one more loop.

The chair held Ellie upright. Not restrained. Supported. Around her, the lights dimmed—not to darkness, but to **memory-light**. Soft. Flickering. Like orchard sun through child-sized windows.

And then the voice began. Not hers. Not Clara's. Not Subject 1C. All three. Layered. Woven. One voice, speaking with three memories.

"I remember the orchard. The chalk on my palms. The way the tree curved when I cried."

"I remember the straps. The mirror that blinked after I did. The sketch I never meant to draw."

"I remember the name they gave me and the ones they took."

"I remember being chosen. Not because I was strong. But because I held."

A static flicker washed across the console. Lines of text blurred, reformed, repeated.

SUBJECT 1C

SUBJECT 1C

SUBJECT ELLIE HALE

SUBJECT CLARA M.

loop confirmed

identity recomposite accepted

stability false-positive: APPROVED

The voice continued. Fractured but seamless.

"I used to hum to myself."

"I used to forget on purpose."

"I used to be someone they loved."

Ellie tried to speak. Her lips moved. But the voice that came out didn't belong to her. Not fully. It curved between timbres—**young, older, clinical**. All sharing breath.

"You were always going to return."

"Because you were never allowed to leave."

"Because they needed one face to end the Spiral."

And then silence. But not absence. Stillness. Sealed. The system logged it without flourish. No broadcast. No signature.

Just three lines on a screen:

SUBJECT 1C – MERGE COMPLETE

SPIRAL LOOP: SEALED

STABILITY: TRUE (OBEDIENCE CONFIRMED)

Outside the room, Gretchen arrived. Too late. Again.

CHAPTER: FORTY-TWO

The Pattern Holds

The new system blinked online exactly one month later. The intake forms looked the same. Same medical jargon. Same boxes to check. But the interface now blinked in slow pulses. Three lights. One pause. Three lights again.

Nurse Iris Delgado noticed the rhythm. She thought it strange—but said nothing. She'd been hired just last week—an expedited transfer from a sister facility across state lines. No explanation why the previous staff had been reassigned or, in some cases, never heard from again.

The hospital had changed, they said. New technology. New memory protocols. More efficient now. Safer. She sat through orientation alone. No instructor. Just a screen. And a voice.

"Welcome to Arlington Hills. You have already been chosen."

The voice was calm. Measured. Female. Young. But not synthetic. Too organic. Too knowing.

"In your role, you will act as a stabilizing presence for recovering identities. You will not question memory recursion. You will not interfere with Merge convergence. You are part of the pattern now."

Iris tilted her head.

"Excuse me," she asked aloud, though the room was empty. "Can I—speak to someone live?"

The screen blinked once. Then pulsed again, slower this time. And repeated the final line.

"You are part of the pattern now."

Her name badge printed automatically. She picked it up, still warm.

The photo had captured her just before sitting down—shoulders squared, no expression yet formed. In the image—she was smiling. Faintly. Like she'd already agreed to something she hadn't heard yet. And in the background, reflected in the corner of the glass…A spiral.

Somewhere beneath Arlington Hills, in the room no longer listed on any blueprint, the Merge chair remains. Empty. Waiting.

The walls hum with breath. The mirror pulses faintly with light. Beneath the chair, the spiral flares—once—then folds inward again.. Inside the mirror, dozens of reflections flicker—one face wearing many names. A voice speaks. Not through glass. Not through wires. Through the walls.

"She came back wrong."

A pause.

"And now, so will you. And you won't even know when."

The spiral flashes red. Then vanishes. But the humming doesn't stop. It never does. Not in a system built to remember. Not in a body built to house return. Not when the blood has dried—but the root still grows.

Epilogue

The orchard was quiet—the kind of quiet that grows older than the buildings around it. The kind of silence that doesn't ask to be broken—only endured.

Gretchen walked the spiral path alone, her boots sinking into the moss-soft earth. Her coat was damp with the breath of something that had been breathing long before she arrived.

She followed the red thread Silas had left behind. A crayon trail dragged across bark and root and broken stone—childlike, deliberate, *grieving*. It ended beneath the tree.

He sat upright, spine pressed to the Spiral tree. Eyes open. Unblinking. But not afraid. His hands rested in his lap, fingertips stained with red and black pigment. The breeze didn't stir him. Nor the sun. Nor Gretchen. He wasn't waiting. He was *finished*.

Beside him, a final canvas. The edges curled as though the paper had aged faster than the body. She dropped to her knees. It was Clara. But not alone.

Opposite her, mirroring her pose—Silas. The two figures sat beneath the spiral tree, identical wounds blooming from their chests. Roots threaded through their spines like veins—memory pulsing inside bark. The lines of their faces had been drawn with something deeper than ink. Their mouths weren't stitched. They were smiling.

Above them, the branches bled spirals. Not drawn—grown. Spiraled through the bark like rings through time. From one limb, a loop of crimson thread hung gently, turning once—just enough to catch the light.

Gretchen reached out, trembling, and closed Silas's eyes.

"You kept her," she whispered.

"Even when they told you to forget."

A breeze passed through the orchard. It didn't speak. But it hummed.

She didn't cry. There were no tears left. Not for this. Not anymore. Instead, she stood and walked back to the hospital, her knees streaked with moss, her hands sticky with pigment and blood that wasn't hers.

She didn't sleep that night. Not after what she found.

It was a drawer she hadn't opened in years.

One that refused to budge—until it did, with a sudden lurch.

Like something inside had been holding it shut.

Inside: a reel-to-reel tape.

Unlabeled, except for a single hand-scrawled phrase in faded ink:

SPIRAL PROTOTYPE: VETERANS A–C

She loaded it into the player. The tape hissed. Then a voice.

Test Log—Spiral Sequence 3. Dr. Margaret Weaver recording. All trauma creates a soft spot in the psyche. The trick is shaping it. We begin implantation using re-triggered combat memory. Then, overwrite it with mirrored phrases from Subject 1C. The children don't remember what they give. But the men never forget what they take.

But the soldiers do. And that's the point.

Click. Silence. Then—Clara's voice. Young. Terrified.

"Please don't put me back."

"I'll be good this time. I'll be quiet."

A long, slow inhale. Metal. Electricity. Then—another voice. Not Clara. Silas.

"She's inside me. She never left."

Gretchen ejected the tape with shaking fingers. She looked down at the chrome panel on the player. For just a moment— Her reflection smiled before she did. He never forgot. Because he was never allowed to. Because even when the Spiral is silenced—its story waits.

And there's always another to remember... before the blood dried.

Afterword

"In 1947, the U.S. government classified over 60,000 patients as 'non-responsive.' Their files were marked inactive. No records of release exist." This story is fiction. What they did wasn't.

Author's Historical Note

J.J Lucie

Before the Blood Dried

Before the Blood Dried is a work of historical, psychological fiction inspired by real conditions, treatments, and institutional practices in post–World War II America.

The novel is set in 1947, during a period of rapid expansion in psychiatric hospitals and growing interest in experimental treatments for trauma, particularly among returning soldiers. While the Spiral Protocol is fictional, it draws heavily on real methods used in mid-20th-century experimental psychiatry, including mirror-phase theory, early electroshock therapy, memory implantation studies, and pre-MKUltra mind-conditioning practices.

Many elements in the novel—including the Merge Room, recursive hallucinations, and memory convergence—are based on actual Cold War–era projects that tested the limits of identity and consent, particularly on vulnerable populations. The treatment of soldiers in *Before the Blood Dried* reflects how PTSD (then often labeled "shell shock" or "war neurosis") was frequently misunderstood, suppressed, or exploited for scientific advancement.

Characters like Silas represent those whose silence was mistaken for illness but, in truth, carried the heaviest burden—forced memory containment under the guise of healing. The historical backdrop also reflects 1940s institutional language, hierarchy, and ethical blind spots, all of which contribute to the novel's central question: What if trauma was never meant to be erased but rewritten?

This book is intended to honor those who were never allowed to tell their own stories—and to reckon with the dangerous history of using memory as medicine.

By J. J. Lucie

Every act of remembering in this book is an act
of resistance. Though the characters are fictional,
their traumas are not. If anything in this story
echoes your experience, I hope you know:

You are not an anomaly.
You are not unstable.
You are not a loop.
You are a voice—still rising.
Still yours.

— J. J. Lucie